PENUMBRA

BY SAMANTHA BENNETT

Dear Grandma Hill,
Love you so very much!
May grace shine upon you!

TRIBUTARIES PRESS

This is a work of fiction. The characters, incidents, and dialogues are products of the author's imagination and are not to be construed as real. Any resemblance to actual events or persons, living or dead, is entirely coincidental.

Penumbra

Published by Tributaries Press
Orlando, FL

ACKNOWLEDGMENTS

So very many people have influenced the writing of this story. I cannot possibly thank you all, but I would like to thank a few of you in writing. Please know that if you've ever shown me a bit of unwarranted love, then you've played a role in the authoring of this novel.

Heather Ostalkiewicz—What a friend you are. You introduced me to the word Penumbra and have taught me so much about the character. Your wisdom and friendship have left me and my story changed.

Joy Givens—Thanks for your humor, attention to detail, and belief in this story. I could not ask for a better editor, business partner, and friend. Thank you for investing so many hours into the crafting of Penumbra. I think you're swell.

Leslie Santamaria—Your gentle suggestions and many edits have made this story stronger. Thank you for being such a champion of Penumbra.

Jessica Bennett and Ellie Beckler—Thanks for lending your talents and brilliance during such busy life seasons. You both helped bring Penumbra's world to life. Thank you!

Josh Grosshans and Christopher Jenkins—Thank you for lending your expertise on this project!

Melina Hill, Crystal Gettings, Susan Yarborough, Janice Bennett, Jenna Sartor, Dave and Cheri Hill, Brandon Hill, Sarah Holke, Beverly Cunningham, Tina Irwin, Adelphi sisters, and the SOC writers group—All of you have encouraged me in a unique way during the writing of this story. Thanks much!

Melinda Hill, my mom—Thank you for all the trips to the library and TCBY. You introduced me to books and encouraged my imagination. I am forever grateful!

Charlotte Bennett, my daughter—You are such a little wonder. I can't wait for you to read Penumbra one day and meet the characters that bounced around my mind while I carried you. You are such a gift to know!

Jon Bennett, my husband—Can you believe we did it? I say "we" because this story is as much mine as it is yours. Thanks for all the ways you invest in me and my dreams. Oh, the adventures we've had and the ones to come!

My God—Thank you for loving me into a new person, day by day. This whole story and process was such a gift. Thank you, thank you!

To Jon, mi amor

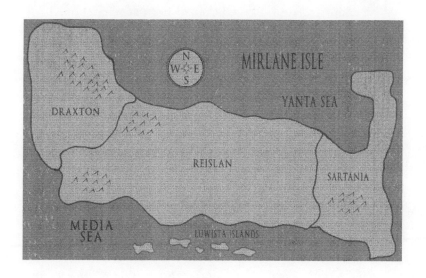

CHAPTER ONE

Norla flinched as a pair of foremen stomped behind her, whips in hand. She quickened her pace and hoped the men wouldn't taunt her. If she lost her temper, her back would have no time to heal from yesterday's lashing before another. Thankfully, the foremen's voices drifted away from her, down the mountain's slope, as Norla climbed upward.

At the summit, Norla dropped her bag of limestones onto the giant pile of rocks and risked a moment's rest to savor the view. The Prumta Savannah unfurled in every direction below her. Unlike the mountain, trampled by generations of slaves in tattered slippers, the savannah rippled with unsullied grass. Farther east, Norla spotted the beginnings of King's Forest, lush with giant trees. Beyond that, soaring up from the greenery, the forested slopes of Vaskel Mountain pointed to the heavens.

Norla's chest tightened, and she wrapped her arms around her blue dress. The distant beauty only reminded her of the mud underfoot and ashy taste of dust in her mouth.

Another girl ambled toward the pile of rocks. Norla didn't know her name, but she looked familiar. Her family lived in a hut a few lanes down from Norla at the mountain's base. The lass was young, barely seven years of age, and her arms already shook with exhaustion.

"Walk slower to the rock quarry and quicker on your return trip," Norla said, taking the girl's burlap bag from her. She dumped the rocks into the pile and returned the bag. "An empty load's easier to carry than a full one."

The girl scratched her arm, covered in grime and limestone dust. She peered up at Norla, and her young eyes flickered in

8

recognition. Averting her gaze, she scurried away without a backward glance.

Norla stiffened but watched as the lass descended the slope, moving at a slower pace than she had come. Foremen often ignored the practice, but not always. They brandished their whips for far lesser offenses. The girl would just as likely be whipped for sport.

A cold autumn wind slapped Norla's cheeks and toyed with her loose hair. She shivered and surveyed the scores of slaves milling around the half-finished temple for King Vaskel, ruler and god of Reislan. The familiar sounds of hammering and sawing filled the air as Norla spotted her mother's muscular frame.

Mia straddled a scaffold, chiseling one of the temple's white columns. Although wind tugged at the long hair escaping Mia's bonnet, she focused on the column with unflinching concentration. No other mason was as skilled. The Linyad architects adored Mia's talent; they protected her from the whip, and some even sneaked her books as reward for her work. And though Mia's status didn't save Norla from whippings, it did protect her from the foremen in other regards.

Norla felt a flicker of pride watching her mother's skillful hands as they carved King Vaskel's solemn face. The stone image seemed as cold and lifeless as the real king. Norla had burned incense and prayed to the king countless times, pleading for freedom. But not once, in all her sixteen years, had she felt heard.

Her mother still prayed to the king. At night, when Norla pretended to sleep, Mia would creep off her mat and set the small statue of King Vaskel on their table. With a bowed head, she would pour out her heart to the king's marble likeness. Norla never understood her mother's words, but she heard the desperation in Mia's whispers. She probably prayed for Norla's father.

Over their suppers of porridge, Mia would talk of completing the temple within the decade. She hoped it would outshine any ruler's shrine found in the mountains of Draxton, the beaches of Luwista to the south, or the orange groves of Sartania to the east. Norla had to admit that the temple on King's Mountain would surely be the largest and most ornate throughout the four kingdoms on Mirlane Isle.

Norla bent to retrieve her bag and noticed a foreman approaching her mother. He shouted something that sent Mia scurrying down from the wooden scaffolding. She dropped to her knees, but the foreman grabbed her by the arm and jerked her to her feet.

A silent scream filled Norla. How dare he touch Mia! Didn't he know who she was?

Rage boiled in Norla's belly, rising up her throat. The emotion powered her feet into action. She hiked up her blue dress and sprinted toward her mother. Heavy mud seeped into her burlap slippers, but Norla didn't slow until she stood beside her mother.

"You work slower than any other mason on the mountain, woman," the foreman said. His clean-shaven cheeks and puny frame revealed his youth. He was obviously new to the mountain; he would serve his two years as foreman and then move to a more reputable post in the Reislan military.

"I want to honor King Vaskel," Mia said, keeping her head bent in submission. Still, her powerful frame dwarfed the short foreman.

"How could your sluggishness honor our king?" he asked.

"Because her work is better than any other mason here," Norla answered. Even if the others had forgotten to explain Mia's status to this foreman, surely he could see the artistry of her hands.

The foreman's mouth parted. He cast a furtive look to see who was watching. Norla followed his gaze and found everyone ignoring them. She tried not to think of how many times she too had pretended to ignore a foreman exercising his authority.

"Do you know to whom you speak, slave?" the foreman asked Norla. He stepped closer, and Norla smelled his sour breath.

"You're of the Linyad class," Norla answered. Her voice trembled. She was barely able to control the anger coursing through her veins. "You're my superior in every way." She looked him straight in the eye and cocked her head to the side. "But you're not quite nobility, are you?"

The foreman's eyes flashed, and Norla knew she had hit her mark. The inevitable whip stings would be worth it.

Mia stepped in front of her. "Please, sir. She's my daughter."

Norla's smirk dropped. What was her mother doing?

Norla edged forward, putting a foot in front of her mother, but Mia's strong arms blocked Norla from advancing.

"Then you should have raised her better," the foreman snapped. His whip cracked. Mia grabbed her shoulder and crumpled to the ground.

"No!" Norla screamed.

Another crack.

A trail of fire burned across Norla's shoulder. Her eyes stung. She squeezed them shut before the tears came. She would never cry with a foreman watching.

With her eyes closed, Norla didn't see the horse-drawn cab until it was practically upon her. The only warning she heard was the foreman's gasp.

~~~

Heaviness descended on Pallo's shoulders the moment he departed from Vaskel Palace. He wished he hadn't played Gen in chess last night. Then he wouldn't have lost the wager and found himself bounding across the mossy floor of King's Forest for a trip such as this.

"Cheer up, Pallo." Gen laughed from across the carriage. "It's inevitable for both of us. We might as well make this fun."

Pallo cocked his head to the side. "Would you think it fun if you had lost the wager?"

"I would have enjoyed the chance to leave the palace."

"Why don't I believe you?"

"Because I'm lying." Gen grinned and adjusted the magenta feather in his wide-brimmed hat. "Have you considered what sort of lady you would like?"

"No more than you." Pallo returned his gaze to the window. Massive keenwood trees stretched their evergreen leaves above a canopy of yellowing cottonwoods and oaks. Months ago, while he and Gen were still students, a ride through the dark forest would have meant the start of a grand trip. Now, Gen served in the military and Pallo served his family's business interests.

Pallo pulled at the silver embroidery of his tunic. "We should reschedule and—"

"We will not reschedule." Gen leaned forward. "If I recall correctly, you challenged me to a game of chess last night. Did you not?"

Pallo scowled.

"Well said," Gen replied. "And did you not suffer an embarrassing defeat at my hand?"

Pallo had never wanted to throttle his friend so thoroughly.

Gen grinned. "Then it's settled. You are choosing a suryan today. And if you took this more seriously, we wouldn't be selecting her on King's Mountain."

"I chose the quickest option."

Pallo had no wish to prolong the horrible process any longer than necessary. Why did he have to choose a mistress in the first place? Pallo hated the age-old tradition and its purpose of preparing noblemen for marriage. It felt like nothing but another link in the chain binding him to the palace.

The carriage slipped out of King's Forest and mounted gentle hills. A few mossy oaks and prickly banyan trees dotted the horizon, though no vegetation was as plentiful as the swaying grass. In an hour, they would reach the barren mountain rising in the distance.

Pallo found freedom in the ripples of surrounding grass. The wild beauty of the savannah's edge was quite different from the manicured order of the palace gardens. It reminded him of his family's olive orchard on the coast. Although he hadn't visited his family's castle in months, Pallo easily envisioned the olive trees' silver leaves blowing in the balmy wind. He doubted he would see those trees again until next harvest—not now that he represented his family at court.

The sound of quiet snoring broke Pallo's reverie. He grinned at the way his friend's chin drooped onto his magenta tunic. Gen never had been able to stay awake long on carriage rides.

Pallo didn't wake him as they passed into Weltang Village at the base of King's Mountain. Rows of mud brick huts lined the grimy road, like cramped mushrooms. Pallo wrinkled his nose. The place smelled of sweat and urine and made his skin itch. Gen stirred with a yawn, and Pallo guessed the stench had awoken him.

Crowds of slaves gawked as the opulent carriage ascended the mountain. Pallo squirmed at their nearness. He noticed the dirt staining their arms, the stoop of their shoulders, and the holes in their slippers. Despite the short distance he had traveled, Pallo knew he had truly entered another world.

Pallo looked to see if Gen felt the same uneasiness, but Gen kept his gaze carefully fixed on the silver staff in his hands.

As they neared the summit, Pallo noticed a girl in a tattered blue gown. She stood opposite a foreman with an older woman beside her. Her uncovered black hair swirled around her like birds taking flight. Although she was small, her passion seemed large enough to consume the entire summit. Pallo had never seen such a lady.

"She's beautiful," Gen said. "Her hair is so... untamed."

Pallo turned to find his friend admiring the same girl.

Gen grinned. "She's perfect for you."

Pallo's pulse quickened. He had no intention of speaking to the girl with the burning eyes. He would sooner boot the drivers from their seat and drive the carriage back himself.

"Not her," Pallo said. "We will postpone—"

"You like her," Gen argued.

"I don't even know her. And she's probably spoken for."

"I saw no bonnet on her head. She is ripe for your choosing."

Pallo considered smacking Gen with his staff. Instead, he risked another glance at the lady. She and everyone near her, besides the foreman, had knelt in the dirt. Pallo's presence had clearly interrupted work on the summit.

Gen tapped the roof of the carriage twice with his staff, signaling the drivers to stop the horses. He leaned forward, his face growing serious.

"You would honor her greatly, Pallo," he said. "And spare her a life of poverty."

Still, the girl would forfeit her place as someone's future wife. As his suryan, she would be respected—he would see to that. They would never marry, though; tradition prevented such unions between Uyandis and Weltangs.

"She would bear the children of a lord," Gen continued. "And not just any lord, a count."

Children. Pallo's stomach turned. They were planning the girl's future without even knowing her name.

Pallo thought of Lania, his half sister through his father's suryan. Everything about Lania had glowed. Her freckled face, her mischievous smile. He had considered her his sister, his equal in every way—despite his mother's constant reminders that Lania belonged to a lower class.

"They're waiting," Gen said, nodding toward the window. "Would you rather I speak for you?"

"I would rather pick another lady." Pallo raised his own silver staff and tapped the ceiling twice. The carriage jolted to life. Pallo looked Gen straight in the eye, daring his friend to contradict him.

Gen kept Pallo's gaze and tapped the ceiling, bringing the carriage to a halt.

"Then I will have her," Gen said.

A rush of heat stained Pallo's chest. He measured Gen's challenging stare and knew his friend was most likely goading him. Gen was even less eager than Pallo to assume the financial responsibility of a suryan. But Gen's eyes flickered with determination. His friend was stubborn enough to uphold his threat if it meant protecting his pride.

No. The word rumbled fiercely through Pallo, and he knew his answer.

"I will take her," Pallo said, though the words sounded strange to his ears.

Gen slapped Pallo's knee. "Good for you. Let's descend." Gen popped the carriage door open and gestured for Pallo to exit first, his eyes laughing. "After you, Count Belany."

Pallo stared at the open door. He had successfully negotiated with two wealthy merchants earlier in the week, yet he felt like a callow youth when faced with the prospect of talking to this slave girl.

Pallo tightened the sash around his waist and smoothed his trousers. He would handle this as he did all his professional dealings. With a shove from Gen, he bounded out of the carriage and onto the muddy summit.

Limestone dust swirled around him, stinging his eyes. Pallo saw that a crowd of bowed slaves had formed around the carriage. Mothers and fathers pushed their daughters forward. They had most likely guessed the purpose behind a trip like this.

"Greetings!" Gen said in a boisterous voice, following Pallo from the carriage. "I am Lord Trilstoy and this is Count Belany." He cast a sideways glance at Pallo, urging him to speak.

Pallo sucked in his breath and looked at the girl. Her blue dress was covered in mud and grime. A long tear ran along the dress's arm, and loose threads hung from its tattered hem. Instead of a sash, she wore twine around her waist. Mud coated her burlap slippers and ankles, and her caramel skin was scarcely visible through the ashy dust coating her skin like sweat.

At the nape of her neck, a raised scar peeked up beneath her soiled gown. The wound didn't look fresh, but Pallo's stomach clenched.

He swallowed and cleared his throat. "I have come to choose a suryan for my household," he said, gazing at the lady's bent head. "And I have made my choice."

Chapter Two

Norla's face stung. She felt his presence above her. His rich voice spoke with the unmistakable authority of nobility.

"Continue with your work," the voice commanded, with the slower, smoother speech of an Uyandi.

Norla heard the sounds of others rising to their feet, muttering words of disappointment.

"Back to work," a foreman called. His whip hissed through the air.

Norla flinched. A hand reached down and touched her throbbing shoulder. His hand. A ruby ring wrapped around his middle finger.

He's chosen me, she thought.

Norla sank deeper into the mud as tears stung her eyes. She knew what would be required of her as a suryan. She would leave one yoke to fill another.

"You may rise," the count said. He released her shoulder and waited, no doubt expecting her obedience and gratitude.

"Rise, child," Mia whispered, beside her. She took Norla's hand and, together, they rose. Norla kept her eyes down, unwilling to look at her new captor.

"You honor us greatly, Count Belany. My daughter is not spoken for." Mia's voice trembled with emotion, and Norla had the disgusted feeling that her mother was pleased.

"What is your daughter's name?" the count asked.

"Norla," Mia said, squeezing Norla's hand.

Norla curtsied but kept her gaze downcast. If she looked up, he would see her tears.

"Norla." The count's deep voice wrapped around the word and sent shivers down her arms.

"Let's have another look at her face," the other Uyandi said. The lord's hand grazed her cheek, before the count slapped it away.

"Don't touch her, Gen," the count commanded.

Norla shrank back and wondered if her captor looked as fierce as he sounded. She risked a glance and found the count glaring at the lord. The pair was an intimidating sight to take in. They both wore feathered hats and purple sashes, indicating their nobility. And though the lord was more muscular, the count stood taller than any man Norla had ever seen.

Both had tanned skin, which surprised her. The few Uyandis she had seen always had skin of pearl. Clearly, the men before her had not restricted themselves to palace life.

The count turned to her then, and the directness of his blue eyes stilled her breath.

"You will be an esteemed member of my household." His tone was cold and formal, as if they were discussing business ventures instead of her future. "Does that please you?"

Of course it didn't please her. Norla wondered why an Uyandi would care about pleasing a Weltang anyway. Maybe he wanted to appear kind in the presence of an audience. But no amount of kindness would cover the true purpose behind such a visit—to take what didn't belong to him.

"You honor us, Count Belany," Mia answered. She gave Norla's hand a soft squeeze, but Norla refused to lie. Instead, she narrowed her eyes and glared at the Uyandi. Let him feel her anger. She wouldn't ease his conscience with pretty words like her mother had.

"You picked a lady with fire," the lord said, with an approving grin.

The muscles under the count's jaw flexed. "Do you know what I offer?" he asked.

Norla nodded. Every man and woman on this mountain knew about the type of arrangement he spoke of. Most girls burned candles to King Vaskel in their huts, asking for the life of a suryan. Norla never had. As Mia's daughter, she knew the kind of agony such a life would bring. Mia had paid dearly for loving another woman's husband.

"You'll live at Vaskel Palace surrounded by riches," the count continued. "Anything you desire will be yours."

"Anything?" Norla asked.

The count gave a brief nod. "I'll deny you nothing in my power to give."

Norla eyed him, so stiff and formal. She wondered what he had the power to give. Freedom for her and Mia? She had heard rumors of other Uyandis offering freedom elsewhere in the kingdom. Maybe this nobleman would free Norla's mother—and her.

Norla frowned. No, the man would never free his suryan. But Norla felt certain she would be able to escape from the palace. Unlike Weltangs, nobles weren't prisoners in their homes. Once the count freed Mia, Norla could escape. They could make a new life together far from the mountain.

Norla felt a flutter of excitement. Even the hope of such a future made Norla feel more alive than she'd felt in months. Squaring her shoulders, she met the count's gaze.

"I accept your offer," she said. For Mia, she added silently. She considered saying, "much thanks" or "you honor me," but she doubted the words would ring true.

The count's eyes flashed with something like relief before growing serious again. "I'll come for you this evening," he said. "All will be supplied for you at the palace." He studied her for the briefest of moments before turning to the foreman. "See that the lady leaves the mountain immediately."

The man scurried to his feet, whip in hand, and gave an eager nod. "Of course, Count Belany."

The count turned to Norla. "May King Vaskel's grace shine upon you." He removed his hat to reveal cropped brown hair and bowed before replacing his hat.

"And you, Count Belany," Mia replied.

Norla said nothing, but curtsied in response.

The lord laughed and gave her a deep bow. Norla glared, which only brought a wider smile to the man's ruddy face. Typical Uyandi arrogance.

She forced another quick curtsy, and the count shoved his companion toward the cab. He gave her a final look before disappearing into the cab himself.

Norla watched the cab descend, scarcely aware that the sounds of hammering and sawing had resumed. She was leaving the mountain.

~~~

Mia took Norla's hand and guided her down the mountain's slope as if she were a child. People watched, wide-eyed, as she left. Word had already trickled towards the village.

"You shouldn't have taken the whip for me," Norla said.

Mia's brown eyes crinkled in a smile. "And you shouldn't have interfered."

Norla bit her lip to keep from arguing. "Did he strike your shoulder?"

"Yes, but I'll survive. And you?"

Rolling her shoulder, Norla found the pain had subsided. "I'll survive."

At the mountain's base, they took the muddy road through Weltang Village. The place was deserted except for young children and the elderly who watched them. No one paid Norla or Mia much attention, and Norla welcomed their indifference. She was too tired to fight back if one of the older women cursed at Mia and her.

A rat scurried by her feet, but Norla hardly noticed. She had grown accustomed to their unending presence. But she doubted she would miss them. She would miss only Mia—and Chestel, but she already missed him.

With a pang, Norla remembered her best friend's parting months ago. A duke had purchased Chestel and a small group of other men to work in his province in the west. Norla had discovered the news too late, and when she'd rushed to his hut, Chestel had already gone.

"Count Belany will come at dusk, I imagine," Mia said. She walked with a lightness Norla had not seen in years. "We don't have much time to prepare you."

"Prepare me?" Norla gave a hollow laugh. "The only clothes I own are on my back." Besides, she didn't want to spend her last moments preparing for *him*.

A sinking sensation spread through Norla's middle. She would leave her hut so soon, the only home she'd known. She would leave Mia.

The panic rose, but Norla exhaled slowly, grasping for composure. She wouldn't break down. She would savor her time left with Mia.

"I'll think of something." Mia picked up her pace and assessed Norla with a flick of her eyes. "In the meantime, you should wash."

"I washed this morning."

"Wash again, and make sure to clean your hair. The count couldn't keep his eyes off your locks."

"Fine." Norla hurried forward, wanting to leave Mia and her happy chatter behind. Didn't her mother care that this would be their last afternoon together?

When they entered their hut, Mia went to her reed-stuffed mat on the dirt floor while Norla glared at the washbasin. Norla found the idea of cleaning unnecessary. The count would still see her as a dirty Weltang.

Mia came to Norla's side and gave her a quick kiss on the cheek.

"Wash, my child," Mia said. "I'll return soon."

With a smile, she disappeared out the door and left Norla alone in the hut. Norla wanted to follow her, to share her pain with someone who understood heartache far more than she. Mia had cried herself to sleep for nearly a year after the slavers took Tylon, Norla's father.

At first, Norla had thought it would be easier for Mia with Tylon gone. As another Weltang woman's husband, Tylon had never married Mia. And unlike Uyandis, slaves took no suryans. Mia had been a mistress without honor.

Every time Tylon visited their hut, another wave of gossip would crash. The man brought nothing but shame and heartbreak in his wake.

Even after his departure, the villagers had remembered he was never Mia's husband. Many enjoyed reminding Norla and Mia of it daily. They all rallied around Tylon's wife, a honey-haired beauty whose easy laughter made her a favorite. The woman had smiles for all but Mia and Norla—and she raised her two sons and daughter to follow her example.

Norla's throat tightened, and she swallowed a sob. She wouldn't waste her afternoon in grief. She knelt beside the washbasin and splashed water on her face and neck. The cold pricked her skin, triggering a shiver down her spine. That would have to do for a bath. She had no plans of subjecting her whole body to that water.

Once Norla had washed, she lay on her bed—a reed-stuffed mat and brown woolen blanket. She propped herself on her elbows and surveyed the familiar scene: the wooden table separating her mat from Mia's, the bench and washbasin by the door, the hole in the thatched roof for fires during the winter. Whether Norla's plan failed or succeeded, she would never see her home again.

She had never imagined missing this place, with its smells of sweat and smoke. But she wouldn't cry herself to sleep tonight like Mia had done. Norla had made that vow long ago.

Leaning back, she welcomed the familiar stick of reeds beneath her back and closed her eyes. She wished her mind would still. If she had no thoughts, then maybe she'd have no feelings either. Maybe if she slept until Mia returned...

It felt like moments later when the door creaked open and Mia slipped in, carrying a bundle of gray cloth. Unfolding it, she revealed a crisp brown dress, a blue apron, and a spotless shift. Judging by the quality of the wool and linen, Norla guessed the clothing had been worn little, if ever.

"They'll be large on you," Mia said. "But they'll have to do."

"Where did you find them?" Norla rose and rubbed her smarting shoulder.

"Never mind that," Mia said.

Norla narrowed her eyes. Slaves weren't able to simply produce new dresses. They received new garments once a year, in the spring. Mia must have gone to the village trading post and sold something.

A rush of heat stained Norla's face. *No.* She sprang to Mia's mat, reached under her straw-stuffed mattress, and pulled out nearly a dozen books. Her shoulders sagged with relief. Mia had not sold her precious library.

Then Norla's eyes went to Mia's pillow. Holding her breath, Norla reached under the soiled square and found nothing.

"Mama," Norla whispered. She knew what that book of poetry meant to Mia. Countless times, Norla had awoken at night to find her mother reading sonnets. Norla had even memorized the swirling pattern of crimson flowers on the book's hardcover.

"Your poems?" Norla asked.

"I couldn't have sneaked a stack of books to the post," Mia said, her face firm. "And that one book bought what I needed. Besides, you represent our family when you go to the palace. Now come, child." She motioned for Norla to join her beside Norla's mat.

Norla obeyed, wishing she felt Mia's joy. While her mother looked radiant, Norla boiled with nerves. If her plan failed, it was likely Norla would never see Mia again.

Mia tugged at Norla's dress, and Norla stood still, letting her mother remove her dress and shift. Mia clucked her tongue and led Norla to the washbasin.

"Oh no," Norla protested. "I already washed."

"Not enough," Mia said. She grabbed a rag, dunked it in the freezing water, and squeezed it over Norla's back.

Norla gasped, but Mia didn't stop. She cleaned Norla's swollen shoulder and tender back with gentle fingers, and then scrubbed every inch of her skin until it stung red. Mia even attacked Norla's callused feet, wiping away grime that had probably gathered months ago.

Norla's hair came next. With soapy water, Mia rinsed the day's dust and mud from Norla's long locks. Although Norla despised the purpose of the washing, she did enjoy it when Mia massaged her scalp to free any remaining dirt.

After bathing Norla, Mia took the wool blanket from Norla's mat and dried her, head to toe.

"I asked about your count," Mia said, fitting her in the new dress.

Norla clasped her hands and said nothing. She did not want *him* to intrude on her last few hours at home. Closing her eyes, she focused on the warm feel of the fabric and tried to forget about the price of the new clothes.

"He'll be a duke one day, Norla, one of the most powerful men in the kingdom. And Belany Province is supposed to be beautiful. It's on the coast with an olive orchard."

Mia grabbed Norla's burlap slippers and banged them together. A bit of mud fell off, and Mia scrubbed the rough threads with her rag. Despite Mia's best efforts, mud still coated the shoes.

With a sigh, Mia motioned for Norla to sit on her mat. Norla obeyed, and Mia wiped Norla's feet before slipping them into the damp burlap.

"I wish your father were here today," Mia said quietly.

Norla stiffened. Her mother rarely talked of Tylon, and when she did, she inevitably gave way to tears.

"Don't hate your father, Norla." Mia tied the blue apron around Norla's waist.

"I don't." The lie came easily enough. Norla didn't want to reveal the depths of her rage—or how much Mia's unconditional love sickened her. If Norla kept lying, maybe her mother wouldn't see how wretched Norla was.

"You're like him," Mia said, smiling.

Norla frowned. If Mia had meant to compliment her, she'd missed the mark entirely.

Mia's smile widened, as if she had read Norla's thoughts. "When he was your age, he had such passion." She shook her head and turned her back to Norla. "But a Weltang with dreams is bound to be miserable," she added softly.

Norla remained still, hoping her mother wouldn't break down. She'd hate her father even more if thoughts of him ruined her time with Mia.

"You can dream now, child." Mia faced Norla. "Don't you see? Your life… " Her voice cracked.

Norla's heart broke at the hope she saw in Mia's face. Why was Norla unable to feel that hope? She saw more chains instead of freedom. Her mother ought to be the one traveling to the palace, not her. It seemed so unfair that Mia should never see the home of the king she served so faithfully. Slaves weren't permitted to travel unescorted beyond the village's stone wall.

"Mama, I'll ask the count for your freedom," Norla said, stepping forward. "Then I can escape and we—"

"You'll do nothing of the sort," Mia said, her face suddenly fierce. "You'll please Count Belany and think nothing of me." She moved into the gap between them and gently took Norla's face in her hands. "He has the power to make your life miserable or full of beauty, child."

A loud rap hit the door.

Norla and Mia jumped. No one visited their hut since Norla's grandparents had died, except Chestel, and he had left six months ago. Mia and Norla exchanged a look. With a shrug, Norla went to the door and opened it to reveal a familiar face.

His pale blue eyes met hers.

CHAPTER THREE

Pallo stood still, breathing in the sight of the lady who had consumed his thoughts all afternoon. Damp hair framed her caramel cheeks, curling at the ends. Her dark eyes flashed, and the fire in them stirred Pallo's blood.

He swallowed and quickly removed his straw hat. Gen had better respect his wishes and wait in the carriage; Pallo was in no mood to entertain a spectator. Norla's presence was unnerving enough.

Pallo had planned to come alone, but when he had arrived early at the palace stables, he had found Gen already waiting for him. His friend had anticipated Pallo's eagerness and outsmarted him. It had not been the first time.

Peeking beyond Norla, Pallo noted the dirt floor, sparse furnishings, and crumpled mats on the floor. Pallo shifted on his feet and averted his gaze. He had never felt more aware of his silk tunic and silver staff. If he'd had any sense at all, he would have changed into his woolen sparring tunic and trousers before coming.

"Good day, Count Belany," Norla's mother said. Although she still had the slight accent of a Weltang, she spoke remarkably smoothly for a slave. "You're very welcome here." She moved Norla aside, providing enough room for Pallo to enter. He obliged, ducking his head to keep from bumping the thatched roof overhead. The older woman's beaming face somehow lessened Pallo's uneasiness. She had a warm way about her. Her daughter, however, looked resentful of his very presence.

Pallo quickly returned his gaze to Norla's mother. "Much thanks, my lady." Her dark eyes reminded him of Norla's, without the fire. "What is your name?"

"Miamra. You can call me Mia."

"Thank you," Pallo said, meaning it. The woman's kindness put him at ease. He wondered if Mia and Norla lived there alone. He had expected to meet Norla's father and siblings.

Gathering his courage, Pallo turned stiffly to the girl. She stood just inside the door with her eyes on the ground. Her frame was even smaller than he remembered. "Hello, Norla."

"Count," she said, keeping her gaze downcast.

"I've brought my carriage for you." Pallo hated the formality of his voice, but Norla's reserve inflamed his nerves.

"Doesn't he honor you?" Mia asked her daughter.

"Yes, Mama." Norla hesitated, then met his eyes. Pallo froze, watching her full lips in anticipation.

"I'm honored to be your suryan," she added.

"The honor is mine," Pallo said.

She shifted under his stare.

"Well... " Pallo said. His palms grew clammy. He hadn't any idea how to proceed. No one had prepared him for the actual task of removal.

"Yes, it is time," Mia said. She bowed to Pallo and turned to Norla. "Goodbye, child. I'll miss you every day."

"You may visit her," Pallo said.

Both women turned to him, eyebrows raised.

Pallo's throat dried. He realized he had broken the custom. A beautiful Weltang suryan would be granted entrance to Vaskel Palace—but not her visiting family members. Pallo had already promised, though, and he would not renege on his word.

"I'll arrange for you to see each other as often as you like," Pallo said. He would find a way.

Norla eyed him with fierce skepticism.

"That's generous of him, isn't it, Norla?" Mia asked.

Norla's cheeks darkened with color. "Very generous," she said flatly.

As he moved toward the door, Pallo felt Norla's coldness mounting.

"Good day, Mia," Pallo said. He cleared his throat. "Your family may expect many blessings from me over the years." He reminded himself to ask his friends what sorts of gifts were appropriate.

"May King Vaskel's grace shine on you," Mia said.

"And you," Pallo replied. He glanced at Norla, hoping to find noble words that would dignify the occasion. None came to mind.

"Shall we?" he asked.

Norla kept her gaze downward and nodded. Mia embraced her daughter and stepped back, leaving behind the smell of soap and fabric. Norla's eyes glittered with tears, but before Pallo had the chance to offer any comfort, she ducked her head and fled through the door.

Pallo squeezed the hat in his hands. It had been foolish of him to suppose he could bring dignity to such a parting. He was taking a girl from her home. And no amount of tradition or precedence could alter that fact.

~~~

Damp winds blew, rippling Norla's brown dress and toying with her wet hair. Oddly, she didn't feel cold as she surveyed the cab, with its two gloved drivers and giant horses. The gilded box looked so much like a cage.

Norla didn't glance back, but she felt the count's presence behind her. She wondered what he thought of the muddy lane at her doorstep. His boots had probably never greeted such muck.

The count didn't speak as he reached past her and opened the cab door. He offered his hand, but she mounted the step without his help. Sitting, she took note of the silky cushions and carpeted floor. Typical Uyandi extravagance.

"Greetings."

Norla looked up to see the brawny lord from earlier. He sat across from her, leaning forward with an easy smile. Norla frowned. She had hoped to present her few requests to the count immediately—one for Mia, and one for her. But she didn't want to speak of such things with an audience present. She knew what role waited for her at the palace, and if she didn't have the chance to speak to the count, he would expect her to play it.

The count sat next to her and sighed. Norla inched away. He placed his hat in his lap and ran a hand across his cropped brown hair.

"Did you meet the lady's family?" the lord asked.

"Her mother is most hospitable," the count answered.

Norla sank deeper in her seat, wondering if he meant to chastise her. Mia had been far more welcoming than she.

"I'm sure any lady related to Norla must have charms indeed," the lord said. He reclined against the cushion and winked at his friend.

Norla glanced out the window and fought to keep her anger in check as the cab rolled on. She would not let a spoiled Uyandi rattle her. They rode past rows of mud-brick huts and into the wild savannah beyond. Norla's heart lightened. She had never set foot beyond her village before.

As children, she and Chestel had dreamed of leaving the mountain for great adventures in distant lands. Chestel had often joined Norla and Mia after supper, when Mia would read from her storybook about Elyarn Isle, the sparkling isle across the sea and beyond their realm. Unlike other villagers, Chestel hadn't looked at Mia differently because she knew how to read. He had even sat in on a few of Mia's reading lessons, when she would write letters on the hut's dirt floor with a stick.

According to Mia, there was a time when all Weltangs knew how to read. But Norla doubted that. She had trouble imaging anything but whips and stones in her ancestors' lives.

Up ahead, trees thickened on the horizon. King's Forest. Her skin tingled in anticipation. She inched her hand out the window, letting the wind lick her fingers.

"It appears the lady enjoys travel as much as you do," the lord said.

"So it would seem," the count said, with a hint of amusement.

Norla quickly drew her hand back inside, vowing to act more collected from that point forward.

The cab followed the cobbled path under a canopy of lush leaves. Norla kept her head inside but craned her neck to see crisscrossing branches form a green tunnel over the pathway. Up ahead, trees and sandberry bushes cleared to reveal Vaskel City.

Norla's eyes widened. She had never seen such elegance. Buildings with stones painted in purples, greens, and blues lined the road, all with silver shutters, and all at least five stories high. Women in flowing dresses and feathered hats strolled out of a milliner's shop. Men with satin cloaks and jeweled staffs disappeared into a noisy inn. The entire street buzzed with warm energy despite the autumn wind.

"I could bring you here sometime, Norla," the count said, "if you'd like."

She turned, finding his blue eyes much too close. She moved toward the window and peered outside.

"Bring her to the bakery," the lord suggested. "The baker's wife prepares the best cream puffs in Reislan. You see, milady, I am a reputed pastry connoisseur." He shot Norla a knowing smile, which she didn't return.

"Both here and abroad," the count added, chuckling softly.

Norla had never imagined a serious man like him would chuckle.

The lord smirked. "If you are referring to the incident in Sartania last spring, I had nothing to do with that shop's fire."

The count pressed his lips together. "Of course."

Norla glanced from one to the other. Neither succeeded in hiding their grins. They clearly found it entertaining that flames had devoured a shopkeeper's business. And she doubted they had helped the him rebuild his livelihood.

The scenery outside gave way to leafy trees and mossy ground. Tilting upward, the cab began to climb Vaskel Mountain. Norla's pulse quickened. They would reach Vaskel Palace within moments, and she had yet to speak with the count.

Up ahead, trees cleared and Norla beheld the palace on the summit, glittering in hazy sunlight. The building's twenty-story marble façade curved on all sides, forming a loose circle of pale purple towers. White shutters lined the palace's many windows, all flung open to reveal sheer curtains fluttering in the autumn wind.

Norla had never beheld such beauty. On clear days, she had seen glimpses of the twinkling marble from the summit of King's Mountain. But she had never imagined the wonder resting atop Vaskel Mountain. It seemed unfair for Norla alone to see it, when Mia would have appreciated the craftsmanship far more.

On the sprawling front lawn, white marble walkways weaved between clusters of oaks and keenwood trees. Nobles strolled along the paths in bright cloaks and feathered hats. Gems of every color sparkled on their hands, their necks, their slippers and hats.

Norla suddenly wished her hair wasn't so wet. Her fingers went to the apron that had cost Mia dearly. Norla wondered what the Uyandis would say when she descended from the cab in her woolen dress. Not that their opinions mattered.

Without warning, the cab came to a stop before Vaskel Palace. Norla gripped the cold windowsill. She needed to present her requests to the count before it was too late.

"My rooms are not far, Norla," the count said. "We can go there directly."

"Will I see you both at dinner?" the lord asked.

The count shook his head and propped the cab door open, revealing a grand staircase leading to the palace's silver front doors. The lord and the count departed first.

"I don't wish to overwhelm her," the count said quietly to his friend. He held his hand out to assist Norla, and as his warm skin touched hers, a jolt tingled down her back. She quickly released his hand. She didn't need his help down from the cab.

"Why would dinner overwhelm her?" the lord asked.

Norla stepped onto the marble path and noticed a pair of ladies mounting the stairs with purple sashes around their waists. They glanced over their shoulders and smiled at the count. When their gazes met Norla, they halted. With wide eyes, they leaned towards each other and began whispering.

Norla glared, but the count stepped in front of her before the women noticed. She felt the familiar anger boiling in her middle. She had spent her whole life wanting to seek revenge on such nobility. She and Chestel used to plot different scenarios as she walked him back to his hut after lessons with Mia. In one of their imagined plans, they had shot flaming arrows from the village all the way to Vaskel Mountain. The entire forest and palace had blazed with fire.

Norla took a deep breath. She wasn't a child anymore. She would have to hide her anger until the count freed Mia.

"Look at them, Gen," the count whispered. He nodded at the women on the stairs. "If Norla comes to dinner, she'll face far more than that."

"Of course she will," the lord said. "She'll have to face them eventually, so why not now?"

"I would rather wait until she's comfortable."

"You brought a Weltang to the palace, Pallo. When do you think she'll feel comfortable here?"

Norla clenched her fists. They spoke as if she weren't even present.

"Bring her tonight. It will be good for you both," the lord said, resituating his hat over his blondish cropped hair. He climbed the stairs and greeted the ladies with a dramatic bow that made them both laugh. He extended his arms to escort them, and both accepted his offer. Together, the trio disappeared through the front doors.

Norla realized the lord had purposely cleared the noblewomen from the stairs for her. She frowned. He needn't have bothered.

"Would you care to dine in the Great Hall, Norla?" the count asked. His eyes searched her face but revealed nothing of his own opinion. "I'd assumed you would rather not, but the decision is yours."

Norla glanced around the lawn and found clumps of Uyandis and their Tintal servants all watching her. She already felt painfully aware of her slave status. She doubted dinner would make things worse. Besides, she had no plans of entering the count's rooms before they spoke.

"I'd like to see the Great Hall," Norla said, keeping her eyes on her hand. "But would we be able to speak at dinner?"

The count raised an eyebrow before nodding. "Of course." He held out his arm for her. "This way."

Norla hesitated. She didn't need a guide up the stairs, but she couldn't deny the trembling in her legs. She'd make such a fool of herself if she fell in front of the gawking nobles.

Grudgingly, she took his arm and noted the hard muscles that tensed at her touch. Why did this nobleman have the body of a slave?

Once they walked through the palace's wooden doors, Norla found herself in a giant entryway with marble floors. A chandelier hung from the vaulted ceiling, splashing the butter-colored walls in warm light. Three archways divided the room, one leading forward into the palace's circular middle, one to the right, and the other to the left. The count turned right and guided Norla along the black marble floor.

Along the way, they passed several men and women. A few of the ladies didn't wear purple sashes, and Norla knew they were suryans. Although they walked with each other and with noblemen, they were never in the company of Uyandi noblewomen. Norla felt their stares, but she didn't return them.

The count ducked into an arched entryway, and Norla hesitated. She would have expected the entrance to the Great Hall to be a bit greater. Through the arched door, they ventured into a dimly lit hallway with dark blue floors and peach-colored walls. Norla's stomach knotted. Was he still leading her to the Great Hall?

At last the count came to a wooden door. Norla tentatively followed him through it, and her blood went cold. She was standing in a bedroom—not a dining hall. Swaths of cream and silver netting covered the four-poster bed. A violet-colored couch sat under the window, with a silver table beside it. A wardrobe stood with doors ajar, waiting for its mistress.

"This will be your room," the count announced. He strode to the closet, flinging the doors open to reveal dresses of velvet and satin and silk. Dresses fit for a suryan.

"I need to speak with you," Norla blurted.

The count turned, shoulders stiff. "Of course."

She held his gaze. "On the mountain, you said you'd give me anything in your power to give."

"I meant it," the count replied.

"So you are a man of your word?"

"I aim to be."

"Then I have two requests." Norla's ears pounded. "I ask that you free my mother."

The count hesitated. "I cannot promise that. Only King Vaskel grants freedom, and I have never seen him do so."

Norla shook her head, unwilling to believe him. "I've heard tales of other Uyandis freeing slaves."

"Those are rumors, nothing more." The count's voice grew quiet, as if he sensed the despair his words invoked. "Vaskel only honors freedom that he alone grants."

The air seemed to thicken. Norla's lungs tightened as she pressed her palms together. If she had known that, she never would have left the mountain so willingly.

"Norla," the count began, his voice softer than she had yet heard it, "I shall go to King Vaskel and make your request, but I cannot guarantee his response."

Norla searched his eyes, wanting to believe him. He was probably spouting pretty words to appease her. But even the chance of Mia's freedom meant she hadn't come to the palace in vain.

"Thank you," she said. Her throat felt thick with emotion. She wished they weren't alone. The count's searching gaze missed nothing.

He moved in closer. Each step triggered a fresh wave of nerves in Norla.

"What is your second request?" he asked.

Norla clasped her hands together, squeezing until her fingers ached. This request was for her, and she would know all too soon if he would honor it or not. She took a deep breath.

"I'd like another night to myself, before becoming your suryan."

CHAPTER FOUR

Pallo blinked. Norla's words had pierced the heart of the tension between them. None of the ladies at court had ever addressed him with such boldness. Still, he had to answer her question.

Clearing his throat, he met her gaze. "Of course. I shall respect your wishes."

She nodded, her fists loosening. Her eyebrows were still gathered in a frown, and Pallo knew she didn't believe him. Well, she would learn soon enough that he was a man of his word. He had no plans to disappoint her—or himself.

"Much thanks."

Pallo saw Norla quickly move her shaking hands behind her slim back. The girl fought to appear as strong as a sword's blade. He knew trained soldiers who showed more weakness than she did.

He gestured to the closet. "If you still wish to attend dinner, there are plenty of gowns for your choosing. Tomorrow, a seamstress will make the proper alterations for you."

"All right," Norla said.

"I'll come for you once I've changed," Pallo said. He bowed slightly and Norla stepped deeper into the room. She placed as much space as possible between them, as if the thought of his touch sickened her.

With a frown, Pallo turned to leave. He had never met someone so utterly repulsed by him.

~~~

True to his word, the count rapped on the door several minutes later. He wore a turquoise tunic over silk trousers, with his purple sash in place. Norla wondered if she would ever look as natural in the nobility's fine fabrics. She wrapped her arms around the tight bodice of her satin dress and wanted to change back into her tunic. The silk stockings restricted her legs, and the satin slippers hardly seemed sturdy enough to walk in.

She had felt like an imposter when the Tintal maid had appeared and laced her into the heavy dress. The woman had hardly said two words. Apparently she had felt assisting a Weltang was beneath her. Norla's back and shoulder, still tender from whip marks, had ached at the woman's harsh hands, but Norla hadn't made a sound.

The count cleared his throat. "You look lovely," he said brusquely. Even when complimenting her dress, he sounded like a man conducting business.

"Thank you," she said.

The count eyed the curves of her olive-colored dress, and Norla's face grew hot. Foremen had looked at her like that. She was a commodity to such men, nothing more.

Norla swallowed and pulled a sweep of hair over her shoulder, running her fingers through it.

"I could send a maid to attend to your hair," the count said.

Norla froze. She had never thought her loose hair would be inappropriate. She probably looked completely feral to this count—her blistered hands especially. She had asked the maid if she might wear gloves to dinner, but the woman had clucked her tongue in disapproval.

"Gloves aren't worn indoors this early in the season," she had replied, as if Norla were an utter fool. "Only after the olive harvests will *noble* ladies wear them."

Norla hadn't made another request.

"Others might stare," Pallo explained. "That is the only reason. Personally, I prefer your hair down."

Norla raised her eyebrows.

"Not that I prefer your hair," he said quickly. "Although, I do *like* your hair."

Norla fought the nervous urge to smile. She had never seen an Uyandi look awkward, and his discomfort had a disarming effect on her. He seemed less intimidating when he was caught off guard.

"When does dinner start?" she asked.

"Presently."

"Then I'll go with my hair down," Norla said. Everyone would see her as an outsider anyway. In addition to the nobles, there would be Linyad merchants and Tintal servants at dinner, but Norla was almost certain she would be the only slave. No need to conceal her differences. She did not wish to blend in, only to secure Mia's freedom. Hopefully the count would ask King Vaskel right away.

The count offered his arm, and Norla accepted. Its firmness still surprised her. Maybe he had served in the army. A few noblemen served in hope of increasing their land holdings.

Keeping his pace slow, the count led her through the halls of his rooms and into one of the palace's main hallways. Other couples and families strolled along the black marble. Everyone, even the Tintal servants dressed in sage tunics and dresses, stared at Norla.

She kept her gaze focused on the long hallway ahead. Let them stare at the Weltang. She had grown accustomed to stares long ago as Mia's daughter.

The count walked her through a set of double doors leading into the circular palace's main hallway. Windows with open shutters lined the way. The air teemed with the smells of leaves, damp moss, and late blooming flowers. Through the windows, Norla spotted one of the palace's gardens.

Candle lanterns dripped from plush trees nearly twenty feet high. The lush branches lined marble pathways, weaving in between trickling fountains. But these candles didn't smell like the ones made from tallow back home. The nobility preferred beeswax.

"This way," the count said, gesturing to the open double doors just ahead.

In the Great Hall, gigantic chandeliers hung from the vaulted dome ceiling. Five tables, each long enough for eighty people, spanned the length of the room. Satin cloths covered the tables and their matching chairs. Clusters of candles lined the centers of the tables, illuminating silver plates heaping with spiced meats, stuffed vegetables, and sweet breads. Individual bowls, filled with olive oil for dipping, stood at each place setting.

Norla's stomach ached with hunger at the smell of the rich food. She hadn't eaten since before dawn, and this would be the first meal of her life that consisted of anything besides porridge and crusty rolls.

Despite the hundreds of nobility sitting at tables and milling through the hall, the room was eerily quiet. Everyone moved and talked with stiff restraint. Maybe the tight dresses contributed to the air of confinement.

"Where is King Vaskel?" Norla asked the count.

"He tends to arrive late," he said. She noted the irritation in his voice with surprise. She had assumed all the nobles adored their king.

Norla hoped that King Vaskel didn't arrive too late. If he did, the count wouldn't have the opportunity to present her request.

"Do you think you'll be able—" she asked.

"Pallo!" a girl's voice exclaimed.

Norla felt the count's arm muscles tighten as a tall girl hurried to them. She wore a white dress trimmed with green feathers that matched her catlike eyes, and a purple sash of nobility hugged her curvy waist. Like the other nobles, she wore an opulent evening hat, swathed with satin, silk, and more feathers.

Norla didn't understand why the nobles thought feathers were so fashionable. They looked completely ridiculous.

"Where have you and Gen been all afternoon?" the feathered girl asked. "The two of you left without a word." If this Uyandi noticed Norla, she didn't show it.

The count shifted on his feet. "I've been introducing the newest member of my household to the palace." He turned to Norla. "Fira, may I present Norla, my suryan."

The girl's eyes widened. Her mouth parted. "I didn't know... " Her voice trailed off, and she turned her full gaze to Norla.

"Norla, this is Lady Effira," the count said.

Norla had never seen anyone so beautiful. Freckles dusted Effira's pale skin and pink cheeks. Blond curls fell from a high bun, framing her face. Thick lashes lined the lady's eyes, which were coolly surveying Norla.

"May King Vaskel's grace shine upon you," Effira said curtly. She turned back to the count. "You and Gen shouldn't have left me behind. You promised I could accompany you on any day trips."

"We traveled to King's Mountain, Fira," the count said quietly. "I assumed you wouldn't wish to join us."

Effira pursed her lips and smoothed her green feathers. "I would rather choose for myself."

"Pallo!" a familiar voice called.

Across the hall, the lord from earlier sat at one of the long tables, waving them over.

Norla felt a flicker of relief at seeing the ridiculous Uyandi and his angular face. He wore a silver tunic that matched the feather in his silver hat. How strange that this man, of all people, would make her feel more at ease.

The count offered his free arm to Effira, and her eyes filled with warmth as she took it. Did the count notice?

Together, the three of them joined the lord at his table. He rose to his feet and gave the ladies a low bow.

"Welcome, my dear Fira and fair Norla," the lord said.

"Much thanks," Norla said, relaxing slightly.

"So this is the Weltang?" asked a blond man sitting beside the lord. He grinned at Norla. "Why have I never thought to pick a lady from the mountain? Well done, Pallo."

With a shake of his head, the man sipped from his goblet. "It seems unfair you should steal the hearts of all the ladies at court, and then keep this beauty for yourself. A better man would share the wealth."

Norla's ears tingled. The man spoke as if she were a possession to trade. She had expected nothing less from Uyandis. She had to bite her lip to keep from snapping at him.

As if he sensed her tension, the count leaned towards her. "Ignore him," he said, nodding toward the blond. He spoke loudly enough for the nobleman to hear. "You have far more manners than he."

The blond snorted and took another sip from his drink.

"And these are Gen's older brothers," the count continued. He pointed to three men, all with the lord's muscular build and deep brown eyes. They were so immersed in their conversation that they didn't hear the count's introduction, which suited Norla just fine. She had already met her fair share of nobility for the evening.

As Norla's eyes darted across the glowing hall, she felt the weight of several more stares. But one stare lingered longer than the others, with a bold intensity that held Norla's gaze. The man looked about Mia's age, and he kept an auburn beard.

Something about him separated him from the others. His silver and indigo tunic was impressive, as were his jeweled hat and sash. Norla could scarcely imagine the cost of so much topaz, amethyst, and agate.

But the man's distinction didn't stop there. He drew glances from all in his presence. He didn't seem to notice the attention he roused, though; his dark eyes remained fixed on Norla.

She wished desperately that he would look away. More people were staring at her now because of him.

"Look who is watching your suryan," the lord said to the count.

The count turned. He drew his eyebrows together and pressed his lips. "I should have expected this."

"Expected what?" Norla asked.

The count looked down at her with a smile that didn't reach his eyes. "You have drawn the king's gaze."

~ ~ ~

Pallo reminded himself to remain calm as the king approached, but every muscle in his body wanted to throttle Waylan Vaskel for the hungry look in his eyes.

"Count Belany, who is this gem on your arm?" King Vaskel asked. He did not take his eyes from Norla's face. She inched closer to Pallo, who tightened his hold on her.

"This is Norla, my King," Pallo said. "My suryan."

Vaskel slowly turned his gaze from Norla. His proud eyes assessed Pallo with the same calculation he applied during their sparring matches. Pallo stood straighter, challenging the king's stare with his own. He would not be found wanting. Norla's safety depended on it.

Pallo had heard rumors of how Vaskel treated his many suryans behind closed doors. He shuddered at the thought of Norla enduring such treatment. Although tradition dictated that the king could not take another's suryan, Pallo noticed the glint in Vaskel's eyes.

"Norla," Vaskel repeated. He licked his lips, as if savoring her name. "I would ask my grace to shine upon you, but I see you already glow."

Norla's cheeks darkened, but she held his stare. Pallo was proud of her. Few women or men in the room had the strength to manage the king's direct gaze.

"Thank you, my King," she said. "You are kind."

Pallo wondered if Vaskel detected her sarcasm.

"I am?" The king feigned surprise, and the hall erupted in laughter. Pallo didn't join the others. Vaskel had never amused him, and the king's advances upon Norla only strengthened Pallo's distaste for him.

"Where do you call home, dear Norla?" Vaskel inquired, leaning forward. "I would love to know from what lands Count Belany has plucked you."

Norla hesitated. "Not far, my King."

Vaskel waited, then grinned at Pallo. "She is coy, is she not? Tell me, fair lady, from where do you hail?"

Norla dropped her gaze to the marble floor. "Your mountain, my King."

A burst of murmurs flew about the room. Pallo's stomach twisted. The whole hall was watching Norla now.

"A dirty Weltang," the king exclaimed. "How extraordinary! She speaks so well for a slave. I can scarcely believe it!"

Norla's anger radiated from her like the scent of perfume. Pallo didn't blame her. He was forming his hands into fists, resisting the urge to strike the grin from the king's face.

"My grandfather picked a Weltang girl for his household," Vaskel said, stroking his beard. "I never have. I believe the adjustment to palace life would be far too challenging."

The king took another step forward and tipped Norla's chin toward him. Her eyes glittered with rage.

"I'll help you adjust, dear Norla," Vaskel said. His eyes caressed her face. "Seek me out for anything you desire."

"Anything?" Pallo demanded. The word erupted from him. How could anyone view Vaskel as a god? He was nothing but a corrupt, lecherous man.

Vaskel stepped back, but he kept his fingers on Norla's chin. "Anything."

"Free her mother," Pallo spat. He would slash the man's pretenses and reveal his empty promises for all to see. "This is her desire."

Vaskel's eyes flashed. He dropped his hand from Norla and turned the full weight of his stare to Pallo.

"You speak boldly." The king's voice was as hard as the marble floor. He eyed Norla with a faint grin. "Are you bold enough to win the freedom of your suryan's mother, Count?"

A wave of dread hit Pallo in the chest. Vaskel's coy smile reminded Pallo of the king's expression when he was about to knock the sword from Pallo's hand in a match.

"I believe I am," Pallo said.

Vaskel's grin widened. He rocked forward on his boots, sweeping his hands behind his back.

"Then go to the Andromila Desert and retrieve the Book that Penumbra stole from me," Vaskel ordered. "When you return with the Book, I shall free the Weltang's mother. Does that sound like a fair quest?"

Murmurs rose from the surrounding dinner guests.

The quest was far from fair. All of Reislan knew of Penumbra's band of riders and their murderous reputation. Vaskel had sent countless missions to recover the Book over the last twenty years. No soldiers had ever returned.

The king had effectively sentenced Pallo to death.

Pallo closed his eyes, unable to meet Norla's gaze. How cavalierly he had thrown away her greatest desire. How brashly he had ruined his one chance to ask Vaskel a favor on her behalf. In his anger, Pallo had created the ultimatum before him.

"I shall go," Pallo declared, meeting the king's triumphant gaze. What choice did he have?

"Excellent!" Vaskel clapped his hands. "And do feel free to kill Penumbra while you're retrieving my Book. Treason requires bloodshed, you know."

Pallo knew whose blood the king wanted.

CHAPTER FIVE

Norla's stomach, still empty after barely touching the rich dinner, tightened with nerves as she hurried to keep the count's pace. She kept remembering the king's final words. Treason in all the Mirlanian kingdoms required death.

"You'll die," Norla said. She walked beside the count, past the lush garden she had admired earlier. The candle-lit courtyard looked far less magical now.

"Perhaps." His voice was void of emotion. He probably hated her.

Norla swallowed. She didn't blame him. Because of her, the count had accepted a quest that would likely claim his life. Although she hardly knew the man, she didn't want his blood on her conscience. She had to make the count see reason.

Norla stopped beside one of the hall's open shutters, forcing the count to stop as well. "You wish to die?" she asked, searching his face. The corners of his mouth dipped, dragging his eyes down as well.

"I wish to uphold my family's honor," the count said. "And yours."

"But you'll fail," Norla argued. "The king won't free Mia." After meeting the source of Mia's adoration, Norla had seen nothing but a cruel, lascivious man. "The king wants to make a spectacle of you," she added.

"That is Vaskel's way," the count said. He brushed the sheer white curtains with his fingers. "He's punishing my insubordination. And he's accomplishing another aim to boot."

"What do you mean, another aim?" Norla asked.

The count focused on the curtains, ignoring her.

Norla marched around to face him. "What are you not telling me, Count Belany?" she asked.

His eyes widened, and for an instant, Norla wondered if she had crossed a line by raising her voice to a count. Mia would be appalled by her behavior.

But the count smiled—a genuine smile, void of the courtly formality she had come to expect from him. In the candlelight, Norla saw an unexpected gentleness in his tanned face.

"You," he said quietly.

"Me?"

"The king desires you as his suryan."

"But I'm yours."

"Not if I'm dead."

Norla's cheeks stung as if a gust of winter wind had slapped her. Of course. She had seen desire in the man's eyes, but she hadn't guessed the cost of it. If the count died, she would join King Vaskel's household and never see Mia again.

Her stomach rolled with the realization. Her ears started ringing. She couldn't live as King Vaskel's personal slave. She couldn't. Even the thought of such a life made her flush with fear.

"Norla, I don't plan to die," the count said softly. "Vaskel believes he's bested me, but I'll prove him wrong."

Norla shook her head. "You'll die, and then I'll be… " Her voice gave way, and she knew she'd surrender to tears if she continued.

A muscle in the count's jaw flexed. "*No*. That will not be your end, Norla." He dropped his hands to his sides. "If I don't go, you'll resent me, and my cowardice will blacken the Belany name. If I go, I can free your mother and trump Vaskel for my family's sake."

Norla narrowed her eyes. Penumbra and his men were infamous criminals. Even if the count did have skill with the sword, he was one man—no match for Penumbra's entire band.

"You can honor your family some other way," she said. "They wouldn't want you to die for them. And I promise not to resent you." She didn't mind lying. Let the count believe she would forgive him.

The count gave her a grim smile, and Norla knew he had already made his decision.

"I have the opportunity to aid all of Reislan by retrieving the Book, Norla," he said.

"What is so special about this Book?"

"In the king's hands, the Book can make Reislan the greatest kingdom on Mirlane Isle."

"How?"

"Ancient magic from ancient ages." The count shrugged. "I know nothing more, Norla. The king has been obsessed with recovering it for as long as I can recall."

The count extended his arm toward her. "Let's retire. I plan to leave at dawn. The sooner I go, the less time Vaskel has to embellish his plan."

Norla reluctantly took his arm, and together they walked along the hall lined with candle sconces. The count was so stubborn. She noted the firm set of his jaw. Impossible man! He was determined to die.

Well, she wouldn't remain behind to suffer the consequences of his ill-fated journey. If she stayed, the king would waste no time in claiming her. If she tried returning home, the king would undoubtedly find her and bring her back to Vaskel Palace. And she and Mia had no prayer of escaping from Weltang Village; there were too many foremen on guard. They would let a Weltang return, but never leave.

Norla sneaked a sideways glance at the count. She wanted to help him. She had to, considering how much his death would affect her.

The count led her to his rooms, and into her bedroom. Her hands trembled. The cozy quarters made her painfully aware of her status as his suryan. Would he honor her request?

Norla had little experience with men in this regard. Foremen had eyed her, but Mia's status with the architects had earned Norla protection in that respect. A few of the village boys had begun to leer at her—until Chestel put an end to that with a few fistfights.

The count ducked through the doorway after her, and Norla's insides churned. His nearness unhinged something in her. She reminded herself that the count was her captor, nothing more. She owed him nothing.

He pointed to a bell on the silver table. "You may ring that to summon your maid. She will help you retire for the evening."

Norla nodded, but she had no intention of asking the Tintal for more help.

"Goodbye, Norla." The count's voice was quiet, pensive. His eyes were fixed in resignation. "I'll try not to die," he added with a wry smile.

"See that you don't," Norla said. She felt the urge to smile back, but thought the better of it. They were not friends.

When he exited, Norla exhaled slowly. Her head felt light, and she massaged her temples for a moment to refocus her thoughts. She had to find the count's friend.

She tiptoed to the door and cracked it open. No sounds emanated from the candlelit hallway. The count must have already retired to his bedroom.

Gathering her skirts in her hands, Norla slipped into another hallway with peach walls and prayed she was heading in the right direction. As she passed several doors on either side, she wondered how many rooms made up the count's suite. Maybe she would have to start opening doors.

Then, up ahead, she spotted a wooden door that looked larger than the others. Reaching it, she cracked it open and saw the familiar black marble and cream-colored walls. She felt a rush of relief and ventured into the main hallway that looped around the circular palace's outer chambers.

She needed to find a servant before anyone saw her. Earlier, they had buzzed about the palace in hordes. Now servants seemed as scarce as daylight.

"Norla?"

Norla sucked in her breath. She turned to see the beautiful lady from dinner—Effira—approaching on the arm of a tall, blond nobleman. Several other men followed in her wake, all wearing feathered hats. If the count intended to take Effira as his wife one day, it seemed he would have his share of competition.

"Is Pallo all right?" Effira asked, stopping before Norla. "He left so suddenly after dinner."

"Er, yes, we did," Norla answered. She had hardly eaten more than a mouthful of the spiced pheasant and peppers, because her stomach had been too full of nerves for much else.

The lords stepped forward to appraise her.

"So this is the lady who has caught the king's eye," one of them said. He had the smell of wine on his breath.

Effira pursed her pink lips. "Yes, this is the lady who will cost Pallo his life."

The words stung, and judging from Effira's steely glare, the effect was intentional.

"You are so serious tonight, lovely Effira," another nobleman said. "Pallo might succeed. If anyone could, it would be him. Only the king can beat him with the sword."

"It will take far more than a skilled swordsman to retrieve the Book," Effira said. She rested her cold eyes on Norla. "Why isn't Pallo with you?"

"He retired," Norla said. "I am, er, looking for a servant."

"Why?" Effira asked.

"Well," Norla hesitated, knowing she didn't owe Effira an answer. The lady's Uyandi attitude rattled Norla, but she swallowed her retort. The count's life depended on her. "I'm trying to help the count," Norla said.

Effira's eyes flickered. She turned to the noblemen with a sweet smile.

"Would you be so kind as to leave us? I wish to speak with this suryan alone." She spoke with an authority that didn't match her smiling lips.

"Couldn't we stay?" the blond nobleman said, leaning forward. "You're both so lovely."

Effira ducked her head and smiled up at him from long lashes. "Perhaps another time, Leondo," she said.

Leondo frowned but bowed goodbye. "How can we deny your wish, Lady Effira?" he asked. "Come, lads. We'll leave the ladies to their own affairs."

Effira kept a smile on her face until the men disappeared down the hall. Then she turned to Norla with a doubtful scowl.

"How do you intend to aid Pallo?" she asked.

"He's leaving tomorrow at dawn," Norla said. "I thought if the count's friend knew, maybe—"

"Gen would accompany Pallo?" Effira finished for her.

Norla nodded.

"Of course Gen would," Effira said. "Pallo knows this, which is undoubtedly why he intends to leave at dawn. He wishes to save Gen from trouble."

"But the count needs help," Norla argued. "It's an impossible task alone. With assistance, he might stand a chance."

Effira wrinkled her mouth to one side, deep in thought. Her emerald eyes were dazzling in the flickering light. What did the count think when he looked into such a lovely face? Norla had never been more aware of her dark skin and muddy eyes.

"You care about him," Effira said. It wasn't a question. She turned abruptly and walked away, calling over her shoulder, "I'll deliver your message to Gen."

Norla watched her go, feeling Effira's chilly parting all the way to her bones. But as much as Effira loathed Norla, she seemed to care very much for the count. Effira would deliver the message.

"Wait," Norla called after the lady. "I want to speak with the lord myself."

~~~

Pallo dreamed of Norla that night. She sat beside a stream, dipping her arm into its brilliant blue waters. Fish the color of rainbows darted through the stream, sunlight splashing off their fins. But at closer look, Pallo discovered hundreds of snakes swimming among the fish.

His heart pounded. He had to warn Norla. But as he moved toward her, she lifted her arm from the water. Dozens of fang marks lined her skin. Her eyebrows lifted in surprise, as if she had not felt the bites.

Pallo felt his chest constrict. He sprinted to her and, kneeling beside her, took her small hand in his. She looked up at him, her dark eyes stripped of their usual hardness. They brimmed with tears.

He gingerly raised her wet skin to his lips and felt her shudder. Carefully, he sucked the venom from one of the snakebites and spat the poison into the grass. He moved from bite to bite, straining in effort, yet Norla's body slackened against him.

Pallo's arms grew weak, and he knew the snakes' poison had seeped into his blood. His vision blurred. The burning began at his lips and blazed like a wildfire through the rest of him. He gathered Norla in his arms and cried out.

~~~

Pallo awoke feeling sluggish. He considered seeing Norla before he left, but feared waking her. If she discovered him in her bedroom, she would undoubtedly question his motives. He had seen the way she tensed when he had wished her farewell last night. Her coldness stung, but Pallo knew he would never draw her respect by force.

Pallo quickly dressed in a woolen tunic, trousers, and riding cloak. He grabbed his hat and strode down his hallways, out of the palace, and through the front gardens to the stables. He held his head high as he walked.

The purpose of his journey was noble, after all. He welcomed the opportunity to provide his kingdom with the much-needed stability the Book would bring. Pallo had grown up with the constant threat of war from Reislan's Draxton neighbors to the west and Sartanian neighbors to the east.

Nearly all had lost ancestors in the Great Wars, which had raged sporadically for nearly two centuries.

Only in the last sixty years had Mirlane Isle known peace. King Waylan Vaskel's grandfather, Benteen Vaskel, had been an influential and powerful leader who had hated the relentless wars. Through his strategic diplomacy, he had coaxed the other kingdoms into signing a treaty. Reislan had granted Draxton and Sartania some of its bordering provinces in exchange for exclusive trading rights with the wealthy Luwista islands, which in turn had become an independent kingdom.

Now that the kingdoms had reached a strained peace, travel was encouraged. Pallo and Gen had always found safe passage on their journeys, but they had each sensed the mistrust behind the polite welcome from inn owners in Drax-ton and Sartania. As an ally, Luwista was Pallo's favorite kingdom to visit. The white beaches and salty air reminded Pallo of his family's castle on the coast.

Pallo would much rather be traveling to Belany Castle than to the Andromila Desert. He and Gen had ventured into the desert's hot sands two summers earlier. They had hoped to spot one of the many Andromilan tribes—nomads who spent their lives traveling the desert. But Gen had complained of the heat, and they had turned around long before reaching Gracehen Oasis, where the tribes met to water their herds.

This oasis was Pallo's present destination as well. At the watering hole, he would question the tribes to divine the location of Penumbra's latest lair. Then he could slip through Penumbra's camp and retrieve the Book unnoticed. He and Gen had plenty of experience blending into different settings when needed—though Gen despised removing his hat.

Pallo neared the stables and paused for a moment to admire the purple light of dawn. The oaks and keenwood trees sparkled with dew and carried the mossy smell of autumn. How grand it felt to be outdoors.

As promised, Pallo's servants had instructed the grooms to have Pallo's horse ready. He had considered asking a few servants to accompany him, but all his men had families. It would not be right for them to risk their lives on such a journey. No, he would travel alone. As a solo rider, he stood a better chance of going unnoticed.

A groom with graying hair gave Pallo a brief bow and held out the reins of Senna, Pallo's dappled gray mare. Senna had been intended for light riding and breeding, but Pallo had allowed his sister to ride the mare in secret. And Lania's riding had been far from light.

Reislan custom discouraged ladies from equestrian activities; horsewomen were "disgraceful and far too masculine," in his mother's words. But when Pallo had watched Senna and Lania fly across the sand, spraying water in their wake, Pallo hadn't seen his sister disgraced. He had seen her *alive*.

Even now, three years after Lania's death, Pallo still thought of his sister when he looked into Senna's wide brown eyes. They had always shared a spark for adventure.

The familiar ache stirred in Pallo's chest. He pressed his forehead against Senna's muscular shoulder and heard the horse neigh softly. Pallo rubbed her coat and smiled. Senna had a way of comforting him like no other. The mare had taken to Pallo from the start, nurturing him along in the art of riding as any mother would train her young. When asked how he had learned to ride so well, Pallo would always reply, "Senna taught me."

Pallo stroked the groove in Senna's muzzle. "Ready for another adventure, my girl?"

The mare bobbed her head and whinnied in agreement.

Stepping into the stirrup, Pallo swung himself onto Senna and evaluated the saddlebags. He had requested that the servants fill them with watered wine and dried meats, beans, and vegetables. If he rationed properly, he would have plenty.

Pallo slipped on his riding gloves and fit his hat securely in place. With a nod to the groom, he guided Senna onto the marble path leading through the front lawn and into King's Forest. Together, the pair traveled under a tunnel of leafy branches, through the deserted lanes of Vaskel City, and into the savannah.

In an hour's time, he neared the silhouette of King's Mountain in the morning light. The faint sound of hammering spilled from its slopes into the savannah. Slaves were already at work. Like a line of ants, they traveled to and from the rock quarry a mile north of the mountain.

Norla's luminous eyes and slight frown drifted across Pallo's mind. He pictured her hands, scraped and bruised, heaving bags from the quarry to the summit. Such had been her life, year after year.

Pallo felt a strange twinge in his middle and brushed Senna's sides with his feet, prodding her into a canter. Cold wind combed through his hair and sent the tails of his cloak flying. With another soft squeeze, Senna accelerated into a gallop. Pallo crouched low, closed his eyes, and savored the powerful sensation of Senna's rib muscles beneath him. And her speed. He felt as though he were soaring above the grass, bounding into the sky.

Senna wouldn't keep this pace long. But for a moment, they both enjoyed the freedom of her gallop.

Then Pallo heard it. The sound of pursuit.

His eyes flew open. Behind him, a horse-drawn carriage was chasing Senna. By the looks of it, the jeweled carriage belonged to a fellow Uyandi. In fact, the carriage looked remarkably like his own. And the driver wore a purple riding cloak and an extremely tall hat with a matching purple feather.

Pallo cursed. He knew one lord in particular who enjoyed matching his feathers and tunics. Pallo reined in Senna and waited, his jaw clenching.

As the carriage neared, Gen brought Pallo's workhorses to a stop.

"Good morning, Count Belany!" he exclaimed from the driver's bench. "What a lovely morning for a ride."

Pallo blinked. "How?" he demanded.

"Your beloved." Gen grinned and nodded back at the carriage.

Pallo tightened his grip on Senna's reins, triggering a toss of her head. Did Gen mean Norla? She was safe at the palace,

54

Pallo told himself. She lay in her bed, and he would see her again after the journey. Still, he had to make sure.

He jumped from Senna and strode to the carriage door. Popping it open, he was greeted by Fira's wide green eyes, under a broad-brimmed hat.

"I'm coming with you, Pallo," she blurted. "You cannot send me back."

Pallo's shoulders relaxed. Fira would be difficult to persuade, but the thought of arguing with her seemed far less daunting than challenging a girl he hardly knew. Then he spotted a glimpse of black hair. Fira was not alone in the carriage.

CHAPTER SIX

"Why are you here?" the count demanded.

Norla shrank back at the force of his voice.

"We're coming with you," Norla said. She forced herself to relax on the cushion, as if his presence didn't affect her.

"You're mistaken," the count said. The taut lines of his face, the stiff set of his shoulders under his dark blue cloak—everything about him revealed his frustration.

"We're here to help you, Pallo," Effira said, leaning forward on her seat. "You're a fool if you think you can manage without us."

Norla blinked. She never had imagined that a lady wrapped in a fine velvet cape would speak so frankly.

"Fira, I have—" the count began.

"I won't see you die," Effira snapped, jutting out her chin. She held his gaze, but her eyes began to mist. She ducked beneath the wide brim of her straw hat.

The count's gaze softened. "I don't plan to die, Fira," he said, "and you know quite well that a lady of the court cannot join an overnight venture with Gen and me. Your reputation would be shredded."

"I've seen to that." Effira dabbed her eyes with a cloth that matched her satin gloves and sat up straighter. "My maids believe I'm visiting my family's manor in the north. Word will spread quickly enough."

The count shook his head, and Norla guessed Effira still risked much by leaving with him. Undoubtedly, rumors would swirl about her timely departure.

"Is this your doing?" the count asked the lord, who had joined him at the cab door. "You cannot seriously mean to join me, Gen. Do you remember our last trip to the desert? You begged me to turn around before we reached the oasis."

"I came down with pneumonia," the lord replied, his eyes darting to the ladies. "And besides, what else will I do until your return? Stay at the palace or my family's castle? I would go mad."

"What about your family, Gen?" the count asked, quieter. "Would you leave your brothers behind, with so little chance of returning?"

The lord scoffed. "I'm the youngest son, Pallo, or have you forgotten? My family cares little of my affairs. Besides, I have no intention of failing. We'll return with the Book, maybe even slay Penumbra, and become heroes throughout the land." He slapped the count's arm with his gloved hand, as if the whole feat would be accomplished in a few days' time.

The count's scowl deepened, and Norla began to wonder if her plan would succeed. She had never met anyone as stubborn as this towering nobleman. His deep blue riding cloak made his shoulders seem broader than she remembered. She wondered how many others had bowed to the count's will when met with that scowl.

"I'm your friend, Pallo," the lord said with a sigh. "I have another month before I must return. Accept that, won't you?"

The count studied his friend for a long moment before nodding. "All right, Gen," he said.

The lord grinned and turned to mount the driver's seat behind the horses. "I am a captain now, after all. You'll benefit from my military brilliance."

The count smiled and shook his head. "Of course. But we won't bring the ladies with us."

"My apologies, Pallo, but I struck a deal with Norla," the lord said, swinging himself onto the seat.

"What sort of deal?" the count asked.

"I wouldn't have known of your departure if it weren't for her. The ladies are coming, Pallo. It's already decided."

The count's cheeks reddened, as if something inside was preparing to burst.

Norla swallowed. It was not that she blamed the count for his anger. She would have been furious if someone had addressed her in such a way. But she knew he stood a better chance of succeeding with the lord's aid—and she would not let the count risk his life for her without at least trying to help.

"This is my decision, Gen," the count said, striding toward the driver's seat. His hard voice and imposing posture was all Uyandi. Images of foremen and their whips filled Norla's mind. She shuddered and rubbed her temples, willing herself to remain composed.

The lord shook his head in apology. "I gave Norla my word. She said you'd fight me on this, and I promised to defend her."

"She did?" The count stomped around to the cab door and peered at Norla. His dark gaze warmed her skin. She had seen the count upset with the king, but his emotions felt far more powerful when directed at her.

"You were extremely busy last night," the count said quietly.

Norla nodded. She wondered if she ought to defend herself, but if she had judged correctly, she wouldn't have to.

The count swept his hat from his head and rubbed the back of his neck. In the morning light, his brown hair shined with flecks of honey. His fingers lingered at his neck's base, twirling an imaginary piece of hair. Norla wondered if he had once worn his hair long.

At last, he smiled grimly. "It appears you've bested me, Norla. But if you ride as my travel companion, I think it is only fair that you call me Pallo."

Norla blinked in surprise.

"Do you agree?" he pressed, watching her closely.

She knew that she needn't agree in order to accompany the count; she had outmaneuvered him, and they both knew it. But part of Norla still wanted to grant the count's request. The man was risking his life for Mia, after all, and it seemed like such a small appeal.

"All right," she said. "Pallo."

He closed his eyes briefly, lips pressed together, and then gave her a quick nod before closing the cab door.

Exhaling, Norla sank against the plush cushion. Her heart beat wildly. She had only said his name, she reminded herself. She called Effira by her given name, and that hadn't affected Norla. Still, something had shifted between her and Pallo, and she didn't know how to shift it back.

The cab started, and before long they rode past King's Mountain, into the vast Prumta Savannah to the west. Norla peered across the cab and found Effira staring out the window, wrinkling her mouth to one side. Her green cape and purple dress made her golden hair and creamy cheeks all the more striking. And a subtle cinnamon smell seemed to linger around her.

The Uyandi lady had defied so many of Norla's expectations. Effira was willing to venture into the Andromila Desert. And although the lady had taken precautions to preserve her reputation, Norla guessed that Effira still risked much by accompanying them.

Effira made no effort to converse, which suited Norla fine. She preferred the silence. Closing her eyes, she thought of Pallo's words. For an instant, he looked as though he saw her as an equal. Had she truly bested him? Norla smiled at the prospect.

Norla kept her gaze to the window and breathed in the sights of the countryside. They rode past creeks and farms where cows and goats grazed in pastures and Tintal workers were busy planting rows of winter barley and wheat. Weltang slaves most likely joined in the labor. The richest Uyandis bought slaves from the mountain for their territories. Squinting, Norla wondered if she rode past her father. From this distance, it would be impossible to tell.

Without warning, Norla's stomach rumbled. She had awoken hungry from not eating dinner the night before, and she'd been so consumed with her plans, she hadn't eaten that morning. Since the food and drink had been packed outside,

Norla would have to wait until they stopped. She would rather die than have the Uyandis think her a weakling.

Throughout the morning and early afternoon, they stopped every couple of hours to let the horses graze. Pallo and Gen ventured off to give Norla and Effira the privacy to relieve themselves. Norla expected the proper lady to fuss and scoff at having no chamber pot, but Effira didn't complain once.

Since Pallo was in a hurry to reach their campsite by evening, he and Gen declared they would eat lunch as they traveled and stop only briefly for breaks. In the cab, Effira sipped from her leather canteen and snacked on smoked meat, a fig, and a large biscuit that smelled of honey. The bread's fine texture was so different from the thick bread Norla typically ate. Effira didn't offer to share, and Norla didn't ask. She had grown accustomed to hunger on the mountain.

The sun dropped lower in the sky. Effira dozed on and off, and Norla assured herself they would stop soon for supper. Even slaves on King's Mountain broke for supper. How strange to think that only a day earlier, Norla had been heaving stones up the mountain's muddy slopes. She would never know that kind of labor again. Soon, she would either be victorious in freeing Mia and herself... or dead. Either option sounded better than returning to the foremen's whips and villagers' stares.

The cab began to slow, and Norla surveyed the surrounding sea of tall grass. Streaks of orange and red trailed across the dusky sky, like bursts of fire across a blue field. When the cab halted, Effira rocked forward. Righting herself, she ran her fingers through her hair, pinched her cheeks, and bit her lips. Norla blinked. In a moment's time, Effira had managed to look freshly rested and powdered.

Gen swung the door open and extended his arm. "Ladies," he said.

Effira rushed forward and stepped down with his assistance. "Pallo," she called, disappearing from sight.

Gen grinned at Norla. "Come and see the campsite Pallo has chosen," he said.

Norla took his hand and stepped into the knee-high grass. It tickled her slippered feet and bare legs, and she savored the new sensations. Thankfully, she had refused to wear the new slippers and stockings Pallo had provided at the palace. The less she took from him, the better.

Pallo strode to her before she even released Gen's grasp. He took her hand and guided it to his arm.

The leather of his gloves reminded Norla of the foremen's gloves. She had never understood why those men needed gloves to yield a whip, yet the masons and builders were required to work barehanded.

"You look exhausted," Pallo said. He surveyed her face with a frown. "Didn't you sleep?"

Norla had the urge to smile at his candor. She glanced down and smoothed her wrinkled apron and dress. The rest of her probably looked just as worn out.

"I'm fine," she said. Her stomach rumbled and Norla walked forward, forcing Pallo to keep pace with her. She avoided his gaze easier when they were moving.

Up ahead, she noted a loose ring of oak trees with underbrush lining its edges. Gen was busy collecting fallen branches, while Effira was freeing the workhorses from their harnesses. She murmured to the brown geldings as she worked, stroking each of their necks.

"She'll groom them every morning and night," Pallo said. "Ladies aren't encouraged to know much of horses, but Gen and I have taught her the basics of grooming."

He watched Effira with a fond expression that looked far too private for Norla to share. Of course he fancied her. Every man in the palace probably did.

Norla untangled herself from Pallo's arm and went to help Gen gather branches. She welcomed the prospect of physical activity numbing her mind.

Gen paused as she moved closer to him. "Are you ill, Norla?"

"I'm fine," Norla said, snatching a branch.

Gen laughed. "Pallo certainly picked a hot blood."

Ignoring him, Norla bent down to pick another branch. And another and another, until her head throbbed. Squatting on the ground, she pretended to search for a branch and waited for the dizziness to pass. Grass brushed her arms and chin, like a feathery blanket.

Pallo's black boots and trousers appeared just before her. He knelt to meet her eyes.

"Norla, what's the matter?" he asked, mere inches from her face.

Norla closed her eyes, fighting the dizziness that Pallo seemed to increase. Just then, her traitorous stomach let out a loud growl. She winced.

Pallo's eyes narrowed. She felt his tension as he stood and faced Gen.

"You told me that you packed food and wine for them in the carriage," Pallo said.

Gen held his pile of sticks in front of him like a shield. "I did." He opened his mouth to speak, then snapped it shut. His face paled. "It was outside the carriage, in the rear, with the tents... The ladies couldn't reach it."

Pallo glanced from Norla to Gen, then back to Norla, before letting out a deep sigh.

"We'll eat promptly," Pallo said. "And the ladies eat first."

~~~

The small band gathered around the campfire at the center of the oaks. A cold autumn wind blew, stinging Pallo's cheeks. He laid three woolen blankets down in a semicircle around the fire. As he sat on one, he looked to Norla, but she didn't seem to notice him as she slipped onto the empty blanket.

Fira, however, chose to share Pallo's blanket. Gen sat on the other blanket and bent over a journal, scribbling away with a quill pen. He had brought the leather journal on all of their travels. Once, when Gen's spirits were high with drink, he had confessed his dream of becoming a famed writer. As the youngest of four sons, Gen knew his dream of great renown would require some creative maneuvering.

Pallo unpacked dried lamb's meat and honeyed biscuits and passed around portions. Next, he produced a jar of olive oil, his favorite addition to any meal. This oil came directly from his family's orchard, and a single drop of its tangy, fruity flavor flooded Pallo with memories of warmer nights and easier days.

When Pallo offered the jar to the others, Norla blinked and then refused. Her lips pressed into something like a smile, and Pallo wondered what she found so amusing about olive oil. He rarely had a meal without it.

While everyone ate, Gen regaled the group with tales from his post on Reislan's eastern border. Gen's storytelling usually involved reenacting sword fights, wild gestures, and any other generally large movements. This night was no exception.

Gen had worked himself into a sweat by the time he had finished his tale about a tavern mistress in the Axum Mountains. Pallo decided not to correct his friend's rendition of the story—it had been Pallo, not Gen, who had beaten the lady's brother in a sword fight in the city square.

While Gen's familiar voice filled the camp, thoughts of Norla filled Pallo's thoughts. He didn't look at her often; when he did, she ate more slowly. But he could hear how quickly she drank her wine and chewed her meat.

Pallo shook his head. Norla had been under his care for only a day, and she had spent much of that time hungry and thirsty. What a dreadful protector he had turned out to be. His only thought had been of reaching this cluster of oaks by dusk.

Pallo had failed Fira as well. He was surprised she hadn't complained. Norla was accustomed to hardship, but Fira had been surrounded by servants since birth. She had traveled with Gen and Pallo before, of course, but only on day trips and always with plenty of provisions. He had clearly misjudged Fira's strength.

Perhaps the party could bed at Yintpa Castle in two nights' time. There, the ladies could enjoy fresh baths, warm food, and plush beds. Duke Yintpa would certainly show them hospitality, as he and Pallo's father had been friends at university. And Yintpa Castle wasn't far off their path. Pallo was sure that Fira, in particular, would welcome the noble treatment after such journeying.

Taking another sip from his jug, Pallo wondered how Fira would feel about the present accommodations. Tradition dictated that Pallo and Norla would share a tent. Theoretically, such an arrangement wouldn't upset Fira. Pallo had never encouraged or pursued her romantically during the course of their friendship. Still, if Pallo felt awkward with the arrangement, he imagined Fira did as well. Gen, however, was clearly too immersed in stories and wine to notice the potential strain of their situation.

Pallo decided to use his friend's orating to his advantage. He rose to his feet and silently slipped through the tall grass to the carriage. Senna and three of the workhorses were lying beside it, while the other stood nearby, munching on grass.

"Enjoying a rest?" Pallo asked Senna as he unpacked the tent bundles and lanterns from the carriage.

Senna lifted her nose, nickering a defensive response.

Pallo held up his hands. "I meant no offense. You deserve it, my girl."

He returned to the camp and began assembling the three woolen tents along the outskirts of the fire. The quicker the transition from fireside to tent, the less time there would be for the ladies—and him—to feel awkward. Thankfully, Gen continued his tale about swimming through shark-infested waters from one Luwista island to another. The ladies listened raptly, and Pallo marveled at Gen's ability to tweak inconvenient facts. For example, in this particular story, Gen had not exactly swum through infested waters. He had ridden in Pallo's sloop.

Pallo worked quickly to set up the three tents, digging sticks and pegs in the ground and attaching giant cloths. He then carpeted the inside of his square tent with silk blankets and pillows, and set a candle lantern in the middle. A single slit in one side served as the door.

The thought of Norla sharing this warm tent with him made his pulse thump. He imagined her small form draped across the silk blankets, her flushed cheek against a pillow, and the curves of her body traced by her simple gown. Despite himself, he felt his blood stir.

He had honored her request last night, and she had said nothing of the following night. But Pallo had noticed the girl's exhaustion, despite her best efforts to conceal it from him. If he had any honor in him, he would make no advances tonight.

Pallo exhaled slowly, willing himself to relax. He had to exert patience where Norla was concerned—however sorely he wished to do otherwise.

As he strode to prepare the inside of Fira's tent, he noticed the camp had grown silent. Everyone was staring at him.

Gen chuckled. "Eager to retire, Pallo?"

Pallo's cheeks burned. "I'm exhausted from a long day of travel," he snapped. "Aren't you?"

"Of course." Gen's eyes flitted from Norla to Pallo in amusement. Norla kept her face focused on the fire, but its flickering light danced across her skin, betraying a deep crimson blush. Fira wouldn't look at him.

Pallo fought the urge to strike Gen, and instead, prepared Fira's tent with plenty of blankets, pillows, and a lantern. He worked quickly, knowing that each passing second was painfully long for everyone present—except Gen.

After readying Fira's tent, Pallo threw a few blankets into Gen's tent and dropped the lantern by the tent's slit. His friend would have to ready his tent himself.

Pallo then strode toward the fire and offered Norla his free arm. "Shall we?" he asked.

Norla hesitated before rising to her feet. "Very well."

"Goodnight," Pallo said to his friends. Fira nodded briefly, keeping her gaze on the fire, while Gen gave a mock salute and a wink.

"Goodnight, Count Belany and fair Norla," Gen said.

Pallo led Norla away as Gen added, "Sleep well!"

Pallo's back stiffened, but he didn't turn around. Snapping at Gen would only prolong the situation.

When they reached the tent, Pallo held the slit open while Norla crawled inside. He followed, and as he assessed their tight quarters, his cheeks warmed. The woolen room was impossibly small. Norla sat on the opposite side of the tent, as far away from him as possible. And yet, she was easily within his arm's reach.

Norla folded her legs against her chest and refused to look at him. Despite her stony expression, he noticed her arms were trembling. For all her bravado, the girl was clearly frightened and freezing. Unlike Fira, she wore no cape to protect her from the elements. He would have packed something for her if he had known of her intent to join him.

He eased his cloak from his shoulders and offered it to her. She shook her head in refusal, still shivering.

She seemed so much smaller in the tent than she did outdoors. He ached to hold her, to comfort her.

"Norla, I—" he began.

"How long have you lived at the palace?" she asked. Her voice sounded high and uneven.

Pallo cocked his head to the side. Why would Norla care of such matters?

"I have lived there permanently since spring," Pallo answered. He reluctantly dropped his cloak and lay on his side. His muscles ached from the day-long ride. "Before that, I spent the school years at Vaskel University and summers at home."

"At your castle?"

Pallo nodded.

"And that's where your family lives?" Norla asked. She still wouldn't meet his gaze.

"Yes." Pallo noticed the way her fingers nervously worked at her apron. He needed to assure her she was safe in his presence. "Norla—"

"Why doesn't your family live at the palace with you?" she asked.

Pallo sighed. He removed his hat and dropped his head to the silky blanket, rubbing a hand over his hair. Talking of his family made his head throb.

"My sister is dead, and my parents manage our province in the south." Pallo closed his eyes; he didn't wish to see Norla's reaction to his admission. And there was so much he hadn't revealed. His father's constant searches for the wreckage. His mother's adamant belief that Lania wasn't dead despite the size of the storm—and then her inevitable acceptance.

There had been a funeral, but with no body they had sent an empty boat to sea. The province priest had prayed for Lania's spirit to find the House of Belany in the realm beyond the sea. But the prayer had meant little to Pallo. His sister had brimmed with life; it was impossible to imagine her in death.

"I'm sorry about your sister," Norla said softly.

Pallo propped his hand on his head. Norla was staring at the lantern, her face relaxed in thought. A glimpse of Norla stripped of her defenses. He drank in the sight of her unbound hair, her flushed skin, her fathomless eyes, like pools of brown topaz.

He savored the image, thinking she looked somehow softer.

If he held her, would she understand he meant only to warm her?

CHAPTER SEVEN

Norla held her breath as Pallo breached the space between them. She saw the desire in his eyes and knew her presence on this trip had signaled an invitation. Maybe if she kept him talking she could delay the inevitable another night.

"What plan do you have to retrieve the Book?" Norla asked. She hated the tremor in her voice.

Pallo frowned. "Why do you fear me, Norla?"

Norla pressed her palms together. She had to find a way to escape the tight tent quarters. She would rather face the cold night than the warm tent with Pallo. His black tunic clung to his chest, illuminating each curve of muscle.

"I don't fear you," she said.

"Norla," he said, his eyes soft.

His plea warmed Norla like flames from the campfire, igniting heat deep inside. And then a sharp wave of anger shot through her.

"You ruined Mia's chance at freedom," Norla whispered fiercely. She didn't want the other Uyandis to hear. "You let the king trick you."

Pallo's eyebrows shot up. His face blanched. "I know. And I'm sorry."

"That doesn't change anything," she snapped.

"Norla." Pallo rose and leaned forward on his knees, his eyes intent upon her. "I ride now to right the wrong."

Norla clenched her hands in tight fists. She was scarcely able to control the emotions churning inside her.

"And when we fail, what then?" she asked. "You've ruined everything."

Pallo's eyes flashed. "There's still hope, Norla."

68

"No thanks to you."

A muscle throbbed at the base of Pallo's jaw. "I'm risking my life for your mother."

"So I should grovel at your feet? Give myself to you out of gratitude? After all, Mia is *only* a Weltang. Her life isn't worth much."

"I never said that," Pallo said, his voice deepening with anger.

"You didn't have to." Words surged up in Norla like a geyser's spray. "How many slaves work on your orchard, Pallo? You're a spoiled Uyandi like the rest of them."

Pallo's gaze flickered. "I'm sorry my Uyandi blood is so offensive to you, Norla." He snatched his feathered hat and the nearest blanket. "I won't press my presence on you any further."

He swatted the tent flap aside and disappeared into the night.

Norla sat in stunned silence. Her whole body shook despite the tent's warmth. She had completely lost control. And in her fit, she had attacked a man who was risking everything for her greatest desire. He had even told her of his sister. Norla had felt privileged to hear his admission, and yet, moments later, she had beaten him away with words.

She had never felt so utterly alone.

~~~

Norla awoke early the next morning to find Pallo asleep beside a dying fire. In sleep, he looked younger. At peace. So unlike the man who had stormed from the tent last night.

She had expected him to return to the tent after their argument—to claim what rightfully belonged to him. He was an entitled Uyandi, and she would never let herself forget that. She'd had plenty of reminders, down to the generous jar of olive oil he had packed.

On the mountain, Chestel had vowed he and Norla would taste the expensive oil one day. She had shaken her head at his ridiculous promise, knowing full well a slave would never taste the liquid gold of the nobles. Even few Linyads dined with olive oil, so why would a Weltang hope to taste it?

Yet Pallo had packed an entire jar of the oil for his travels.

After waiting hours for him to return, she had calmed and drifted to sleep, only to dream of masked riders pursuing across sandy plains as she rode Pallo's mare. No matter how hard she rode, the riders had advanced, nearly capturing her before she awoke in a sweat.

Norla shivered and brought Pallo a blanket from their tent. She draped it over his long form and wondered how he had managed to fall asleep in the cold night. Norla felt a flicker of guilt but reminded herself that he had chosen to sleep there.

Rising, Norla saw Effira emerge from her tent. She had changed into a yellow dress, but still wore her green cape over her shoulders. It was strange seeing the lady without her hat. Effira's eyes immediately went to Norla's tent, and then to Pallo before spotting Norla.

Effira raised an eyebrow in question and came over to Norla. "Why did he sleep outside?"

"He chose to," Norla answered. As she bent to collect sticks for the fire, she felt Effira's stare.

"Are you not his suryan?"

"In title, nothing else." Norla saw no point in pretending a relationship existed when it didn't.

"I see." Effira peered at Pallo, and her fingers went to her hair. She brushed curls from her face and began braiding her honey strands.

Norla felt a pang of jealousy but pushed it away. Effira was a free woman. If Norla gave way to envy, she would never escape that trap. Effira would always win.

Effira turned away, then stopped. "I'm sorry about yesterday," she said.

"Yesterday?" Norla asked.

"I assumed you had eaten while I slept. I never thought to share with… "

"A Weltang," Norla finished.

Effira nodded and gave Norla a small smile.

As Norla watched Effira return to the fire, she ached for Mia. How Norla longed to speak with someone who considered her an equal. Instead, Uyandis surrounded her. She had always felt the distinction, but since last night, her loneliness had magnified into an acute throb.

Still, she had sentenced herself to this. The heart of this venture belonged to her. Hopefully she had not ruined Mia's chance at freedom by angering Pallo. Hopefully he would still want to retrieve the Book for his own sake—if not for hers.

~~~

The next day of riding passed quickly. Pallo avoided speaking to Norla; he preferred silence to her lashing words. No one spoke much over their supper of dried beef, squash, and biscuits, not even Gen, who sat comfortably on a ridiculous pile of pillows. Apparently hours on the driver's bench had not agreed with his backside.

Gen wrote in his journal, dipping his quill pen into the ink bottle every so often and frowning constantly. When Fira asked to see the journal, Gen laughed and tucked it away. Pallo had never asked, but he had been sorely tempted on more than one occasion to take advantage of his friend's negligence after drinking.

Norla hardly looked at Pallo as she ate. He fought with all his might not to think of her, but his mind continually rehashed their argument from the night before. Norla con-sidered him a failure, an Uyandi *pig* that had ruined her mother's hope of freedom.

Pallo sipped from his jug. Well, he would prove her wrong. He would stop at nothing to retrieve that blasted Book.

As the others finished eating, Pallo told them his plans to break their journey at Yintpa Castle. Norla said nothing, but Fira clapped her hands in delight, and Gen nearly spilled his ink bottle out of excitement.

Though his friends' excitement encouraged Pallo, he still felt a dull ache.

He didn't look at Norla as he helped Gen prepare the tents, and then made his own bed beside the fire. He avoided even bidding the girl goodnight. He had faced enough humiliation at her hand. Gen offered to share his tent with Pallo, but the thought of any tent chafed in Pallo's present mood. He preferred the vast sky for a ceiling.

~~~

A new wind blew from the west the following day. It smelled faintly of sand and heat, and Norla knew they were surely nearing the savannah's edge. Effira's eyes darted from the window to Norla most of the morning. Unlike before, Effira offered Norla plenty of food and drink—even though Norla had her own supply of watered wine and olives. She definitely preferred the Uyandis' fare to her diet on the mountain.

Today, the Uyandi lady wore a deep green dress that matched her cape and her eyes. Norla still wore her brown dress from Mia.

"What will your mother do when she's freed?" Effira asked, leaning forward slightly. "Will Pallo employ her as a maid?"

Norla stiffened. "No."

"But why? She isn't a Tintal, but Pallo could make an exception. Wouldn't you want to see her every day?"

Norla studied the lady's intent gaze and knew Effira was genuinely curious. Norla leaned against the cushion and remembered the blissful silence in the cab the previous two days.

"Mia has other plans," Norla said. Effira didn't need to know that it was Norla who had the plans. And if Norla succeeded, she and Mia would venture south to build a new life on the Luwista Islands. Boats traveled often enough from Reislan's southern coast to the nearer islands.

"What is your mother like?" Effira asked.

"Like?"

"What are her interests?"

72

Norla felt an unexpected throb in her throat. She pictured Mia surrounded by books on her dirtied mat. As a young child, Norla had spent long days in her grandmother's hut while Mia worked on the mountain. The old woman saw to Norla's needs, but hardly spoke to her. Norla had assumed the woman blamed Norla for Mia's ostracism.

But then Mia would return in the evenings and sweep Norla away to a hut brimming with stories of distant lands. Chestel would tell his parents he was playing leapball with his cousins and join them. Together, Norla and Chestel would listen as Mia's voice painted tales of beauty and adventure and everything the mountain lacked.

Mia read to them about Elyarn Isle the most. According to ancient storytellers, the faraway isle was as old as time. Its lands glittered with flowers so vibrant that a passerby could taste their juices just by smelling them. Waters from hidden mountain springs doused the skin with just a glance. And the sprites... Norla had found the stories of those immortal creatures most dazzling of all.

But each year on the mountain had made it harder to journey with Mia to her sparkling isle beyond the sea.

"She likes stories," Norla said. She crammed a handful of raisins in her mouth and turned to the window.

Although Norla felt Effira's gaze, the lady miraculously left Norla alone for the rest of the afternoon.

When the sky grew dusky, a light mist replaced the afternoon rain. Night approached quickly, and then, through the water-streaked window, Norla spotted a cobbled path lined with torches.

Outside, Gen and Pallo let out whoops of joy, and the cab lurched forward. Norla knew the Uyandis were eager to have castle walls around them once again. Of course, she secretly welcomed the prospect of a proper bed as well. She could still feel the way her bed in the palace suite had enveloped her so wonderfully.

Fiery lanterns whirled past the window and illuminated the outline of a modest castle ahead, not more than four stories high. As they approached the limestone façade, servants poured from its double front doors. They wore sage trousers and tunics, and gray sashes and flat caps. On their waists they carried swords.

Norla's skin tingled. Something was wrong. As the cab came to a halt before the front entrance, the servants formed a circle around Senna and the cab.

Norla exchanged a glance with Effira, and both of them went to the door. They descended onto the wet stones just as Pallo spoke.

"Why do you greet his guests in this manner?" he said, to no one in particular. He remained seated on Senna. "I'm a friend of Duke Yintpa's and wish to speak with him."

A female servant on the top step laughed. "An interesting request," she said. Her dark red hair was unbound beneath a flat gray cap and hung past her shoulders. Like the other female servants on the steps, she wore a sage dress and gray sash. "But there is a new master of the house now."

Mist chilled Norla's cheeks. She considered the servant's confident smirk and wondered how much that smile concealed. The woman slouched and yawned as if the whole scene already bored her. Despite her weary expression, she looked only a few years older than Pallo. And she spoke in the slower, polished tongue of a noble.

"We demand to see this new master," Gen said, standing from his seat on the cab. He rested his hand gently on the hilt of his sword at his waist and glared at the nearest servants. "Move aside, or I shall move you myself."

"What a temper," the lady said, and clapped her hands. "I wouldn't make another threat like that, grand Lord." She smiled, but her tone sliced like a blade. Another two dozen servants emerged from the entrance behind her. The lanterns on either side of the double-doors reflected flames upon their swords.

Norla's stomach flipped. Pallo and Gen were proficient swordsmen, but they had no hope of overcoming such numbers. Effira had shown greater resilience than expected during their travels, but Norla doubted the lady knew anything of fighting. And Norla had fought back against the foremen occasionally, but she had no prayer of defending herself against a sword.

"I'll honor your request," the lady said to Gen. "This could be entertaining to watch." After giving him a lazy smile, she disappeared into the two-story castle.

"What should we do?" Effira asked.

"Attack," Gen said, inching his sword from its sheath.

"Don't be a fool," Pallo said. "We have no hope of overcoming so many." He scratched behind Senna's ears, but the mare kept her head high and stiff. "We must wait and speak to this new master."

"What if he's a renegade servant like the others?" Gen asked. "What if he chooses to kill us and take the ladies for himself?"

Pallo glared at Gen, but then gave Norla and Effira a quick glance that betrayed his fear.

"We wait," he said, quieter. "We have no other move, Gen."

Gen let out a groan, but slipped his sword back in place. He sneaked several glances at Effira and Norla as they waited for this new master to make his appearance.

"We cannot let them take the ladies," Gen said.

"I will die before that happens," Pallo said.

"As will I," Gen added quickly.

As Norla watched the two, she realized they cared for her—a Weltang—to some extent. And in a small way she cared for them, too. She didn't want to see either harmed.

The servant woman with the crimson hair returned. Behind her, a man emerged, dressed in the same sage tunic and trousers as the other men. His body was strong and tanned, and he wore his hair long. He looked much younger than Norla had expected, nearly the same age as her.

He moved down the stairs as his dark gaze assessed the scene, making quick calculations. As he came closer, Norla's breath stilled. She hadn't seen those familiar, defiant eyes in months.

His lips parted in shock. "Norla?"

Norla exhaled. "Chestel."

CHAPTER EIGHT

Norla rocked on her feet. She had not seen her best friend since a slaver had taken him from the mountain six months earlier. He looked taller and broader, but his brown hair was as unruly as ever. His rebellious eyes still glimmered with mischief.

Her throat tightened as Chestel bounded toward her and swept her up in his thick arms.

"Norla," he whispered, holding her close to his woolen tunic. He smelled of hay and wind. She squeezed him tighter and tears slipped down her cheeks. Everything would be all right now, she told herself. Her best friend was here.

When he pulled back, Norla saw her own tears mirrored on his cheeks. They both laughed and wiped their faces.

"I can't believe it," Chestel said, stepping back to look at her. "Destiny's brought you to me."

"No, I brought her to you," Pallo said, striding to Norla's side. "I am Count Pallo Belany of Belany Province." He threw the words at Chestel like punches. His blue eyes blazed.

Chestel stepped forward, his hand moving to the bronze hilt of his sword on his waist.

"How do you know this lad, Norla?" Pallo asked, holding his own sword's hilt.

Norla moved between the two of them.

"She doesn't answer to you," Chestel said to Pallo. Although his height didn't match Pallo's, his presence did. "Who's this man to you, Norla?"

Norla hesitated. "I'm his suryan."

"His what?" Chestel growled. He whirled around to the lady at the top of the stairs. "Roella, you said the girl's a maid."

Roella shrugged. "Does it matter if she's a mistress or a maid?"

Chestel glared at Pallo, who returned his stare with equal animosity.

"She isn't your suryan anymore," Chestel said in a low voice.

"Who are you to make such a statement?" Pallo challenged. Gen strode up behind him, eyes dark as he glowered at Chestel.

"He's my best friend, Pallo," Norla said quietly. "We were slaves together on the mountain."

"We don't have slaves here." Chestel gestured to the men and women encircling the cab and horses. "We're brothers. Equals." His lips parted in a wry smile. "And anyone who doesn't understand our code's an enemy."

"That's madness," Gen exclaimed.

Pallo moved closer to Norla, wrapping her arm around his free arm. Chestel's eyes flashed. The muscles in his square jaw flexed.

Norla dared not move; she felt wedged between two rocks. Chestel deserved her allegiance. Countless times, he'd made her laugh after a foreman's whipping, helped defend Mia from the gossipers, and listened to and shared her dreams of freedom.

Still, Pallo didn't deserve betrayal at her hands. He might be entitled and hopelessly Uyandi, but he'd proven himself, in her chamber at the palace and in the tent on the savannah, to be a man of honor.

"I won't let you take Norla from me," Pallo told Chestel. "She's my suryan and under my protection."

Chestel's face relaxed. Norla knew the look well; Chestel had won his way.

"Then you defy our law," Chestel said. He waved three of his comrades forward. "Take him to the dungeon."

Pallo tightened his grip on Norla's arm. "What will you do to her?" he asked.

Chestel raised his eyebrows. "Worried about her? You're the one who used her."

"Pallo isn't a criminal," Norla said, stepping forward.

Chestel and Pallo turned to her in surprise.

"He's an Uyandi," Chestel protested.

"Yes," she agreed.

Chestel gaped at her. Murmurs rose among the circling comrades.

"Protecting her count," Roella said from the top of the stairs. "What a good little mistress."

"You know nothing of me," Norla snapped at the lady, her face burning.

"I can't make exceptions, Norla," Chestel said. "If a man thinks he's above the rest of us, he isn't one of us." His eyes pleaded with her, and Norla knew he expected her allegiance.

"What about you lot?" Chestel asked Gen and Effira. "You choose equality or prison?"

"We shall never be your equals," Gen spat. He raised his chin in a valiant pose that made Norla's throat tighten. Gen, with all his airs and ridiculous ways, didn't deserve the dungeon. None of them did.

"And you, Lady?" Chestel asked Effira.

"Will you harm the horses?" she asked.

Chestel frowned.

"I shall go with Count Belany and Lord Trilstoy," Effira said, "but I insist you care for the horses. They must be groomed twice a day, every day." She held her head high, waiting for Chestel's compliance.

Chestel blinked. He surveyed her silk dress and blonde curls with obvious frustration. Unfortunately, Effira looked remarkably like the part of the entitled noblewoman.

"I'll see to the horses," Chestel replied curtly.

Norla knew he meant it. When they were younger, Chestel had often dreamed about riding a horse one day.

Effira reached into her cape's pocket and pulled out a glass vial that smelled strongly of cinnamon.

"This will help if they have sores," she said. "I made it myself from elpine herbs." She stepped forward and placed it in Chestel's hand. "You must apply the ointment liberally."

Chestel bristled but accepted the vial. He nodded to the nearest comrades. "Take the three of them to the dungeon. And divide their supplies among the comrades."

Pallo glared at Chestel, but said nothing. As the comrades came forward, he gave Norla's arm a quick squeeze.

"I'll find a way from this mess, Norla," he whispered. "I promise no harm will befall you."

Norla assessed the honesty of his gaze, the passion in his voice. He meant every word. He still considered himself her protector. She felt the sudden need to defend him further, but she suspected her words would do no good against Chestel's army of comrades.

She offered Pallo a grim smile as the comrades took his sword, bound his hands, and led him toward the castle's door behind Gen and Effira. He glanced back at her, and she held his pale blue gaze until one of the men pushed him toward the stairs.

"He thinks himself in love with you," Chestel said. He glowered after Pallo. "I should kill him."

~~~

Chestel led Norla up a winding staircase and along a dim stone hallway.

"How long have you lived here?" Norla asked. "Aren't you free to come home?"

Chestel cleared his throat and kept his gaze forward. "We'll have time to talk soon, but first let me show you your room."

Norla frowned. Chestel was hiding something, but he wouldn't talk until he was ready. He had always been determined to do things his way, whether that meant organizing a village-wide game of leapball or hiding rocks in the foremen's bags when they weren't looking.

They passed an array of candle sconces and framed paintings before reaching a closed mahogany door. Chestel stepped forward to open it, and then held out his hand with a boyish grin.

"My lady," he said, in a mock Uyandi accent.

Norla laughed in spite of herself. Oh, how she had missed Chestel's accents. If the foremen had been particularly fond of their whips on a given day, Chestel had never failed to make Norla forget her troubles with one of his ridiculous accents.

Norla moved forward to wrap her arms around Chestel's thick neck.

"Thank you," she whispered.

Chestel chuckled and hugged her in return. "For what?"

"For being here." She had felt like a bird caught in rain since Pallo had taken her from the mountain. Chestel was the first bit of sunlight she'd felt in days.

"You haven't even seen your room yet," Chestel said. "Wait and thank me then."

Norla pulled away to find Chestel's eyes glittering. He nodded ahead, and Norla stepped through the doorway. The room's rich mahogany dresser matched the four-post bed and side table. Powder blue linens covered the bed and shaded the windows. An open wardrobe in the corner revealed fresh sage tunics, trousers, and dresses made with the finest wool.

"It's yours, Norla," Chestel said. He assessed the room with his chin raised in pride. "What do you think?"

"It's beautiful," Norla said.

Chestel strode to the wardrobe and grabbed handfuls of the fresh wool. "Wear as many as you want." He laughed. "Wear two at once!"

Norla smiled as Chestel went around the rest of the room, pointing out every furniture item and having her sit on the plush bed. She tried to mirror his excitement, but she could not stop thinking of Pallo and the others in the dungeon. Were they cold? Would they be fed? Norla doubted her uneasiness would disappear until Chestel freed the Uyandis.

"Did you ever think we'd actually do it, Norla?" Chestel was saying. "We dreamed about taking adventures like this."

Norla nodded. "It's incredible."

"Come with me." Chestel grabbed her hand. "I'm going to prepare a hot bath for you."

Norla shook her head, alarmed. "You don't need to do that." He'd have to take a great deal of time for such a task.

"I want to." Chestel squeezed her hand and led her into the hall, past several doors, and into another room with a marble bathing tub, sink, and a pink cushioned settee under the single window.

Norla exhaled slowly and skimmed her fingers along the tub's silky surface. She had never seen a tub before, and this one looked like a work of art from one of Mia's storybooks. It sat on four bronze claws and shined like fresh snow in the lamplight.

"I bet they have bathing tubs like this on Elyarn Isle," Chestel said.

Norla grinned. "It's fit for a sprite."

"Then you're a sprite tonight," Chestel said, dark eyes shining. "I'll return!" He dashed out of the room before Norla had the chance to protest.

Sighing, Norla sat on the settee and waited. She let her mind drift to younger times, when she had believed Mia's words about the faraway isle. Norla and Chestel would dance around the hut, pretending to fly alongside wind sprites after a ball thrown by the king of the sprites, King Lumin. Mia would sing along until the children collapsed on Norla's mat in exhaustion. Then they'd ask about all the different sprites and the powers they held in their voices. Norla's favorite had always been the song sprites; their rich voices painted the air with colors more dazzling than any found on Mirlane Isle. But Chestel had always preferred stories of the warrior sprites, who commanded their swords with a word.

Chestel reappeared with a bucket of steaming water. He dumped it into the bathing tub and hurried out only to return again and again, for what felt like an hour.

Norla had so many questions for him—she wanted to know how he had come to be master of the house, why he hadn't returned the mountain, and so much more. But Chestel seemed determined, almost fanatical, about drawing a hot bath for her. He allowed no distraction. By the time the bath was properly filled, his brow was damp and he had rolled up his tunic sleeves.

On his last trip, Chestel brought Norla a bar of soap and a fresh dress and shift. He clumsily laid the clothing on the settee next to Norla and cleared his throat.

"I'll, er, see you at dinner," Chestel said. "Take the winding staircase down to the main floor. You should find the dining hall easily enough."

"All right," Norla said, standing. Chestel turned to leave, his cheeks flushed, and Norla added, "Much thanks, Chestel."

Chestel gave a quick nod over his shoulder and shut the door behind him.

Norla chuckled at his hasty departure and removed her dress and shift. She grabbed the soap, stepped into the hot water, and instantly felt her muscles relax. She sank lower into the water and rested her head against the bath's back, inhaling deeply. The soap smelled subtly of lavender, and the extravagant scent underscored the oddity of the situation all the more.

Her last bath had been with a dirty rag and freezing water. Now she was sitting in a bathing tub. In a castle. And she had come with Uyandis.

An image came to her mind then, of Pallo and the others huddled on a cold floor somewhere beneath her. And suddenly Norla wanted nothing more than to finish her bath. She scrubbed her skin as ruthlessly as Mia would have, washed her hair in the soapy water, and slipped into the cotton shift. She put on the sage dress and pulled her damp hair into a braid.

Finding the dining hall was as easy as Chestel had said. Once she had reached the main floor, she followed the sound of boisterous talk and laughter. Chestel sat at the head of the long table, where two dozen comrades all ate together. Roella sat to his left, and Chestel waved Norla over to the open chair directly to his right.

Roella didn't speak as Chestel prepared a plate of broiled pheasant and spiced potatoes for Norla. The dinner reminded her of the rich palace food, a far cry from porridge. Although it smelled of clove and pepper, Norla didn't have much of an appetite. She kept wondering if the nobles would eat in the dungeon. She had to convince Chestel to release them.

Chestel placed a bowl of olive oil topped with herbs before her. His eyes shone.

"I promised," he said.

"You did." Norla tried to muster the enthusiasm he expected. She gave him a broad smile, dipped a cube of potato into the bowl, and took a bite. The smooth, tangy oil filled her mouth with the subtle flavors of fruit and earth—the tastes of spring. She thought of Pallo, and her stomach turned. Was she eating the olive oil from Pallo's saddlebag?

Chestel let out a booming laugh. "Can you believe it? We're eating like a couple of lords, you and me."

"Yes, it's wonderful," Norla said, trying to gain control of her thoughts.

Chestel frowned. "Are you all right? You don't seem like yourself."

"I'm fine," Norla said.

Chestel's dark eyebrows gathered in concern. "I know it's a big change, but you're free of him, Norla. Free."

"Ah yes, our fearless leader, granting another lady her freedom." Roella chuckled and took a long sip of ale from her mug. She tipped her head to the side in a mocking smile. "How kind you are, Chestel."

Chestel surveyed her with a slight frown. "You're drunk."

"But I'm *free*. Isn't that right?" She ran her finger around the rim of her mug. The large chandelier above the table cast shadows under her hazel eyes. "And now you're free, sweet little Norla."

"That's enough, Roella," Chestel snapped.

Roella's eyes flickered with apparent surprise, but she maintained a lazy smile as she slid back her wooden chair and stood up.

"All of this invigorating conversation has worn me out," she said, holding her mug. She turned to the rest of the comrades, all lost in their own conversations. "Good night, comrades. May King Vaskel's grace shine upon you!" she spat.

"And you," the nearest men and women replied. Roella winked at Chestel and slipped across the stone floor toward an arched doorway. As Roella sauntered across the stone hall, Norla noted how many men watched her, including Chestel. Unlike the others, though, his gaze looked more tired than admiring.

As Roella disappeared through an arched doorway, an elderly man rushed in past her. His back was stooped as he hurried forward, as though he carried an invisible bag of stones. Had he worked on the mountain? He didn't look browned enough.

Chestel sat up straighter and motioned for the man to take Roella's free chair. The old man shook his head.

"There ain't time to sit," the man said. "That count's demandin' he speaks with the lady."

Chapter Nine

"Wendel, you don't have to take orders from lords anymore," Chestel said. "You've got the keys to the dungeon."

"I knows that," Wendel said. "But they won't shut up. That one with the matchin' coat and feather's the worst."

"Ignore him," Chestel said. He narrowed his eyes on Wendel's gray sash. "Where's your sword?"

"It's more pains than it's worth," Wendel said. "Besides, them lords is locked up."

"It's more intimidating for a guard to be armed."

"I don't cares about looks," Wendel snapped.

Chestel let out a frustrated sigh and pointed to Roella's chair. "Take a break and eat with us."

"Fine," Wendel grumbled. He ambled to Roella's chair, and Chestel prepared him a heaping plate of meat and mug of ale. The old man grunted his thanks and dug into the pheasant first. He stared at the table as he ate, not once glancing up.

"Sorry about Roella," Chestel said to Norla. He stabbed a potato cube with his fork. "She's a troubled lady."

Norla smiled at Chestel's succinct description.

"Why does she hate me?" Norla asked.

Chestel hesitated. "She doesn't like you defending that count. Roella's mother was a Linyad—and Duke Yintpa's suryan." He bit into the potato and chewed. "The duke didn't treat Roella or her mother very well."

"Roella's the duke's daughter?"

"Yeah, and his only child. He died four months back, so now Roella oversees the province. She isn't the legal heir, of course. But she doesn't see it that way."

"What about the duke's wife, or Roella's mother?"

"Both dead." Chestel took a sip of ale, shaking his head.

Norla sat back in her chair. As the daughter of a duke, Roella had royal blood in her veins. But as the daughter of a Linyad woman, she would never be considered equal among the Uyandis. Or the Linyads. She fell somewhere in the middle.

"So Roella thinks she's freed you all?" Norla asked. The royal court would never recognize the freedom Roella supposedly granted. Not when she wasn't the rightful heir. The province would pass to the duke's brother or another male relation, however distant, instead of Roella. The court probably hadn't learned of Duke Yintpa's death yet.

"Yeah." Chestel sipped from his mug. "She said we could stay or go. Either way, we're free."

"Then why haven't you come home to us?" Norla asked, leaning forward.

Chestel's cheeks darkened. "I, eh… " He shoveled another bite into his mouth and chewed slowly. Norla waited. She wouldn't let him escape her question. She had watched Chestel's parents, siblings, and cousins mourn his parting.

"I'd be a slave again," Chestel said. "The king won't honor the freedom Roella gave me. But I did mean to come back."

"What made you stay?"

Chestel's eyes darted to Wendel and then down the length of the table. The old man was still staring at the table, seemingly lost in his own thoughts, and the other comrades were engaged in conversations. Chestel cleared his throat and leaned forward. From that angle, Norla saw the dark stubble on his browned chin and cheeks.

"Roella," Chestel said in a low voice.

"Is she your lady?" Norla asked.

Chestel swallowed. A war of emotions played in his eyes.

"She was so broken after her father's death," he said. "Asked me to be master of the house. She doesn't want the title, but she makes the decisions."

Norla pushed a bite of pheasant across her bronze plate with a fork. She envisioned it all happening. Roella's heartbreak. Chestel's hope to rescue her.

"She isn't my lady anymore," Chestel said. His dark eyes searched her face. "You believe me?"

"Chestel, who am I to judge your lady?" She gave him a genuine smile. "I only want your happiness."

Chestel frowned. "You don't care if I'm with her?"

Norla squirmed in her chair. Did Chestel expect jealousy from her? Without warning, Pallo's serious gaze came to mind—and his rare, relaxed smile.

Chestel leaned forward. "Let's start over, Norla. We can forget about Roella and the count."

Norla took a bite of peppered potato to keep from answering right away. She wondered if forgetting was that easy.

"It'll be like that Uyandi pig never touched you." Chestel reached out to squeeze her hand.

"He never has," Norla replied, staring at his hand.

"What do you mean?"

"Just that. Pallo's never touched me."

Chestel's mouth dropped. His lips parted in a triumphant smile. "All the better!" he exclaimed. He pushed her mug towards her. "Let's toast."

Norla grabbed her mug and clanked Chestel's, but the ale had no taste for her. It felt odd celebrating Pallo's honor with someone who thought so little of him.

"What brought you to Yintpa Province anyway?" Chestel asked.

"We're searching for Penumbra."

Norla bit her tongue. She hadn't meant to divulge so much, but she hadn't seen Chestel in months. And there was so much to tell him. Words escaped from her like a leak.

Chestel raised his eyebrows. "You're after the Book? You mad?"

Norla toyed with her fork. Now that she had let slip the heart of their journey, she saw no sense in concealing the peripheral details.

"King Vaskel arranged the mission to kill Count Belany," Norla said.

"Why?" Chestel asked with a smirk. "Is the count this disagreeable to everyone?"

Norla didn't return his smile. "The king wants me as his suryan. He hopes to kill Pallo and take me for himself."

Chestel eyes flashed. "You aren't the king's to take."

"I agree. That's why we aim to ruin the king's plans by fetching the Book."

Chestel shook his head, his long hair swaying beneath his flat hat. "You won't succeed, Norla. Penumbra's riders stalk the desert, murdering some and selling others as slaves to Draxton." He lowered his voice. "And the trip to Draxton is a brutal one. The snatchers pack you in trunks with only a slit for air and gruel."

Norla felt a swell of nerves. She hadn't thought of slave snatchers before. The desert sounded far more dangerous when Chestel described it.

"We'll avoid the snatchers somehow," Norla said, assuring herself.

"Only way to avoid snatchers is to join up with a band of nomads. Snatchers don't bother as much with crowds. They like to pick off the lone travelers."

"Then that's what we'll do," Norla said. "Chestel, we have to try. The king will trade for the Book. If we succeed, he'll free Mia."

Chestel puckered his lips, clearly lost in thought. "The king values this Book very much," he said quietly after a moment.

"Yes, he's sent many, many campaigns to find it." Norla squeezed Chestel's arm. "We have to continue, Chestel. You can't keep the Uyandis prisoners."

"Norla, don't you see?" Chestel's voice rose, trembling with excitement. "If the king'll free Mia, maybe he'd free more. You, me, my family, maybe even the whole class!"

Norla sat up straighter, startled by his words. "The king would never free all the Weltangs. He treasures his temple too much."

Chestel leaned forward, cupping her shoulder with his hand. "I think he treasures this Book even more."

"Chestel, I'll see about the king freeing you and your family as well. I really will. But he will never free every Weltang."

"What about yourself, Norla?" Chestel challenged. "Why aren't you including yourself in this bargain?"

Norla's cheeks warmed. "Because Pallo made the bargain, and a nobleman would never free his suryan. It's ridiculous to ask. Besides, I'm going to escape on my own." She paused. "But I really could include your family, Chestel."

Chestel shook his head. "That's not good enough."

Before Norla had the chance to argue, Chestel whipped his head to Wendel, nearly unsettling his gray cap.

"Can you send word to all the comrades on duty?" Chestel asked.

"Chestel, you're not even listening!" Norla said. Her cheeks pounded with heat. She wanted to strike him. Chestel had always acted like a runaway horse when an idea stoked his passion; it had kept his spirit alive, despite the whip scars lining his back. But this idea of his was far more dangerous than any mischief he had attempted on the mountain.

"Have them meet here, Wendel," Chestel continued, oblivious to her. "All right?"

"Yeah, yeah," Wendel said. He pushed himself up with his arms and shuffled out the room, muttering under his breath.

"We'll leave immediately," Chestel said, more to himself than to Norla.

"Tonight?" Norla exclaimed.

Chestel grinned. "Easier to avoid snatchers at night. And the faster we ride to Gracehen Oasis, the sooner we can join a band of nomads."

Norla jumped out of her chair. Chestel's lunacy would get him killed—and keep Mia enslaved.

"Well, I'm not going with you," Norla snapped.

Chestel blinked and focused fully on her for the first time since she had mentioned the Book.

"I wouldn't expect you to face the snatchers," Chestel said, his voice quieter. "You can wait for me here at the castle."

"It's not that. You're ruining Mama's chance at freedom, and you don't even care."

Chestel took her hand in his. His skin was warm to the touch. "Norla, I love Mia like my own mother. I'm doing this for her. But I want to do it for the other slaves as well. Don't you see that?"

"I owe the Weltangs nothing," Norla said. She looked Chestel straight in the eye, letting him see her resolve. If anyone knew of her hellish life in the village, it was Chestel.

"Start a new life with Mama and me," Norla offered. "Once the king frees my mother and your family, I'll escape and we can all flee to Luwista."

Chestel's expression softened. His lips parted in a sly smile. "You would want that?"

"Of course!"

He watched her for a long moment, and Norla sensed his struggle. He had defended her from the villagers since he was a child, but he had always been one of them. Chestel was loved by all, despite his strange friendship with the outcast.

Norla saw the moment she lost him—his gaze hardened with determination.

"No… I have a greater duty," Chestel said firmly.

A knot welled in Norla's throat, but she nodded. As much as she didn't want to, she understood Chestel's choice.

"I won't come with you," Norla said, staring at her plate.

"Fine," Chestel said in a crisp tone.

"Are you going to leave the Uyandis imprisoned?" Norla asked.

Chestel's lips curved into a snarl. "Let the nobles rot in the dungeon where they belong."

Chestel rose to his feet and quieted the table. As he described his plan to his comrades, Norla thought again of Pallo. Her eyes strayed to the doorway through which Wendel had disappeared. The old man held the key to the dungeon.

~~~

Norla sat on the bed's fine woolen coverlet. Her hands shook with anticipation. It was well past midnight, but she still heard men talking in the hall. She had to wait until they disappeared before leaving the castle room Chestel had designated as hers.

Norla still chastised herself for not anticipating Chestel's reaction to the information she had so carelessly let slip. In the past, Norla had desired the same end as Chestel. Even now, it made sense for her to desire the same end. Instead, she thought only of freeing Pallo and the others.

She had learned from Chestel that Wendel would stand guard in the dungeon overnight. Norla guessed Wendel would be alone and unarmed. Although she didn't like the idea, Norla knew she'd be able to overcome the old man. She had learned some tricks from fighting the foremen. And Wendel wouldn't have a whip to fight her off.

Norla listened and realized the hall had quieted some. Much of the castle had begun to retire after their meeting with the master of the house. Chestel's fevered speech had drawn little interest from his comrades. Most of them were Tintals, and although they wanted equality with the Uyandis and Linyads, they weren't prepared to risk their lives for the Weltangs.

Norla wondered how many had actually departed with Chestel. Regardless, he had gone. He was determined to free the whole Weltang class and wouldn't change his mind until he had accomplished his goal—or died trying. Norla swallowed. Her mind flashed with images of masked snatchers with raised swords...

Norla rose to her feet. She would free the Uyandis, for their sakes and for Chestel's. They needed each other on a mission such as this.

With a determined nod, Norla grabbed the bundle she had prepared for Pallo, Gen, and Effira. She had packed a few garments for the Uyandis after learning their supplies had been pilfered and divided among the comrades. The garments were a far cry from the velvets and silks the nobles were accustomed

Penumbra

to, but Norla guessed they would welcome any relief from their soiled clothing.

Reaching the door, Norla put her ear to the mahogany wood. She heard nothing but the faint howl of wind against the castle walls. With a shiver, she stepped into the dark hallway and crept toward the winding staircase leading to the main floor. The leather boots Chestel had given her made little sound on the stone floor.

The main floor was deserted.

Norla hurried through the darkened dining hall. Moonlight shone through the arched windows, splashing the room in an eerie glow. Out one of the windows, Norla's eye caught the silhouette of a rider near the horizon. He wore a dazzling silver cloak and raced toward the castle.

CHAPTER TEN

In an instant, the rider in silver had vanished. Norla stepped forward and squinted. She was sure she had seen the rider approaching, but the cobbled path to the castle now lay empty. It made no sense.

Well, he wasn't one of Penumbra's riders. She knew that much. Those men remained in the desert, far from the border. And comrades guarded the castle's perimeter at all times.

She exhaled slowly and continued forward, through the darkened kitchen and into one of the servants' passageways. The candles in their sconces had burned out, and Norla could scarcely see two feet of the stone floor in front of her. Still, she kept shuffling forward. The longer she took in freeing the Uyandis, the greater distance Chestel put between them.

At last, Norla spotted an arched doorway up ahead with stairs leading downward. She felt a fresh pulse of energy in her exhausted legs. Hurrying forward, Norla heard the faint sound of snoring. She wanted to clap her hands for joy. With Wendel asleep, she would be able to steal the key without a fight.

Norla held her breath and sneaked down the stairs. The only light in the miserable dungeon came from candle sconces in the hallway beyond the bars.

Wendel sat on a wooden chair with his head against the stone wall and his mouth wide open. His face looked even more wrinkled in slumber. A sage tunic covered his arms, but Norla wondered if he bore whip scars like she did. He was not from the mountain; his pale skin revealed that much. Maybe he had been a mine worker.

"Norla?" a familiar voice whispered.

Norla snapped her head toward the iron bars farther down the hallway. Her insides swirled at the welcome sound, and her feet carried her to Pallo.

~~~

As Norla hurried over to him, Pallo exhaled in relief. She appeared unharmed. It was foolish for him to have thought otherwise. In the brief time Pallo had seen the Weltang boy, it had been clear that he cared deeply for Norla.

Through the flickering candlelight, Pallo assessed her new gown and dampened hair with a frown. Seeing to her needs was his responsibility.

"Are you all right?" Norla whispered, approaching him.

The kindness in her eyes stilled him. He dared not move, for fear of shattering the moment.

She stood so close.

Pallo's skin warmed, and he wondered how it would feel to reach past the bars and touch her cheek.

"I'm all right," Pallo said. He hated the thickness of his voice. "And you?"

"All right," Norla replied. Her eyes shifted behind him to where Gen and Fira slept on reed-stuffed mats. A type of mold that was better left unexamined grew on the grimy floor.

Norla's eyes filled with worry, and Pallo knew that none of them looked their finest. Gen had removed his purple cloak and clutched it protectively on his chest, keeping it safe from the floor. And Fira certainly looked a far cry from the lady who had departed from Vaskel Palace three days earlier. With fraying curls and a dirtied green cape, she would hardly be recognizable at court.

Personally, Pallo felt as crumpled as his tunic. And his eyes stung from exhaustion. He had longed to sleep, but he had stayed awake, not wanting to miss Norla in case she came.

"Have you eaten?" Norla asked.

Pallo nodded and held the bars. Her fingers nearly touched his. If he moved his fingers slightly, he would brush her skin.

"Wendel carries the key," Norla explained. She nodded to the sleeping man behind her. "I had to wait until the comrades retired… and then I had some trouble finding the dungeon."

Pallo grinned. "An admission of weakness?"

"Of course I have weaknesses," Norla said defensively.

"As many as I have?"

She hesitated, and Pallo chuckled.

"You are less flawed than most Uyandis," Norla offered with a wry smile.

"A high compliment."

Norla's smiling eyes held his gaze, stirring warmth inside him. She had never treated him with such familiarity.

"What is your weakness, Norla?" Pallo ventured. He knew what he risked by asking a personal question. If he pushed too hard where Norla was concerned, she would bristle and shut him out.

Norla watched him for a moment, and then glanced at her boots. "I speak without thinking."

"We can all do that," Pallo said.

Norla gave a quiet laugh. "You're far more understanding than foremen on the mountain. They like to punish that particular weakness."

Pallo's grip tightened on the bars. He knew the kinds of Linyads who became foremen. They were typically younger brothers from lesser households—men with something to prove. The thought of any of them harming Norla made Pallo burn with rage.

Norla's life would have been so different if she had been born in Belany Province. Pallo's mother forbade the use of whips and provided slaves with homes equal to those of their Tintal counterparts. Of course, Weltangs received no earnings, but that was the way of the land. His family had committed no great wrong.

Pallo met Norla's gaze and saw a flash of raw pain in her dark eyes.

He tensed, unprepared to see such ache. What could he say to help her? To offer relief to a slave girl he barely knew?

"I'm sorry," Pallo said stiffly. He backed away from the bars. "I should wake the others."

Norla blinked, her expression growing stony. Pallo cursed his cowardice.

"Norla, I—" he began.

"Wake them," Norla snapped. Her skin flushed in the low light.

Pallo swallowed, knowing his response had hurt her deeply. He turned to give her a moment to compose herself. He owed her that at the very least.

When Gen and Fira had roused, their eyes widened at the sight of Norla.

"She came," Gen said.

"I expected as much," Fira said.

"So's did I," another voice added.

Pallo's breath froze. They had been talking far too freely.

~~~

"Best tell 'em what you did, missy," Wendel said, rising with a heavy sigh. The old man looked squarely at Norla.

Norla raised her hands, ready to silence him with her fists before he exposed her failure to the Uyandis. But as the old man ambled forward, Norla felt her ire deflate. Wendel wasn't a young foreman on the mountain. He was Chestel's friend and nearly crippled after a life of grueling work.

"Guessin' Chestel's halfway to the desert by nows," Wendel said.

"What?" Gen exclaimed. "Why?"

"He's after the Book," Wendel said. "Knows how much Vaskel wants it."

"How?" Pallo asked.

"I'll tell you how," Gen said, marching up to the bars. "Norla betrayed us."

Norla backed away.

"Norla wouldn't do that." Effira strode up to Gen, her hands on her hips. "You should apologize for suggesting it."

"How else would the Weltang know about our mission?" Gen asked.

Effira and Pallo exchanged a look. Neither spoke, but they both turned to Norla, waiting.

Norla gulped. Only moments ago, she had wanted to hurt Pallo for his probing question. Now she wanted his understanding. It made no sense.

"It was an accident," Norla said. Her voice sounded so small in the dark, still room.

Pallo winced, and Norla focused on her hands. She squeezed them together, hoping to expel the nerves swirling inside her.

"Why in Vaskel's name would you do that, Norla?" Effira demanded. She grabbed the bars with her grimy gloves.

"I didn't mean to," Norla said. "Chestel's my best friend. I was confiding in him, and it just slipped out."

Effira looked more than angry; she looked hurt.

"But I never would have told him if I had thought he'd go after the Book himself," Norla added. She kept her eyes on Effira. Although the lady's disappointment stung, it was nothing compared to Pallo's. He looked like the wind had been knocked out of him.

"Chestel thinks King Vaskel will free the entire Weltang people in exchange for the Book," Norla added.

"Draxton's queen," Pallo cursed. "Vaskel would never agree to that."

Wendel shuffled toward the bars. "There ain't time for all this talkin'. Chestel's already left, and we've gotta get you fits for travelin' the desert."

Norla raised an eyebrow. No one spoke.

"I'm tryin' to help you fools," Wendel said.

"If you wished to help us, why didn't you release us earlier?" Pallo asked.

"Yes, why did you have us spend half the night on a mat?" Gen asked, rubbing the back of his neck.

Wendel's eyes twinkled, and Norla knew the old man he enjoyed Gen's discomfort. Still, Norla believed Wendel. Instead

98

of hollering for help from his comrades, the man was seeking their trust.

"Why would you help us?" Effira asked. Her emerald eyes narrowed into a scowl.

"I loves Chestel like a son," Wendel snapped, "but that boy's too headstrong. He rides with hardly any helps, and those sands is thick with Penumbra's snatchers. Chestel'll get himself snatched or killed if someone don't help him."

Norla saw reason in the man's explanation. She had feared a similar end herself.

"Snatchers?" Effira asked in a high voice.

"Penumbra's band," Wendel said. "They sells you to Draxton as slaves. That's why's you gotta meet up with a band of nomads at Gracehen real quick."

Effira's face paled. Pallo and Gen were watching her with frowns.

"You needn't come, Fira," Pallo said softly.

"You could remain behind," Gen said. "I bet Wendel would show you a proper room."

Wendel grunted his agreement.

"Of course I'm coming," Effira snapped. She tossed fraying curls from her face.

"No one's goin' anywhere until you agrees to help Chestel." Wendel nodded at Norla. "This lass cares 'bout him. If she's in your party, I reckons Chestel'll have a few allies out there."

Wendel reached into his trouser pocket and produced a tarnished brass key.

"I ain't unlockin' this dungeon until I sets something straight," he said. "Chestel ain't your enemy. He wants the Book, you wants the Book. If I lets you outta there, you're Chestel's comrades."

They hardly looked like comrades. Pallo and Gen clenched their fists in fury, and Effira's face was milk-white with anger.

Wendel turned to Norla. "I'll gives you some time with 'em. Don't let 'em out until they's good and ready to help Chestel."

He dropped the key in her hand and nodded to a locked cupboard on the far end of the hall. "Their swords are in there. Same key'll works the lock."

Norla clutched the key, too surprised to speak. The old man hardly knew her, yet he entrusted her with much.

"I knows you love Chestel," Wendel added, as if he could read her doubt. He shuffled toward the staircase and disappeared from sight.

"Let us out!" Gen exclaimed.

Norla approached the gate as Wendel's words echoed through her mind.

"I won't unlock this gate until you agree that we go as Chestel's friends," she said.

Pallo frowned. Gen and Effira balked.

"Why would we partner with someone like him?" Gen asked.

"Chestel imprisoned us, Norla," Effira said.

"Because he doesn't know any better," Norla said. "You're nobles."

"But we've never harmed him," Gen said.

Norla shook her head in frustration. How would she make three Uyandis understand?

"Maybe you didn't work on the mountain, but you might as well be foremen in Chestel's eyes," Norla said.

Pallo blinked. Gen and Effira gawked at her, as if she had spoken in another tongue.

"I had never even met the lad before today," Gen protested. He looked to Pallo for support, but Pallo was watching Norla. His face hadn't hardened like the others'.

"Is that how you view us, Norla?" Pallo asked, his gaze intense.

Norla squeezed the key in her palm until the metal smarted against her skin. She didn't mean to cause Pallo pain, but her honesty seemed to do just that. She hadn't the slightest idea how to explain herself to him—and she wouldn't attempt it with Gen and Effira looking on.

"Once we're free of this place, we'll offer Chestel an alliance," Pallo said finally. His voice was flat. "If he refuses, I won't renew the offer. Does that sound fair?"

"Yes," Norla said quietly.

"I agree to that," Effira said.

"Fine," Gen said. "But I hope the lad refuses."

Norla wanted to snap back at Gen, but she kept her mouth shut as she unlocked the dungeon and then went to the cupboard down the hall. She heard Pallo's footsteps following her, but she didn't turn around. She had nothing more to say to him, and she doubted he wanted to hear from her anyway.

Norla had just shoved the key into the cupboard when Pallo gasped behind her. She turned just in time to see a man charging down the stairs, sword raised. His cloak was silver.

CHAPTER ELEVEN

Pallo's heart hammered. He recognized the man's distinctive cloak. The opponent was one of King Vaskel's asaltanis, highly trained and ruthless assassins.

Pallo shoved Norla into the corner, flung open the cupboard, and grabbed the first sword his fingers found. Air rushed, and Pallo sidestepped the blow as he whirled around. He tightened his grip on his sword's hilt. His skin was hot, his breath heavy.

"Throw me a sword!" Gen exclaimed.

There was no time. The asaltani advanced, and Pallo countered.

Metal clanked, flashing in the dim light.

Pallo assessed his opponent. The man was tall with a long reach; he might leave his legs exposed.

The asaltani lunged, again and again, with unflinching aggression.

Pallo parried and countered, sweat sticking to his brow. Jolts of nerves shot through his body. He refused to surrender ground. He had to remain between his opponent and Norla.

The man advanced. Pallo blocked the blade and, seeing his chance, countered with a swift strike to the asaltani's thigh.

"Draxton's queen," the opponent cursed, then stilled as sounds emerged from the top of the stairs.

"You's all right down there?" Wendel called. "Plenty of comrades up here to help!"

Without warning, the asaltani fell on his own sword. He collapsed to the floor and lay there, motionless.

Pallo's body went cold. Norla gasped behind him. Fira screamed, but Pallo scarcely heard her over the ringing in his ears. For all his swordplay, Pallo had never seen death before. He knew asaltanis were trained to take their own lives before risking capture, yet he hadn't expected it. His whole body trembled with the shock of the man's blood pooling on the stone floor.

Pallo felt Norla's hand on his shoulder. Turning, he saw her eyes were still wide with terror. His throat tightened.

"Are you injured?" she asked.

"No, I'm unharmed." Pallo leaned his sword against the wall and raked a hand over his hair. His heart still pounded.

"Vaskel be praised," Fira murmured. She gingerly side-stepped the dead man, keeping her gaze averted, and threw her arms around Pallo.

But Pallo kept his eyes on Norla, whose gaze was quickly returning to its guarded expression.

"You should have tossed me a sword," Gen said, as he approached with a scowl.

"There wasn't exactly time," Pallo said, releasing Fira.

"I suppose not," Gen mumbled.

Wendel descended the last few steps and clucked his tongue at the asaltani on the floor.

"Didn't expect that," Wendel mumbled. "Wouldn't a lied about all 'em comrades if I'd known."

"Who was he?" Norla asked.

Gen sighed. "Pallo just fought an asaltani."

"Vaskel's crown," Norla said.

"Vaskel certainly had a hand in this," Pallo said, feeling the flush of anger. The king wished to kill him, and now he had sent an asaltani to ensure the outcome. Asaltanis were an elite branch of Reislan's army. They were chosen among the Linyad class, and those who bore the title rode in Vaskel's personal vanguard.

"I saw him approaching through a window upstairs, but I didn't know he was an asaltani," Norla said. Her voice shook slightly, but her eyes were steady. "He seemed to disappear as I watched."

Gen nodded. "They're trained to be stealthy. And they always ride in pairs. You can assume the other has long since fled. The man who came was probably sent to scout the castle. When he found you… "

"He hoped to take the glory for himself," Pallo finished. He peered up the staircase, knowing the other asaltani was beyond his reach now. An assassin of that caliber was trained to vanish without a trail to follow.

"What if there are more, though?" Norla asked.

Pallo was asking himself the same question, and he knew the likely answer. Vaskel was a thorough man.

"We should be safe during the day," Gen said. "Asaltanis are trained to attack at night, when their opponents are most vulnerable."

"Then we had best wait until daybreak before leaving," Fira said.

Pallo agreed. The thought of more asaltanis hunting them sent chills down his back. He assured himself that he alone was Vaskel's target. The king would certainly want the others returned to the palace alive. But when Pallo thought of Norla's future if she returned without him, his muscles tightened.

Pallo put such thoughts from his mind as he turned his attention to the dead man's body and helped Wendel remove it to a spare servant's quarters.

Once they returned, Fira approached the old man. "I would request a room where I could freshen up before our travels, if you please," she said hesitantly.

Wendel grudgingly obliged and led the group to a hallway behind the kitchen, where a few more small rooms sat vacant.

Pallo washed his face, neck, and hands in a bowl of cold water, enjoying the cool sensation on his skin. It reminded him of the baths he would take in the sea after working in their olive orchard. Unlike other nobles, Pallo's father believed in tending the orchard alongside his men. He saw no point in a man owning land but never working the soil for himself.

Pallo tried to still his mind; his body was exhausted enough without adding mental burdens. He scrubbed the dirt from his skin before drying and changing clothes. Norla had brought him and Gen sage tunics and trousers. He retrieved a small leather pouch from his dirtied trousers and tucked it safely in his new trousers.

He appreciated Norla's gesture with the new clothing, but he wondered if she would display such kindness again. Their conversation had dredged an unfortunate truth to the surface— Pallo didn't want to hear of Norla's past. He would rather pretend her life on the mountain hadn't existed. What a true Uyandi he was turning out to be.

Norla probably hated him. She had said that Pallo and the others were practically foremen in Chestel's eyes. Surely that meant she saw them in the same light.

Pallo felt his hands squeeze into fists, and he forced himself to exhale. He hadn't the power to change his class or his clumsy choice of words. He had to earn her trust again somehow. Perhaps if Norla saw his selflessness in aiding Chestel, protecting him even, she would see him as something more than a Uyandi *pig*.

Shaking his head, Pallo slipped his velvet cloak over the fresh tunic and then strode back to the dim kitchen hallway, where Gen, Norla, and Wendel were waiting. A single candle in a bronze sconce provided some flickering light.

"Thank you for your help, Wendel," Pallo said, extending his hand.

The old man grunted, but didn't take Pallo's hand. "Just find Chestel, and keeps him from harm."

Gen came to Pallo's side and muttered, "That water was downright frigid."

Pallo nudged Gen. Wendel had shown them great kindness and had most likely heard Gen's attempt at a whisper.

"I found it refreshing," Pallo replied.

Gen snorted and pressed his hands over the fresh sage tunic. Unlike Pallo, Gen still wore his own black trousers and sash of nobility under his purple cloak.

Fira emerged then from her bathing room, wearing a sage dress. It was strange to see his old friend and Norla in matching gowns. Of course, Fira still wore her purple sash, velvet cape, and hat.

Although Norla's head was bare, she did wear a new cape. It was highly irritating that Norla had no qualms taking from Chestel when she had rebuffed all of Pallo's gifts.

Fira went to Norla and threw her arms around her. "Much thanks for the clean dress."

She pulled back with a suddenly timid smile, holding Norla by the shoulders. "I'm thankful you thought of us."

Norla nodded stiffly and cleared her throat. She looked to Wendel for help, but the old man only chuckled.

"Follows me," he said. Wendel took them to the kitchen, still deserted in the early hours. He quickly filled baskets with dried foods and watered wine and gave them a brief lesson on desert survival, before leading them to the castle's stables at dawn.

The familiar smell of hay quickened Pallo's steps and cleared the haze from his mind. He had to focus on the mission at hand. He wanted to catch Chestel that day, preferably before the sun got too high. The desert's border was a half-day's ride away, and Pallo did not wish to cross it until he outlined his plan to the others—including Chestel.

Pallo searched for Senna in the stalls but couldn't find her. Then the young groom reluctantly led him to an empty stall.

"The master of the house took your gray mare," the lad said quietly.

Pallo cursed. "That scoundrel!"

Lania was the only other person who had ridden Senna. The poor mare probably felt betrayed.

"Chestel will take good care of her," Norla said, standing at the gate of the empty stall.

Pallo snatched his hat from his head. He hated the way she talked about Chestel.

"That's beside the point," Pallo snapped. He pounded his fist into the stall door. "The lad had no business taking what's mine."

Norla shrugged and backed away from the gate.

"Draxton's queen," Pallo muttered. He had done it again. He went after her to apologize, but she had already joined the others at the stable's front.

"You sure Chestel approves?" the groom was asking Wendel.

Wendel clapped a weathered hand on the lad's shoulder.

"Trust me, Bron," Wendel said gruffly. "We're helpin' the master. Nows, be a good comrade and prepares the Uyandis' cab and 'orses." He motioned for Gen and Fira to pack the baskets he had prepared in the kitchen.

"How many others wents with Chestel?" Wendel asked Bron.

"Just the one," Bron replied.

"One?" Wendel cursed. "That boy's pride'll kill him."

Wendel turned to Pallo and the others. "Now, don't go tryin' to kill Penumbra," he ordered them. "Just gets yourself run through that ways. Nab the Book and makes haste real quick."

"That's exactly what I mean to do," Pallo replied. He was after the Book, not granting extra favors for Vaskel.

Within minutes the party was heading west per Wendel's instructions. Pallo rode a borrowed gelding named Hickory while Gen drove the ladies in the carriage like before.

They rode hard through the morning, breaking sparingly. Pallo kept his eyes on the horizon. He reminded himself time and time again that asaltanis did not attack during the morning hours. But that knowledge did not keep him from envisioning silver cloaks over every hill.

~~~

They stopped briefly for refreshment under a cluster of banyan trees. Pallo and Gen set out blankets. To Norla's surprise, Effira joined her blanket instead of Pallo's, passing a sweet biscuit and some dried figs her way. Norla accepted the offerings with a slight nod.

"We'll cross the desert border in an hour or two," Gen said as he bit into a biscuit. "Wendel said we'll be in range of Penumbra's riders in another day's time."

"We must ride on," Pallo said. "We have no choice if we want to catch Chestel today."

There was no mistaking the grimace on Pallo's face when he said Chestel's name.

"How long have you known Chestel?" Effira asked Norla.

Pallo's eyes met Norla's for a moment. As he dropped his gaze, she focused on chewing the fig's crunchy seeds. In spite of herself, she was becoming fond of Uyandi fare.

"I suppose you met on the mountain, no?" Effira continued. She peered at Norla with rapt interest, and it was clear she wouldn't dismiss the topic without an answer.

"We met in the village," Norla said, "when I was very young."

"How did you meet?" Effira asked.

Norla smiled. "Chestel overheard my mother reading to me one evening. He marched right into our hut and demanded that she read to him, too."

Chestel had adored Mia's book of sonnets as much as Mia herself had. Norla liked the poems as well, but she had always found more beauty in the book's painted cover. The artist had depicted such vibrant red flowers on the leather, winding along the spine in a graceful path.

"I remember you saying that your mother liked stories," Effira said.

Norla squirmed. She hadn't expected Effira to remember anything about her, and the fact that Effira did was oddly irritating. She also didn't want the nobles to take too much interest in Mia. Architects had given Mia those books in secret.

"Did anyone else join your mother's lessons?" Effira asked.

Norla snorted. "Of course not! No one visited our hut."

"But why not?"

Norla recognized her mistake immediately. She had said too much. Again. She blamed Effira. That Uyandi lady was so infuriatingly curious.

"Why didn't anyone visit your hut?" Effira asked.

Silence fell over the group. Even Gen didn't speak. Norla took another bite of fig. The subtle flavors of apple and pear expanded in her mouth, and Norla thought of how much Mia would have enjoyed the fig's rich taste. Even in the savannah, miles away from Weltang Village, Mia's reputation hung in the air like the perpetual limestone dust on the mountain.

"Norla—" Effira asked.

"Fira," Pallo interrupted.

"Because my mother is unwed," Norla snapped. "My father was another woman's husband, and I'm his unwanted daughter."

CHAPTER TWELVE

Norla looked each of the Uyandis in the face, daring them to speak. Let them see her for who she truly was. She didn't care what they thought.

Effira's and Gen's eyes were wide with shock. But Pallo... His face had softened, and his eyes were full of emotion.

Norla felt a throbbing sensation in her throat, and then a rush of heat. She sprang to her feet and marched across the fallen banyan needles toward the carriage. A cold breeze brushed her bare face and hands, and she welcomed the jolt to her senses. She climbed into the cab and shut the door behind her.

Norla's pulse pounded. Her hands shook. Tears stung her eyes, and she fought to gain control. She never used to cry so easily before. What was happening to her?

She managed to compose herself before Effira joined her in the cab.

"I'm so sorry... for prying, I... " Effira began, but her attempted apology died on her lips.

Norla ignored her. She had said enough to Effira for one day.

They rode all afternoon, keeping their rests short. The vegetation grew scarce, until almost nothing but waves of tan sand stretched out before them. The sand was hard and tightly packed, like a beaten path, and a few cacti and yucca trees dotted the barren land. But the greatest change came in the harsh west wind.

When the sky began to fade, the wind intensified. Norla felt it through the thin cracks beside the cab door. She hoped Pallo and Gen were warm enough—and Chestel, riding some-where ahead of them.

Norla's mind wouldn't cooperate at all. She kept remembering the look on Pallo's face under the banyan trees. It had not been mere shock, judgment, or the distaste she knew so well. Oddly enough, it had been something like compassion. No one had ever shown Mia or Norla compassion on the mountain or in the village; it didn't make sense for a count to be the first. But then Norla thought of Pallo's chilliness when she had spoken of the foremen's punishments on the mountain. He hadn't the stomach for the kind of life Norla had known.

Norla returned her gaze to the window. She kept expecting the men to stop and make camp, but they seemed determined to catch Chestel.

Then Gen cursed from the driver's bench.

"Asaltanis!" he screamed.

"We can't outrace them with the carriage!" Pallo's voice shouted nearby. "We'll stop and fight!"

Gen brought the cab to a sudden halt. Norla and Effira held their seats to keep from tumbling as Gen's and Pallo's shouts and the horses' panicked whinnies flooded the air.

Effira's eyes widened. She dove onto the floor and yanked two swords out from under her seat. "I asked Wendel for these." She shoved one into Norla's hands and flew out the cab door.

Norla's heart hammered. She stared at the blade in her hands. She'd never held a sword, and her hands trembled against the cold metal. Still, Norla had muscle enough from hauling rocks to wield the weapon. She wouldn't surrender to the asaltanis without a fight.

Steeling herself, Norla climbed through the door and met the fierce wind. It beat against her face, slamming bits of sharp sand across her skin. Norla grimaced and pulled her cape over her chin and nose.

Up ahead, the sound of horse hooves echoed on the horizon. Two riders approached from the west.

111

"Sartania's king! Both of you, return to the carriage now!" Pallo bellowed at Effira and Norla. He positioned Hickory between the riders and the cab. Gen leapt down onto his feet, sword in hand.

Effira inched closer to the cab's door, but remained outside. Norla stayed planted as well. In truth, she wasn't sure her feet would move even if she wanted them to.

On the western horizon, the pair of riders drew near. But one rode a modest gray horse, and the other sat astride a giant white brute—and it became clear with their approach that their cloaks were not silver. Something about the gray horse seemed familiar... and then Norla recognized Chestel's wild hair.

Norla loosened her grip on the sword's hilt. Her shoulders sagged with relief. Seeing her oldest friend in this strange desert filled Norla with assurance. All would be well now. She just needed to convince Pallo and Chestel to call a truce.

Walking forward, Norla turned her attention to the second rider. The twilight illuminated strands of deep red hair. Roella. Why had she come? And astride a horse, no less. Roella might not be a noblewoman, but custom forbade her from riding.

Pallo led Hickory forward to meet them. "How dare you steal Senna," Pallo snarled.

Norla winced. She would have chosen a different way to begin Pallo and Chestel's truce.

"Why did you bring the women to the desert?" Chestel demanded, guiding Senna to a stop. He wore a gray riding cloak and gloves, looking like a lord. "You mad?"

"You brought Roella," Pallo countered.

"That's different," Chestel said, with a wave of his hand.

"I don't see how," Pallo said.

Roella chuckled and brought her stallion to a stop beside Senna. Like Chestel, she wore fine wool clothing—a gray hooded cape and matching riding gloves. Even with wind and sand swirling around her, Roella looked perfectly composed.

"I don't need a big count to protect me." Roella gave Norla and Effira a condescending smile.

"Neither do I," Effira said, raising her sword.

"Nor I," Norla said. "I wasn't raised in a castle like some."

Roella's eyes widened briefly, before she managed a laugh. "You certainly picked a spirited mistress, didn't you, grand Count?"

Norla stiffened as Chestel shot Roella a scowl.

"Are you appalled to see a horsewoman, grand Count?" Roella asked.

Pallo ignored Roella altogether. "Do you have a plan, horse thief?" he asked.

"Of course." Chestel scratched Senna behind her ears. The mare lowered her head in pleasure.

Pallo looked crestfallen.

"Traitor," he muttered.

"I guess you want to partner," Chestel said.

"I guess *you*—" Gen began.

"Yes we do," Norla interrupted. Her neck ached from looking up. She sincerely wished she had a horse of her own. "We all want the same end—the Book."

"Yeah, but I'm not giving up the Book until King Vaskel frees all the Weltangs," Chestel said.

"That is most definitely not the arrangement," Pallo snapped. He guided Hickory forward until the gelding's nose almost touched Senna's. "If we push the king too far, he could renege and deny Norla's mother her freedom. Mia's freedom is my aim, lad, nothing more."

Chestel leaned forward in his saddle. "You haven't even thought about freeing Norla, have you? You'll free Mia because it serves your purpose, but you don't even notice the thousands more still enslaved. I'm not just looking at Mia."

"Then we'll never agree," Pallo said. The pair studied each other for a long moment. Senna and Hickory imitated their riders, though their gazes seemed far more approving.

Norla knew what was expected of her as a Weltang. The proper course would be to ask Pallo to side with Chestel. Chestel's aim was far nobler than hers. She knew all of this, and yet Norla dared not risk Mia's one chance at freedom.

The villagers had done their best to treat Norla as an outsider since birth. On their morning walks to the trading post for porridge, she and Mia had felt the stares and heard the foul words muttered in their wake. Even Chestel's family had acted civil to Norla only when Chestel was present.

But Chestel had been unwavering. Norla wouldn't deny that. She wanted to offer him her aid for as long as possible.

"We don't have to reach a decision today," Norla said.

Chestel's eyes filled with hurt. "You should know why I ride, Norla," he said.

Norla stared at her hands. Chestel's words felt heavy enough to push her into the sand.

"You've spoken enough, horse thief," Pallo said. His voice left no room for arguments. "We must come to an agreement."

"How?" Chestel asked.

Norla met Chestel's eyes. For so many years, looking into that fierce gaze had given her the strength to wake the next morning. Now, though, he directed his fierceness at her.

"We could travel together until we find Penumbra," Norla offered. "For safety."

"And when we find the criminal?" Chestel asked.

"We part ways. We each give the other their chance to retrieve the Book."

After a long moment of silence, Chestel spoke. "I'd agree to that."

"And I," Gen said. "As long as the lad doesn't try any trickery."

"I agree," Effira said. "Pallo?"

Pallo was watching Norla, his gaze curious. She wondered what questions ran through his mind. What did he think when he looked at her? He knew it all now, knew what kind of girl he had chosen for his royal household.

"You think it wise for us to remain with Chestel?" Pallo asked her.

Norla blinked. He was asking for her counsel?

"Yes, I do," Norla said.

Pallo nodded in his formal manner and narrowed his gaze on Chestel.

"Once we discover Penumbra's whereabouts, we part ways," Pallo said.

"I'm counting on that," Chestel said. "We'll ride hard during the night and rest on the dunes during the day. That'll keep us hidden enough from the snatchers."

"What about asaltanis?" Effira asked. "I thought we were traveling by day to avoid them."

"Asaltanis? From the palace?" Chestel looked unnerved for the first time.

"They came to Yintpa Castle," Norla said. "Just before we departed."

Chestel thought for a moment. "Well, we'll be safer from them if we're moving, anyway," he said. "If we set up camp during the night, we're like a marked target." He cocked his head to the side, daring Pallo to contradict him.

"The lad's plan has merit, Pallo," Gen whispered loudly.

"I know," Pallo muttered. "I agree with him." He swept his hat from his head and rubbed the back of his neck.

Norla sensed his exhaustion. Unlike Gen and Effira, Pallo hadn't been asleep in the dungeon when she had found them. He had been waiting.

"We should leave now," Chestel said.

"But the horses must rest," Effira protested. She had pulled her velvet cape around her face, hiding all but her bright green eyes.

"My horse is fine," Chestel said.

"*My* horse needs rest, thief," Pallo replied hotly.

"We'll rest an hour before departing, Chestel," Norla said. "Listen to Pallo."

Pallo's eyes went to her. His expression softened.

Norla felt her skin flush despite the cold wind. He had acted so formal only moments ago. But when he looked at her like that...

"Excellent plan," Gen said.

"Indeed," Effira added.

Roella chuckled. "I'm afraid Norla has won this one, Chestel."

~~~

Pallo passed out a supper of dried rabbit and squash at their makeshift camp, tucked in the lee of a dune. The giant hill blocked a great deal of the harsh wind. Although they didn't want to draw attention to themselves with a fire, they did use a single lantern for some light.

Gen sat on a blanket to Pallo's right, scribbling in his journal within the cocoon of blankets he had constructed. Fira shivered beside Pallo, and he nabbed a blanket from Gen to drape across her shoulders. She had just finished brushing the horses with Chestel. The lad had actually brought along Fira's ointment for the animals. He had failed to bring the olive oil he had stolen from Pallo's bags at the castle, however.

Chestel and Norla sat on the opposite side of the lantern. Their voices were low, and judging from Chestel's tone, it sounded like the lad was reprimanding her.

Another watched the pair as intently as Pallo. Roella lounged on her side, resting her arm over her hip. Although her stoic expression revealed nothing, her fingers tapped her hip in frustration as Chestel leaned closer to Norla.

Pallo rose and walked past Norla and Chestel to check on Senna. The mare nickered and lowered her head in greeting. Pallo stroked the groove of her muzzle and scratched behind her ears, gently leading her forward a few steps. From this position, he could easily overhear Norla's conversation.

"Tell the count to side with me," Pallo heard Chestel say.

"I can't do that." Norla' voice was strained.

Chestel threw up his hands. "You'd throw away such a chance for Mia?"

"I'm sorry, Chestel. My heart isn't as noble as yours."

Chestel sighed and moved his hand to cup her shoulder. "Then I'll pray that you find the courage to do right before we reach Penumbra."

116

Norla gave Chestel a sad smile, and Pallo guessed she placed little weight in prayers. Chestel, however, seemed emboldened by Norla's smile. He wrapped his arm around her, and she leaned her head against the lad's chest while she ate.

Pallo's pulse throbbed. He had never asked Norla about her relationship with Chestel, but he would waste no more time in doubt.

Pallo gave Senna a final rub and then moved toward them. Norla would most likely refuse his offer, but he had to try.

"Norla, would you care to accompany me on a walk?" Pallo asked.

Norla turned, her eyes widening. Although her expression revealed surprise, she didn't look repulsed or frightened. Pallo waited. He welcomed any progress—great or small—where she was concerned.

"You don't have to go with him, Norla," Chestel said. "You aren't his anymore."

Norla didn't meet Chestel's gaze, or Pallo's. The night's silver light danced on her tanned skin and set her dark gaze aglow. Inky hair spilled over her shoulders in a sea of loose tangles. What a wonder she was.

"I'll walk with you, Pallo," Norla said.

CHAPTER THIRTEEN

"It isn't safe," Chestel protested.

Pallo patted the sword on his hip. "We'll remain close," he said.

Norla felt the sting of Chestel's disappointment as she grabbed a blanket and rose to her feet. She didn't return his gaze. She had grown tired of trying to please her best friend.

Pallo extended his arm. His lips tilted in a small smile, and Norla realized how much she had come to enjoy that smile.

Nothing made sense anymore. She was ignoring her best friend and welcoming smiles from the man who had taken her from Mia.

Taking his arm, Norla sensed the others' stares as they departed—especially Effira's—but she could not feel guilty for emotions that were not hers.

As they walked, plains of sand stretched into the distance, shining silver in the full moon's bright light. The farther they moved from the dune, the greater the wind. Norla pulled the wool blanket more tightly around her to block grains of sand from her skin.

"How are you?" Pallo asked. His voice was soft.

Norla's ears tingled. "I'm well. And you?"

"Quite well at the moment."

Norla let go of his arm and looked back toward the campsite. Although she was able to see silhouettes, she and Pallo were very much alone.

"Norla, I, er... wish to speak of our plans to retrieve the Book," he said.

"All right," Norla said slowly.

Pallo cleared his throat. "Once we find Penumbra, I plan to slip in and out of his band as quickly as possible. I should be able to avoid capture if I blend in and don't linger." His tone had turned oddly formal.

"I agree," Norla said. Their best chance of stealing the Book would be the quietest and quickest.

"Good." Pallo folded his hands behind his back and studied his leather boots. "Norla, I... would speak with you on another matter as well."

Norla surveyed his taut shoulders, his downcast eyes, and knew Pallo shared her nerves. The realization unexpectedly pleased her.

"Do you, er... still consider yourself my suryan?" he asked.

Norla pressed her palms together. She didn't want to hurt Pallo, but she had spent her whole life bound to foremen and their whips. How would it feel to claim no man as her master? How would it feel to follow Chestel's example and assert the freedom she had gained at Yintpa Castle—however unofficial that freedom might be?

"I don't," Norla said.

Pallo's eyes flickered. Norla lifted her hand to touch him, but let it fall beside her.

"You don't wish to return to Vaskel Palace with me, then," Pallo said. He kept his eyes on his boots.

He was clearly speaking more to himself than to her. In truth, she had never planned to remain at the palace with Pallo. She considered telling him so. Maybe it was the desert or the darkness, but Norla felt free to tell him the truth for one moment.

Then Mia's face came to mind. Norla wouldn't risk Mia's chance at freedom for anything—certainly not for a count whose nearness made Norla forget her responsibility to her mother.

"If we retrieve the Book, I'll return with you to the palace," Norla said, carefully choosing her words. "But until then, out here, I consider myself a free woman."

She didn't look at Pallo, and silence stretched between them.

"Do you intend to be with Chestel in the meantime?" Pallo asked. His tone was stiff and brusque.

"That isn't your concern," Norla said. She shook her head and turned to leave, but Pallo caught her wrist. She struggled, but he held her easily. His hand felt massive around hers, like a muscular shackle.

"It is entirely my concern," Pallo said. His stiff façade broke. "Norla, I must know if you've given your heart to Chestel."

Norla didn't owe him an answer, but she felt compelled to reply.

"He is like a brother to me, Pallo," Norla said.

Pallo snorted and released her wrist, leaving a pool of warmth where his touch had been.

"He doesn't look at you as I looked upon my sister," Pallo said.

Norla paused. She had wondered about Pallo's sister ever since he had mentioned her in the tent. She had no experience with brothers or sisters herself. The other children of Norla's father had never seemed like siblings. The two boys had been as cruel as the other villagers, and the girl had ignored her from the start.

"Your sister?" Norla asked.

Pallo eyed her with a strange wariness. Norla waited.

"Her name was Lania," he said at last. His eyebrows were furrowed and his lips pressed tight. "She drowned in a storm three years ago."

Pallo brushed the sand with his boot. "Lania saw things differently than everyone else," he continued. "She didn't see differences between Uyandis and Weltangs, and she refused to worship the Vaskel kings as gods."

"What was King Vaskel's response to her at court?" Norla asked. She doubted the king would stand for such beliefs in a noblewoman. Waylan Vaskel's family had held the throne since the reign of his grandfather Benteen. The supposedly divine leader had united the wealthiest families, all with their own kingdoms, into one large kingdom in order to better defend their provinces during the final Great Wars with Draxton and Sartania.

"Lania wasn't welcome at court," Pallo said quietly. "She remained at Belany Castle."

"Why wouldn't your sister be welcome at court?"

"Lania was neither a noblewoman nor a suryan."

Pallo finally looked up and met Norla's gaze. "She was the daughter of my father's suryan."

Like Roella, Norla thought. Another woman caught in between classes.

"It's just as well Lania never visited court," Pallo said. "They would have mocked her for her visions."

"Visions?"

"Lania saw all of Reislan drinking from the same jar, including the Weltangs."

Norla raised her eyebrows, but tried to keep an open expression. Pallo was watching her, she knew, and measuring her reaction. Honestly, Lania sounded no stranger than Chestel or any number of Weltang idealists.

"Everyone considered her mad," Pallo said. "But I never did."

Norla followed Pallo's gaze into the sea of sand unfurling before them. He looked far more comfortable in the desert than he had looked in the fine palace halls.

"I don't think your sister was mad," Norla said quietly.

The endless sand was calming, despite the wind. She had never felt smaller. And if they were small, maybe the troubles surrounding them were small too.

They stood side by side for several moments, before Pallo's arm slipped around her waist.

Norla inhaled sharply, catching the scent of spices and leather on his cloak. Blood pounded against her ears. She turned and found his eyes locked on hers.

"Norla," he whispered.

The warmth of his breath brought a flush to her chest, her cheeks. Her heart thumped. Her skin tingled. His eyes were hungry and determined, and Norla felt her restraint waver.

Pallo's hands were urgent around her waist now, weaving new sensations into her body. Norla sighed and shivered at his nearness. She wanted to give in to him, to melt away from the shadows stalking her. And yet, she was suddenly angry.

She had opened herself up to Pallo, and he had seized the opportunity to fulfill his needs. With her.

Norla started to push him away—just as the sounds of horses approaching echoed over the dunes.

~ ~ ~

"Draxton's queen," Pallo cursed. He grabbed Norla's hand and raced toward the camp. Norla kept his pace, which surprised him. She had surprised him in many ways already—but Pallo could not think of such things at that moment. If he did, he would cease running and take her in his arms.

Panic surged through him. How had the riders discovered them? They had not lit a fire. It would have been nearly impossible for asaltanis or Penumbra's riders to find them in the great sea of sand.

As they neared, Pallo saw with faint relief that the others had spotted the approaching riders. Roella was mounting her stallion. Gen was already seated on the carriage, waving Norla and Fira to him.

Pallo hustled Norla to the carriage door, where Chestel was waiting. The lad shoved Norla and Fira into the carriage and then sprinted to Hickory. Senna was already at Pallo's side. He mounted her, and with a slight dig of his heels, she accelerated into a gallop. Hickory and Roella's stallion followed close behind, with the carriage in the rear.

They headed south, away from the approaching riders. Wind and sand slapped Pallo's chapped face. His pulse thumped. They had to find coverage soon, as they had little prayer of outracing the riders. His workhorses wouldn't maintain a gallop for much longer.

Over his shoulder, Pallo spied the rugged outlines of riders in flowing robes. The men were not asaltanis, but they were clearly pursuing them. And they were gaining.

A pounding realization flooded Pallo's body. They couldn't outride the snatchers with the carriage. They would have to rely on the greed of their pursuers instead.

"Follow me!" Pallo shouted into the whipping air. "We cannot outrun them!"

Pallo threw his weight to the left and prodded Senna into a sharp turn. He had to position himself between the riders and the carriage.

"We'll fight them off!" Chestel shouted. He and Roella followed Pallo's lead, and when they had all reined in their horses, the carriage lay safely behind them.

Riders approached.

Chestel unsheathed his sword, a defiant grimace on his face.

"Are you mad?" Pallo asked. "We cannot possibly fight so many. We must negotiate."

Pallo pulled a leather pouch from his pocket and squeezed it in his hand. So much depended on the gems within. He had packed the stones in case of capture. He would bribe the snatchers' mercy and promise more gems upon safe passage through the desert. Pallo and Gen had employed similar tactics when hiking the Axum Mountains of Draxton. But he and Gen had never faced Penumbra's snatchers while traveling in Draxton. Pallo pressed the pouch against his chest, hoping to relieve the building pressure. He could not fail.

"And what's in that?" Chestel asked, nodding at the pouch.

"Leverage," Pallo answered. "If you don't interfere, I may very well be able to buy us safe passage."

No one spoke. All listened to the sound of the horse hooves eating up the distance between them and the robed riders. Chestel held his sword and glared ahead in challenge. For once, Pallo felt grateful to have the fiery lad beside him.

And he wouldn't be surprised if Roella knew how to swing the blade sheathed in her saddle.

"I will be the one speaking," Pallo said.

Chestel grunted.

"I will speak," Pallo repeated. "Understand?"

"I heard you," Chestel muttered. Roella rolled her eyes.

Norla and Effira had climbed out of the carriage for a better view. Pallo cursed. They were holding their blasted swords again. He wished the moon's light wasn't so bright. He didn't want the riders studying the ladies too closely; they would fetch a high price among slavers.

The riders arrived in a fury of hooves and robes. Splitting down the middle, they formed a loose circle around the group.

Pallo remembered Roella's comrades applying the same strategy, but their sage tunics had been far less intimidating than the copper robes of these riders.

Pallo shivered at the riders' nearness. He could scarcely look at them without his eyes hurting; the bright moonlight reflected so strangely on their robes.

Oddly, all of the riders save one turned their horses outward, away from their captives, as if they were watching for more intruders. Only the rider nearest to Pallo remained facing him. The man sat astride a giant chestnut stallion with a white diamond marking between its eyes. He held a sword in his red sash, and over his woolen robe he wore a sleeveless copper cloak. A red mitzah cloth covered his hair and fell halfway down his back. And his keen eyes revealed great intelligence.

This was not a man Pallo wanted for an enemy.

CHAPTER FOURTEEN

"We seek safe passage to Gracehen Oasis," Pallo said.

The evenness of his voice impressed Norla. She was scarcely able to control her trembling hands. She doubted her voice would behave any better.

"I see," the rider said. He spoke the Reislan tongue perfectly, with only a slight lilt betraying his origins. His jewel-like eyes assessed the rest of the group with relaxed confidence.

Norla took an instinctive step back toward the cab. She had thought Pallo's gaze penetrating, but his was nothing compared to this man's. The rider was unlike anyone Norla had met. His easy posture, the smoothness of his face, even the way the bright moonlight scattered across his skin... it all seemed wholly foreign.

Clearing his throat, Pallo held out the pouch to the rider. The strange man took the bag, peered inside, and returned it as if the pouch carried no more than dirt.

"You ride to find Penumbra," the rider said.

Norla froze. The man spoke with authority, as if he knew the goal of their trip with absolute certainty. But how could he possibly know?

"We will gladly take you to our master," the rider continued.

A sharp shiver raced down Norla's spine. The man confirmed what Norla already knew. The most dangerous men in the kingdom now surrounded her.

Norla focused on her breathing. She could not let them see her lose her nerve. Penumbra's riders obviously outnumbered them. They had no prayer of escaping. And if the riders considered Penumbra their master, maybe they would await his instructions before acting.

"We welcome your lead," Norla called. She hoped her voice carried over the fierce wind.

The rider's eyes lingered on Norla, and Pallo glanced at her over his shoulder. She held Pallo's gaze, hoping he had reached the same conclusion. Surely he would agree to seem compliant for the moment.

Pallo gave a slight nod. "If you are traveling to meet Penumbra, then we shall gladly accompany you," he said to the rider.

"Otherwise, you'd best let us on our way," Chestel said, raising his sword slightly.

The lead rider turned to Chestel, and Norla wanted to muzzle her friend.

"We are not in the habit of receiving orders from anyone but Penumbra," the rider said.

Chestel stiffened astride Hickory, and the horse shook its head, as if chiding its rider for his brashness.

"We welcome you as our traveling companions," the rider said to Pallo. He shouted a foreign command to his fellow riders, and they turned their horses inward.

Norla sucked in her breath and looked around. She blinked in surprise. A few of the nearest faces were female. All of the riders held their horses' reins with bare hands, and tucked within their red sashes were swords with golden hilts.

"I must first ask your word that no harm will come to our party on the journey," Pallo said.

The rider's eyes flashed. "You are as bold as your young friend." He nodded towards Chestel. "Tell me, why do you seek Penumbra?"

"We've heard much talk of him," Pallo said. "We wish to see him for ourselves."

"So be it. You will find our master near Clovesdell Oasis, not Gracehen. We will help you onward."

Norla grimaced. The riders' "help" ruined any plans of slipping through Penumbra's band of snatchers unnoticed.

The rider's eyes drifted to Roella atop her stallion, and then to Norla and Effira.

"You travel with great treasures," the rider said.

"The ladies are spoken for," Pallo said tersely. "I insist you pass that message to your men."

Roella scoffed. "You really should calm down, grand Count," she said, leaning back in her saddle. "You're making my head ache, and I'm only watching you." She turned her full smile on the rider. "We welcome you as guides. Thank you for the generous offer."

Whatever the woman's opinion of Norla, Roella obviously agreed with her reasoning. Since the riders would take them regardless, it was far wiser to go as apparent guests than as prisoners.

"I'll come as well," Chestel said, his face stretched taut as he assessed the lead rider.

Norla prayed he would say no more. Leaving Effira's side, Norla climbed onto the cab seat to stand beside Gen. He raised an eyebrow but said nothing.

"Shall we leave?" Norla asked. Her voice trembled, and she longed to laugh and simper like Roella. How did the woman remain so collected when surrounded by snatchers?

"Fine," Chestel said, narrowing his gaze on the lead rider. "But I want to speak with you when we break for camp."

The rider rubbed his black beard with a gleam in his eyes.

"So be it," he said.

Norla shuddered. Such a conversation could only end in swordplay.

~~~

Penumbra's snatchers led them north to a nearby camp—a loose circle of tents at the base of a hill.

When the cab came to a stop, Gen jumped to the ground and helped Norla and Effira down. As Norla and Effira walked forward, they found Pallo's arms around their shoulders. Norla stiffened at his nearness, but he had positioned himself to take the brunt of the wind.

Wind howled as they walked. Since their steps were small, it felt like an eternity before they reached a tent flap. Pallo pulled aside the tightly woven fabric, and urged Norla and Effira inside.

In an instant, the howling stopped and the wind ceased. Norla felt the change like a physical force. Tents truly were wonderful.

Giant lanterns hung along the interior rim of the circular tent, and an even larger lantern was suspended from its elevated middle. Pillows, cushions, and blankets lay scattered on a sprawling rug, radiating warmth. The entire place smelled of meat, spice, and smoke.

Maybe Norla would rest for a moment before finding Chestel. Her body, her mind, every part of her, felt as frail and brittle as a reed. She hated such weakness and knew all too well that the only salve was sleep.

With a deep breath, Norla sank onto the orange rug. Effira did the same, and Pallo brought them both blankets. Norla nodded silently in gratitude. She didn't attempt to speak; her teeth were chattering too much.

Pallo looked just as cold. His cheeks and nose were stained a dark crimson, and his hands shook as he removed his gloves and held them in front of the nearest lantern.

"Draxton's queen," Pallo murmured. He glanced from his gloves to Norla's bare hands.

She tried to hide her red fingers under the blanket, but Pallo winced.

"You don't have gloves," he said, more to himself than to Norla. "My ignorance is astounding."

"I'm fine," Norla said.

Pallo closed his eyes, shaking his head.

Norla watched his shivering body and felt his dejection as if it were hers. He had noticed, and that meant something. She gathered one of her blankets in her arms and took it to Pallo, draping it across his shoulders. He turned towards her in surprise, close enough for her to feel the chill of the desert on his cloak.

His eyes softened, and Norla remembered their talk only an hour ago. He had wanted to kiss her. What if she had let him? For an instant she wondered how it would be to know the feeling of his lips on hers. Despite her frigid skin, warmth bloomed inside her.

Norla's ears pounded. She needed distance, space to think. Effira was only feet away.

"Chestel," Norla said.

His name had the effect Norla had desired. Pallo stepped back, his eyes hardening.

"I have to stop him from meeting with the rider," Norla said.

"No one is forcing the lad to have such a meeting," Pallo said. "The choice is his."

"I know, but I won't sleep until I know he's safe."

Pallo's mouth tightened. "You care a great deal for his well-being."

"He's my best friend, Pallo. I've told you that."

Pallo studied her for a long moment, his face impossible to read. "Then he's quite lucky," he said at last. He turned his back to her, warming his hands by the lantern.

Norla watched his stiff back for a moment. She took a deep breath, gathering what little strength she had left, and turned to the door. She purposefully kept her gaze from Effira, whose nosiness was probably bubbling over after this latest interchange.

"Wait... I'll escort you," Pallo said. He didn't sound thrilled by the prospect.

Norla wondered if he sensed her exhaustion. Though she didn't desire his pity, she was thankful for his help against the wind.

Pallo let out a deep sigh and stretched. The motion accentuated the breadth of his shoulders, and Norla watched, transfixed by the man who had suddenly crowded her thoughts. She knew so little of him. She wondered what ignited his passions, what he loathed, what he dreamed about. Did he wonder such things about her?

With a grim smile, he held out his leather gloves. "Take them," he said.

"I'm fine," Norla replied.

"Please, Norla," Pallo pressed. He sounded so weary that Norla relented. She didn't really need the gloves, but she would take them if it helped assuage his conscience.

When she slipped her hands into the gloves' furry linings, she had to admit that the warm sensation was welcome.

Pallo was watching her with soft eyes.

"Much thanks," Norla said quietly.

"I'll come as well," Effira said. "I must groom the horses."

"Fira, let me do that," Pallo offered. "Stay and enjoy the warmth."

"You don't wish for me to accompany you?" Effira's voice was sharp.

Pallo blinked. "Of course you can join us, if you wish."

"Do *you* wish for me to accompany you?"

"Of course." Pallo held out his hand, and Effira hesitated before taking it firmly in hers.

Norla forced her gaze to the tent flap. She wouldn't think about those two at the moment. She would focus on protecting Chestel and ignore the palpable feel of Pallo's presence just behind her.

She slid through the flap and wind licked her face like a hundred whips. Pulling the blanket tighter around her shoulders, she surveyed the circle of tents. There were at least a dozen, and Norla needed to discover which tent held the lead rider and Chestel.

Norla passed a few lantern-lit tents and saw glimpses of horses through the crimson flaps. The great animals chewed on hay and alfalfa while their masters lounged nearby on golden pillows. Effira nodded in approval, and Norla wondered if she would be sharing a tent with Senna that night.

Chestel came striding toward them from one of the giant tents, flanked by Gen and Roella.

"What're you doing out here?" Chestel called over the wind.

"Where are the horses?" Effira demanded.

"They're sharing a tent with some of the riders," Gen answered. "We were just seeing to them."

Effira bit her lip, looking past Gen to the tent.

"They will be well taken care of, Fira," Gen continued.

"Of course they will," Chestel said, his eyes still on Norla. "Why aren't you inside?"

"You can't meet with the lead rider," Norla replied. She hugged her arms across her chest. The blanket blocked some of the wind, but icy licks still beat against her exposed neck and face.

Chestel grinned. "Talked with him before grooming the horses."

Norla's stomach dropped. "What did you say, Chestel?"

"What I had to." He kept his catlike grin and nodded to the tent Norla had just emerged from. "Shall we?" he said in his best Uyandi accent.

"The men are sleeping in a separate tent," Pallo said, stepping up beside Norla.

Chestel's smile dropped. "Of course," he said. "But I'll see Norla to her tent."

"Why don't I join you?" Pallo said.

"Why don't you go back to the palace," Chestel muttered. He extended his arm, and Norla gladly took it. Her skin had grown numb, and she welcomed the warmth. Besides, Pallo already had Effira on his arm.

"How touching," Roella said, brushing them aside as she strode toward the tent.

Norla exchanged a glance with Chestel, and he shrugged.

When they all reached the tent, neither Chestel nor Pallo showed any signs of being the first to leave. In the end, Gen took each of them by the arm and booted them out by force.

"What a bewitching girl you are, fair Norla," Roella said, after the men left. She stretched across the orange rug and yawned. "Don't you think so, Lady Effira?"

Effira's lips twitched. "I don't know what you mean."

"Don't you?" Roella smiled. "Well, Norla certainly does."

"No," Norla said. "I don't."

Roella clucked her tongue. "Then you're both blind."

~~~

They rode north the next day, stopping at several crude wells along the way. Pallo wondered at the strange wells; none were near oases.

"I would never expect to find so many wells in the desert," Pallo said to the lead rider on one of their stops.

"It is unexpected, isn't it?" the rider replied, with a faint grin.

Pallo frowned. He didn't press the subject any further.

The riders offered to share their well water, but Pallo and the others drank from their own jugs and ate their own food. Pallo found the strange riders unnerving; he didn't trust them. He was sorely tempted to try one of the riders' purple berries, though. The mere smell of their tangy sweetness seemed to fill Pallo's stomach.

They didn't pass a single oasis, but they did see two different tribes of nomads. Both tribes appeared on the distant horizon and disappeared just as quickly. Thrice, Pallo thought he saw a pair of asaltanis trailing them. And thrice the silver cloaks disappeared when Pallo looked again. Penumbra's riders clearly encouraged distance from all they encountered.

Gen, however, seemed to be warming to the snatchers. Pallo had overheard Gen asking the lead rider where they purchased their fine wool. Undoubtedly his friend wished to incorporate the fabric into his wardrobe.

Pallo saw little of Norla. She had returned his gloves to him and kept mostly to Chestel, whose company she clearly preferred.

Pallo tried to ignore those thoughts—the thoughts of what might have transpired among the dunes the previous night, had the snatchers not appeared—and focus on the task at hand. If they had any hope of stealing the Book and escaping enslavement in Draxton, they needed to separate from Penumbra's band of snatchers. Unfortunately, the group had no time alone. Riders were constantly present, making it impossible to discuss plans. And even though Pallo and the others remained armed, so did the riders.

That night, Pallo gazed at the tent's woolen ceiling and listened to Gen's heavy breathing. It had been a wonder watching the riders set up camp from the limited saddlebags their horses carried. He still didn't understand how they fit the plush pillows and blankets, let alone the massive tents, into such compact bags.

Five armed riders shared the tent with Pallo, Gen, and Chestel—and all appeared to be sleeping. Since the men made so little noise regardless of whether they were asleep or awake, it was impossible to know.

Pallo had to wake Gen without waking the riders.

Crouching on his knees, Pallo took a few deep breaths to steady his pulse. The air was cold, since the lanterns had nearly died. His breath came out in soft puffs as he crawled toward Gen. A leather-bound journal lay open at his friend's side. Pallo spotted the words "gallant," "sparkling night," and "winged rider."

Pallo shook his head and cupped his hand over his friend's mouth to wake him. Gen's eyes flew open. His arms and legs flailed before he recognized Pallo. When Gen had calmed, Pallo released his hand and motioned to the tent's flap. Gen gave Pallo a dramatic nod and scurried toward the flap. Pallo hesitated. He still had to wake the horse thief, or else Norla wouldn't come with them.

"Where're you going?" Chestel demanded from behind him.

CHAPTER FIFTEEN

"Trying to leave me behind?" Chestel sat straight up, chin high, making no effort to keep his voice down.

Pallo's cheeks burned. The other riders had awakened, of course. Although they didn't stir from their mats, their watchful eyes proved threatening enough. Pallo longed to throttle Chestel.

"Not at all," Pallo said. "I needed a stretch," he added. The snatchers seemed satisfied by the lie—most of them closed their eyes again.

"You know that Norla won't leave without me," Chestel said, easing himself back onto his pillow.

Pallo clenched his jaw. He and Gen exchanged glances before striding back to their cushions. Chestel had thrown the perfect barb, and the lad knew it.

At dinner and supper, Norla and Chestel had shared several laughs. The pair had reached a kind of truce, it seemed, and Pallo had watched their easy friendliness with envy snaking up his spine. He only enjoyed Norla's unguarded ways from afar. Whenever he neared, she grew quiet.

Instead, it was Fira who had kept Pallo company. Together, they had groomed Senna and taken turns guessing which details of their journey Gen had embellished for his memoir. Both of them believed Gen had already written a song or two about their travels for the palace minstrels.

"I imagine he'll write himself as the most dashing swordsman," Fira had said, brushing Senna's side with quick flicks to remove all the sand and dirt.

"He can be rather dashing," Pallo had said, with a wry grin. "Especially when he has an audience."

Fira had laughed. "Well, he isn't the most dashing swordsman I know." Her face had grown serious then, and she'd held Pallo's gaze for a moment before abruptly returning her attention to Senna's coat.

Pallo had understood her meaning, and the realization had filled him with dread. As much as he admired Fira, the thought of welcoming any woman into his household besides Norla was intolerable at present.

Pallo had to speak with Fira. He assured himself that once he had delivered the Book to Vaskel, then he would speak with her—and sort out the rest of his life.

Taking a deep breath, Pallo gazed at the woolen ceiling and turned his thoughts to Penumbra. The man had earned a vicious, if vague, reputation in Vaskel's courts. And, upon meeting Penumbra's riders, Pallo was certain the criminal was even more powerful than Vaskel realized. The riders seemed inhuman, almost ghostly—and wholly unlike the greedy snatchers Pallo had expected. Their calmness was almost more unnerving than bloodlust would be.

Pallo shuddered at the risks ahead. He had encountered dangerous situations in the past, of course, but this trip was different. Norla had placed her hope in him.

~~~

Pallo dreamed of Norla and the stream again. As before, Norla dipped her arm into the deep blue water, with its shining fish and terrifying snakes. And like before, Pallo sucked the venom from Norla's blood, only to grow weaker himself. The poison burned and squeezed Pallo's chest as if the snakes themselves were constricting him.

But this time when Pallo cried out, a figure appeared. The strange man stepped from the stream onto the shore, moving toward them. He wore copper trousers and a sleeveless tunic that revealed bronze arms. Looking closer, Pallo saw faded fang marks lining the brown skin. If the man had lived through the snakes' bites, perhaps Norla and Pallo would live as well.

"We're dying," Pallo said. He barely managed to speak through the fiery pain coursing through his limbs.

"Perhaps not," the man said. His eyes were kind and immutable, capable of much. His easy confidence reminded Pallo of the lead rider.

When the man from the stream stretched out his arms, Pallo shrank back. He didn't know the man from the river, and he wouldn't trust Norla with a stranger.

Pallo turned his gaze back to Norla's limp body. He would save her somehow. He had to.

~~~

Norla sat across from Effira in the cab after their captors had packed up camp the next day. Roella opted to ride with the men, and Norla secretly envied her freedom. If Norla knew how to ride, she too would prefer the freedom of a saddle to the confines of the cab. And judging from the way Effira eyed Roella astride her horse, Norla was not alone in her wishes.

Her stomach churned with nerves. Today, their fates would be decided.

She had exhausted her mind with potential escape plans— and all of them were lacking. Penumbra's riders had not left them alone for a moment. Even at night, female riders had shared the tent with her, Effira, and Roella. They would meet Penumbra as prisoners.

Because of Penumbra's band, though, they were actually moving closer to their goal. The Book was with Penumbra, and they had now discovered the criminal's location. Yet, Norla shuddered at the thought of what awaited them at Clovesdell Oasis. If Penumbra caught wind of their journey's true intentions, or if he simply decided to kill them for sport...

Effira offered her canteen to Norla, and Norla gladly took it. The desert was as relentlessly warm during the day as it was cold at night. Before Norla could take two drinks, Effira offered her olives as well.

The lady was constantly trying to share with Norla. And she peppered Norla with questions about Mia and Chestel far too often. Despite herself, Norla answered most of Effira's questions until she grew weary of the lady's onslaught.

"And what about you?" Norla blurted, when Effira finally took a breath. "Tell me of your family."

Effira blinked and shifted on the silk cushion. "My father is a younger son," she said quietly.

Norla nodded. She knew that younger sons had no castles or governing rights in their families' provinces. They still had grand manors and plenty of servants, though.

"We have a wheat farm," Effira added, with a strained smile. "It really is lovely. It's near the edge of King's Forest. My sister and I used to play in the forest quite often, actually, pretending we were characters from storybooks." Effira's shoulders relaxed, and she took a drink from her canteen.

"My sister always pretended to be a duchess or princess," Effira said. "But I would be a commander in the army, assigned to exotic quests in faraway lands… "

Effira took another drink and laughed. "It's silly, really. Of course ladies aren't permitted to join the military. It was only pretending." Effira paused, her eyes growing clouded. "But not for my sister. She really will become a duchess one day."

Norla raised an eyebrow. Despite herself, she was curious.

"An older count from one of the northern provinces has taken a liking to her," Effira said. "He is more than twice her age, but my parents are thrilled with the match. So is she. He will be a duke one day, and no one expected a daughter from our family to marry so well." Effira folded her hands in her lap and stared out the window.

Norla watched her, feeling something akin to sympathy for the lady. She knew what it was like to be looked down upon by one's peers. But surely no one in Effira's presence could consider her lacking. She would marry as well as her sister. Norla's breath caught as she thought of Effira's most likely match.

Norla had seen little of him since their capture, but she could not bar him from her thoughts. His pale blue eyes had haunted her dreams, teasing her with their depth and mystery. Norla still knew so little of the man. He had revealed nothing of his past, apart from his sister's death. When Pallo had spoken of Lania—his eyebrows drawn, his deep voice growing softer—Norla had ached with him, and yet... they avoided each other.

Norla opted for the comfort of Chestel's company instead. Unlike Pallo, her old friend didn't make her tongue grow heavy. She and Chestel talked little of the present, with all its divisions and complications. Instead, they swapped stories from their days on the mountain.

"Remember when we sneaked into the quarry after supper, and then we had to stay until dawn because a guard took his post while we were inside?" Chestel asked.

"Of course," Norla replied. "We thought that guard would never leave! Mia was so angry. She'd assumed a snatcher had gotten me."

"She didn't let me into your hut for a week after that."

"And only then because you begged her."

Chestel dropped his jaw in protest. "I didn't beg."

"You were on your knees, Chestel. That's begging."

Chestel grinned, before launching into another memory. He obviously hoped Norla's heart would soften. But as much as Chestel tried, he would never be able to erase the villagers' ostracism. Norla wouldn't risk Mia's freedom for the lot of them.

The party made its way across the hard sand and occasional yucca shrubs. The lead rider and a dozen of his men rode at the front. Pallo and Chestel rode behind them, just before the cab, and another dozen riders filled in behind the cab. Such had been the formation the previous day as well.

Wiping sweat from her brow, Norla felt a sudden wave of excitement as she peered out the window. Each step of the horses brought her closer to the Book.

On the horizon, Norla saw a flicker of green through the window. Her heartbeat quickened. Sitting straighter, she squinted. There, in the midst of cacti and scorching sand, was an oasis.

"Do you see it?" Norla asked, breathless. "Clovesdell."

Effira blinked. Her lips parted but no words came out.

When the cab fell under the cover of trees, Norla exhaled in relief. Even though she and Effira were protected from much of the elements, the cab had become like a furnace in the oppressive desert heat. The horses slowed to a walk and followed the beaten grass path into Clovesdell.

The plush oasis put Vaskel Palace to shame. Towering palms covered the oasis in generous swaths of shade. A little lower, plump trees glittered with orange, red, and yellow fruits, blazing like drops of sun against green leaves. Beneath the trees' twisting branches, horses, sheep, and goats grazed on grass.

Ahead, a clearing appeared. Over a hundred nomads and their herds surrounded a gushing spring. At the mouth of the pool, robed women filled jars. Bearded men in brown robes lounged with their feet in the spring. The whole place teemed with the sounds of laughter and splashes.

Norla's heart stirred at the sense of community. The scene reminded her faintly of Weltang Village. In the evenings, everyone would gather along the roads after a long day's work. Typically, Chestel or another lad would initiate a game of leapball, and all the children would join in.

Norla imagined a game of leapball would fit in nicely at the oasis. She felt lighter just being near the desert men and women. She wondered if they knew Penumbra's snatchers were in their midst. Surely not, or they wouldn't be so carefree.

Once Gen had brought the cab to a stop, he helped Norla and Effira down. Like Norla, Effira and Gen seemed unable to keep their gazes from the colorful scene, and she suspected the Uyandis were shocked by the lack of decorum. Children raced around, tagging each other in turn. Men and women sat under open-air tents, chatting and eating slices of cheese and fruit. A dozen riders in copper were interspersed throughout the oasis, looking remarkably like riders from Penumbra's band. Nearby, a group of girls in light blue robes splashed each other near the edge of the spring, earning a disapproving glance from an elderly woman sitting under an open-air tent.

Effira unfastened the workhorse from the cab, and Pallo came to help her. His cheeks were flushed from riding. He looked so *alive*. Norla stared at him for a long moment, until Pallo met her admiring gaze. A smile came to his lips, and she quickly glanced away.

Chestel and Roella dismounted their horses, and together the six of them walked toward the spring.

"Where's Penumbra?" Chestel whispered, casting a sideways glance at the lead rider.

"I'm sure we'll meet him soon," Pallo answered.

"Let's hope so," Chestel said, assessing the camp. He watched as Hickory and the other horses followed Senna to the spring. The animals bent down and took greedy sips, side by side.

"Will someone steal them?" Chestel asked.

"How interesting," Pallo said. "A horse thief worried about horse thievery."

Chestel glowered.

"We'll keep a close eye on them," Pallo added.

A few of the nearest tribesmen quieted at the sight of the foreign horses, and Norla suddenly felt like an intruder. She knew the spring was considered no one's property in particular, yet the mood of the place seemed to stiffen. The nomads' eyes darted from Norla to the riders, following closely behind. Did the tribesmen recognize Penumbra's band?

To Norla's surprise, the nearby tribesmen bowed to the riders. Why would they treat the snatchers with such respect? Maybe they acted out of fear. After all, Norla and her group had obeyed the riders for fear of the consequences.

Norla inched toward the spring's grassy edge, with Chestel and Pallo on either side of her. The setting sun threw its crimson light like flames on the pool's surface. Norla marveled at the water's clarity. Her dry mouth longed for a taste of the spring.

"Where's your Master?" Chestel asked, breaking into Norla's thoughts.

She looked up to see Chestel's back to the spring. He was facing the lead rider with a slight scowl. "Is he here? Did you mean to trick us?"

Norla flinched at Chestel's loud tone. He drew the stare of every nomad within earshot.

"You ask many questions, Reislaner," the lead rider said. His eyes crinkled in something like a smile. "Does the oasis not please you?"

"Haven't traveled this far to see a spring," Chestel said. He threw his hand at the pool, as if it were no more than a puddle. "We came for Penumbra."

"Penumbra is near," a voice said. It came from an open-air tent only a few paces from the spring, where an elderly woman and a younger woman reclined on brown cushions. They both wore deep blue robes.

"But you might not meet the man you were expecting," the elderly woman continued. Her voice was hard, but her eyes had a softness that reminded Norla of Mia. "You have been sorely deceived."

Chapter Sixteen

"Your wicked kiyaza enjoys deceiving many," the elderly woman said.

Pallo raised his eyebrows. He recognized the desert word for "king," and he'd never heard anyone so openly voice their disapproval for Vaskel.

"My dear mama, you should not say such things," the younger woman said to the older. She wore a brown mitzah over her head that fluttered in the wind. "There are many who worship Kiyaza Vaskel as their god."

"And many who do not," the older woman said gruffly. "The kiyaza would do best to step down from that makeshift throne of his."

"Please forgive my mother," the younger woman said to the others. "She speaks her mind, regardless of who is listening."

"So does my mother," Pallo replied, smiling. He remembered the time his mother had called two highly respected merchants a pair of "serpent-tongued swindlers" when they had made an insultingly low offer on the family's harvest a few years back.

Chestel stepped forward. "Where's Penumbra, ma'am?"

The woman turned her gaze to the group of young girls playing in the spring.

"What do they say about him?" she asked.

"That he's the most dangerous criminal in the land."

"He is dangerous, to be sure," the woman said. "But then, not in the way you think."

Pallo watched the old woman with growing favor. Her sharp tongue had reminded him of his mother, but her veiled amusement and gentle eyes reminded him of Lania.

"Madam, what do you think of Penumbra?" Pallo asked her.

Her thin lips parted into a smile that lit her cheeks and lifted her eyes. "Do you know our word *drayza*?"

Pallo shook his head.

"It means a digger of wells," she said. "And I think Penumbra is a drayza like no other."

Pallo frowned. "Penumbra digs wells?" Why would an infamous snatcher dig wells?

The woman nodded. "Some say he enchanted his well water to trick others into following him. Some say his water is no better than the spring at Gracehen or any other oasis. But we know Penumbra's wells come from a different water source." Her eyes drifted to the lead rider, standing behind Pallo and Chestel.

"We can leave directly. The animals have had their drink, and the wind will cool quickly with the approach of dusk." The rider nodded to the westward sky. "The journey is short."

"And Usak will lead you true," the old woman said, grinning at the rider.

"Usak," Pallo repeated.

The rider nodded, his green eyes gleaming.

"We'd better leave the ladies here," Chestel said to Pallo and Gen.

Fira, Norla, and Roella looked sharply at Chestel.

"You forget yourself, Chestel," Roella said, eyes cold.

"We go where you go," Norla said.

"Of course we do," Fira snapped.

Pallo grinned. The lad had tied a rope around his own neck, and Pallo wouldn't lift a finger to help him remove it.

Chestel swallowed. He moved toward them and lowered his voice. "What if Penumbra's a sorcerer? Can't you wait until we decide he isn't dangerous?"

"It's not your decision to make, Chestel," Norla said. She turned to Pallo. "Shall we leave?"

"We shall." Pallo grinned.

Chestel's proud expression had deflated into a pout. "We agreed to split ways before finding Penumbra. We should do so now." Roella stepped towards him, but his eyes went to Norla.

She remained silent while he watched her. Pallo waited.

"I'm not coming with you, Chestel," Norla said finally.

The lad's eyes flashed. "You still side with the Uyandis over your own people?"

"For Mia? Yes."

Pallo tried to hide his grin. The horse thief shook his head, and for once he held his tongue. With a nod to Roella, Chestel strode toward the spring to retrieve Hickory. He did not glance back at Norla.

The others followed Chestel, including Pallo. He preferred to keep the horse thief in sight. As Pallo mounted Senna, he noticed a group of lads admiring his mare's shining coat. Senna noticed, too. Her ears pricked forward and she snorted with pride.

Pallo waved at the lads, and their tanned faces broke into grins. When they returned his wave, Pallo felt himself smile. A part of him wished to remain longer in the lively oasis. It felt more like home than the royal palace ever had.

Once the workhorses were harnessed again, Pallo made sure Norla and Fira had cloaks and gloves. The sun hung low over the horizon, and the wind had grown cooler.

As the group headed west, Pallo guided Senna into a trot. Chestel and Roella pushed ahead, and though Pallo kept them within view, he did not strive to keep their pace. He welcomed the extra time to prepare for meeting Penumbra.

The old woman had fed the seed of doubt in Pallo, mostly because he already believed Vaskel to be a charlatan. The king would lie about anything to ensure the outcome he desired. What if... what if he had lied about Penumbra?

Vaskel had enough influence as king to create a man's reputation, which meant Penumbra could have become whomever Vaskel chose. Perhaps Penumbra did not even possess the Book.

Of course, Penumbra's band of snatchers had been intimidating enough. Pallo had not imagined that. They had threatened Pallo and the others, hadn't they? Pallo strived to recall, but he only remembered Usak offering to lead them to Penumbra. Pallo had assumed the offer was an order, but now he wondered. And the snatchers had let Pallo and the others keep their swords, which had been hardly wise if the riders considered them prisoners.

They reached the summit of a hill covered in yucca shrubs. Below, people were walking in a line across the sand, carrying goatskin jugs and clay jars of every size. Their robes were earthen tones like those worn by the nomads at Clovesdell, and their chatter radiated an air of excitement. Pallo guessed they were tribesmen in search of Penumbra's latest well. Perhaps the wells they had passed earlier had been dug by Penumbra as well.

Led by the riders, Pallo and the others galloped down the southern face of the hill. Their pace had quickened. Penumbra's band of riders was clearly eager to see its leader, and even Pallo felt a strange draw towards Penumbra's well.

As Pallo raced beside the trail of pilgrims, Senna easily passed Hickory. Pallo grinned and gave Chestel a quick wave. The obstinate lad tucked his head and kicked Hickory's sides, but it didn't help. Senna would never allow the gelding to embarrass her.

Up ahead, more people with jars had gathered into a large circle. Reaching the rim's outer edge, Pallo dismounted Senna. Unlike the tribesmen at Clovesdell, these nomads hardly noticed the group of foreigners among them. They were all focused on the center of the circle. Some laughed, many talked, and a few scowled.

Dozens of riders in copper robes and mitzahs sat astride giant horses, facing the outward desert. Pallo recognized them as more of Penumbra's band.

Chestel reined in Hickory, and though the lad jumped down immediately, he too waited for the carriage. Apparently he still hoped Norla would join his cause.

Before Pallo had the opportunity to assist Norla, she had climbed from the carriage seat. Pallo stiffened, but when she smiled up at him, his frustration vanished. She looked radiant in the dusky light.

"We're so near," Norla said. Her voice was barely audible over the pilgrims' excited chatter, but Pallo sensed her warmth.

"We'll free your mother somehow," Pallo said. He spoke the words over and over in his mind, willing them to be true. If Penumbra did indeed have the Book, Pallo would not leave the desert without it.

She gazed at him with a tentative smile, her hair tossing in the wind, and Pallo nearly reached out to touch her.

"Won't find the Book if we stay back here," Chestel said, breaking Norla's gaze. He gave Pallo a smug smile and held his arm out to Norla. "Walk with me, at least?"

Norla's eyes darted from Pallo to Chestel, before she sighed and took Chestel's extended arm.

"He's trying to rattle you," Fira said.

"He's succeeding," Pallo said.

Pallo gave her a grim smile, and the three of them walked forward, with Usak just behind them. Effira held a lantern, shedding light on the people ahead.

The crowd parted to reveal nothing but a crude hole in the sand. Nearby, a rope was looped around a prickly yucca tree and disappeared down the hole. Several of the people closest to the well, including Chestel and Norla, were bent forward in expectation.

The inner ring of pilgrims was far quieter than the outer edges. The quiet stretched until at last a mop of uncovered brown hair emerged from the hole. Then, a face with arresting eyes that reminded Pallo of the turquoise waters at home. Then broad shoulders and two strong arms, pulling hand over hand up the rope. His body appeared next, covered by the same woolen robe the riders wore, and a sash, which held an old shovel. Stripes of mud colored the man's copper robe and white sash. His deeply tanned face looked much younger than Pallo had expected—certainly younger than Vaskel—but something in the drayza's air gave his identity away.

After dropping the rope, Penumbra wiped soil from his forehead and grinned at the crowd. He smelled of sand and sun. His laughing eyes traveled from face to face, before falling on Pallo.

Pallo's skin warmed. Part of him wished to turn away from the man's penetrating gaze, but the other part desired to lean closer. Penumbra looked at Pallo in a way that left him feeling wholly known. It was as if Penumbra could see beyond Pallo the Uyandi count, to the child who had stood before the ocean, lost in dreams of distant isles.

Pallo forgot all about the ache of his muscles and the thirst of his throat.

"Greetings, Reislaners," Penumbra said, amusement coloring his voice. He rubbed the unkempt beard on his cheeks. "I have a feeling you aren't here for my water."

~~~

"Why do you want my Book?" Penumbra asked. He brushed strands of his thick hair from his face, leaving a streak of mud through it.

Norla blinked, the air rushing out of her. How did he know why they had come?

With a start, she realized that Penumbra had directed the question at her. She pressed her hands together and took a step back. The man's dazzling bluish-green eyes gave her pause. He seemed to look inward, to spaces within her. But unlike his riders, nothing about the man seemed foreign. The fading sunlight didn't fall on him in strange ways.

"We have plans to do much good with it," Norla said. The words were true enough, but they tasted small on her tongue. She wanted to say more, to convince Penumbra of her cause. But she doubted more words would come.

The man nodded slowly and turned back to the well. He didn't look like the infamous renegade of Reislan. Instead of a blade, he carried a shovel. And he didn't seem angered or even surprised by their quest for the Book.

Norla glanced around and noticed the robed pilgrims had all fallen silent. They were listening to her conversation with Penumbra. Norla's ears tingled at the thought, and she squeezed her hands tighter.

"Do you know what you'll find on the Book's pages?" Penumbra asked, bending to his knees. He scraped the edges of the crude well with his shovel, forming a smooth circle that was about as wide as a man's height.

Norla shook her head. She doubted anyone knew except King Vaskel—and the man standing before her.

Penumbra laughed softly, a melodic sound. He rose to his feet and reached into his waist sash to reveal a small book bound by something like tree bark.

The Book.

Norla's chest tightened. She was looking at the key to Mia's freedom.

Penumbra held out the Book to her with a casual air. "Here. You can have a look."

Norla tensed. Surely the man had some purpose of his own for allowing her to hold the Book. Could it be cursed in some way? Still, if she intended to return the Book to King Vaskel, she would have to touch it at some point.

She leaned in and accepted the Book. Soil coated Penumbra's hands and the visible part of his forearms. The sight of them reminded her of King's Mountain.

Once Norla had the Book, she quickly stepped back. Chestel moved to look over her shoulder, and Pallo sidled next to her as the others gathered around. Oddly, she found herself leaning towards Pallo instead of her best friend. Days ago, she never would have chosen him as the person to share this moment with her. Now, it only seemed right.

Her breath stilled as she gazed down at the small book, illuminated by the last rays of the sun and a lantern held by

Effira. Its bark-like cover scraped against her palms. She had imagined the Book would be larger and grander—with a silver spine and inlaid gems, perhaps. Yet this book felt light, no more than ten pages in length.

With a deep breath, Norla opened the bark cover to reveal a yellowed page.

CHAPTER SEVENTEEN

Norla blinked. She was looking at a map of the entire Mirlane Isle—Draxton in the west, Sartania in the east, the Luwista Islands in the south, and Reislan, of course, making up the middle band of land. Norla had seen a map of the isle before. Mia used to draw the four kingdoms for Norla and Chestel with a stick on their hut's dirt floor.

But this map missed a crucial part that Mia's maps had never excluded—kingdom boundaries. Although the different kingdom names were written in the Book, the lines dividing them were absent.

Norla wondered at the blatant exclusion. Had the isle ever existed without the division of kingdoms? The kings and queens of the isle's four kingdoms were infamous competitors—they coexisted only for the sake of trade. Every few generations, one royal family would anger another, and the entire isle would erupt in bloody wars. Boundary lines would change, only to change again after the next war. At least, that was how Mia had explained history to Norla.

With a frown, Norla studied the map before her. A single line, marked "Vinelain River," snaked through all three of the mainland kingdoms and each of the Luwistan islands. That made no sense.

She flipped through the rest of the pages in a whirl of confusion. They were also maps, one devoted to every kingdom. These drawings were far more detailed than the first. In addition to mountains, savannahs, rivers, and lakes, these maps showed the giant river winding through the landscape.

"What do you think?" Penumbra asked. He grabbed a jar with handles and held it in his blistered hands.

"It's not what I expected," Norla said carefully. The thief seemed powerful, dangerous even, in a way all his own. The number of followers he commanded was proof enough of that. And with a single word from him, his snatchers would have no trouble surrounding Norla and the others.

"There is no such river," Pallo said, pointing to the yellowed page.

"You've never seen it," Penumbra said.

"We've traveled much of Mirlane Isle," Gen said. "If there were such a river, we would have seen it."

Penumbra's gaze drifted to the well. He turned to the hole and attached the clay jar to a second rope. As he lowered the jar, Norla remembered the old woman at the oasis. She had said Penumbra dug into a different water source.

"The river's underground," Norla said suddenly. "Isn't it?"

"What?" Chestel asked.

Pallo's eyes lit with understanding. "But what headwaters would feed such a river?"

"An entirely different kind of headwaters," Penumbra replied, keeping his focus on the well. "Vaskel would rather keep the Vinelain River and its headwaters secret—which is why he sent you to steal my Book."

Norla's cheeks warmed. Penumbra knew everything about their trip. But how?

"The Book is rightfully King Vaskel's," Effira said in a small voice. She and Gen stood on Pallo's other side. "And we are here in his name to claim it." Although Effira bit the corner of her lip, she kept her chin raised.

Penumbra shook his head, keeping his back to them. "The Book has never belonged to Waylan Vaskel. He doesn't even know what it contains."

"Then why does the king want it so badly?" Chestel asked. He kept his body tilted away from the well.

"Vaskel believes many lies about the Book," Penumbra said. He nodded at the Book, sweat dripping from his forehead. "I came to show everyone what's really on those pages."

"You would reveal this map?" Pallo asked.

"The map is already revealed," Penumbra said. "You'll find it in the path of your keenwood trees, the pattern of hills in your great savannah... The river's course is engraved throughout Reislan and every other kingdom on Mirlane Isle."

Norla thought of Mia's book of poems. The painted red flowers on the book's cover, snaking along the spine in a smooth path. Her ears began to tingle. The curves of the flower path matched the swirling course of the underground river, turn for turn.

"I've seen this path in a painting," Norla said.

Penumbra smiled, and Norla felt something stir deep inside her.

"The river's pattern is a natural part of Reislan's land-scape," the man said. "It's no wonder artists imitate its bends and twists." He returned his gaze to the well, his face brightening. After adjusting his grip, he yanked the rope toward him and heaved the jar to the surface in strong strokes.

The taut muscles of Penumbra's forearms strained. Watching him work, Norla admired his strength. She had never seen anyone so naturally connected to the earth.

"What's so special about this underground river?" Chestel asked.

"See for yourself." Penumbra heaved the jar from the well, spilling water from its sides.

Norla's mouth practically itched at the sight. She had drunk little that day, and every inch of her body craved water... but what if it was enchanted?

People pressed forward, whispering in hushed excitement, as Penumbra held the jar out for a small girl in a blue mitzah. She dipped her hands into the jar and lapped water greedily into her mouth. Penumbra laughed and poured water from his jar into the goatskin jug held by the girl's mother.

The pair murmured their thanks, and when Penumbra handed the mother his jar, she poured its water into her neighbor's jug. Around the circle and down the line, pilgrims passed Penumbra's jar and poured its contents into their neighbors' jugs. Bursts of laughter and excited chatter spurted from them all.

Norla frowned. She didn't understand why the water hadn't run dry.

Within moments, the jar came to Pallo. Since Pallo had no jug of his own to fill, the woman beside him handed him Penumbra's jar to drink from. Norla leaned in closer and felt Chestel press against her, straining to see the water for himself.

Pallo's eyes flickered to Chestel's hand on Norla's shoulder.

"Sartania's king," Pallo muttered, and then looked into the jar. His eyebrows lifted in surprise.

Norla tucked the Book into her sash and peered over the jar's rim. Strangely, the bucket was still full.

Norla's eyes caught Pallo's, and she sensed their simple shared question: How?

Penumbra stood at the well, watching. Norla had no intention of drinking his enchanted water. But she didn't want him to know of her mistrust in him, either.

Taking a deep breath, she dipped her hand into the clear water. Its iciness shocked her skin and sent a shiver down her back.

Chestel's hand tightened on Norla's shoulder. All around her, people drank the water. They bubbled with laughter and conversation, as if a breeze of life had blown through the crowd.

"You shouldn't, Norla," Chestel whispered.

"Let her choose for herself," Pallo said.

"Then why don't you drink?" Chestel challenged.

"I intend to." Pallo cupped his hand and dropped it into the water. His fingers grazed Norla's.

For an instant, Norla forgot all about Penumbra and the Book and the freezing water. Her head felt light. Far, far too light. And her skin was warm. Pallo's touch unhinged something in her, and he did it without even trying. It was frustrating, really.

Norla dared not look at Pallo as she raised her hand from the water. She pretended to drink, but didn't swallow a single drop of water. When Norla lifted her gaze, it was Penumbra's beautiful eyes that found hers first. And somehow, she was certain he knew her bluff.

~~~

As Norla raised her hand to her lips, Pallo did the same. He had a hungry, almost instinctual, pull to the water. Closing his eyes, he let Penumbra's freezing water splash down his throat.

Thoughts of Belany Castle drifted to mind—the white olive blossoms, the coarse sand, and the blue-green water. He remembered the feel aboard his sloop as salty waves misted his skin.

Then he saw Lania aboard the same boat, all alone, in her favorite yellow dress. She glanced over her shoulder, smiling and laughing. Pallo's chest tightened. She was making her ill-fated escape to sea.

Pallo had remembered the imagined scene a thousand times since Lania's death, and each time, he felt the same guilt, like a dripping shroud across his shoulders. If he had been there, Lania wouldn't have escaped alone. Pallo would have helped her. He had known how miserable she was at Belany Castle, trapped inside stone walls with needlework and tea service lessons as her only diversions.

Lania's mother, the suryan of Duke Belany, had been planning Lania's marriage to a Linyad merchant twice her age. Meanwhile, Pallo's mother had decided to present Lania to a distant cousin as his suryan. Both plotting, neither had seen the light dimming in Lania's eyes.

Pallo clenched his fists. Both women had known Lania's spirit was too free for such constraints, and still they had plotted. So Lania had sought escape to the blue shores and spicy winds of Luwista. Only she had never arrived. The sea had claimed her instead.

Pallo's throat throbbed, and another memory came to him. He saw himself three years earlier, reading a book beside Gen in their history tutorial. Gen had yawned and earned a stern look over the rim of the professor's spectacles.

Pallo froze. His eyes moistened. He realized what he was remembering—the exact moment Lania had drowned. Pallo had been miles away from Belany Castle. And he realized something else too. The miles that had distanced Pallo from his sister at the time of her death represented a different kind of separation altogether. He shared no guilt in Lania's death.

Pallo's chest lifted, and he slowly, deeply exhaled. He'd been waiting to do so for three years. When he opened his eyes again, the sun had just dipped below the horizon, and the brightest of the stars had begun to appear.

"Do you approve of the water?" Penumbra asked.

Pallo met Penumbra's exultant eyes. Pallo didn't understand how, but he knew that Penumbra had been privy to what he had just experienced. And Penumbra looked thrilled for Pallo.

Pallo felt his lips tilt into a smile, as if Lania herself had lifted the corners of his mouth.

"Very much," Pallo answered. And he approved of the man who'd given him the water as well. Penumbra was no thief or snatcher.

Vaskel had clearly painted the drayza as a villain for his own purposes. But what could the king hope to gain by de-faming Penumbra and stealing the map, when the drayza himself wished to reveal it?

Pallo shook his head and focused on the vision of Lania. He hadn't realized the constant strain of guilt in his chest until it had finally eased. He wondered if Norla had felt a similar release when she had drunk the water.

Beside him, she studied her hands as wind whipped her wild hair. Her cheeks and ears had reddened, which he had learned meant that she was either angry or embarrassed.

Pallo frowned. How could anyone feel turmoil after drinking such water?

Feeling weighty stares, Pallo found Gen and Fira watching him with wide eyes. Fira was gripping Gen's arm and biting her lip in worry.

Pallo laughed. "You look as though I just died." He handed the jar to Gen and nodded at Fira. "Here."

Gen took it, still wary, but Pallo knew his friend's curiosity would win out. Gen wouldn't let Pallo drink mysterious desert water without him; after all, his memoir would suffer terribly from such a decision.

Fira was already cupping her hand into the water. As expected, Gen followed Fira's lead and the two lapped water from their hands.

In a few moments, their eyes lit up. Their shoulders relaxed.

"Oh," Fira said, her face beaming.

"Yes," Gen agreed. "Hadn't expected that." He exchanged a look with Fira, and the pair laughed.

Pallo understood their joy. He wondered how the water had affected them. What pain had bound them in guilt or fear? Whatever the causes, Pallo could sense the genuine relief in his friends.

But Norla appeared as tense as ever.

Chestel stood beside her. He snatched the bucket from Pallo, gave a quick glance inside, and passed it to another pilgrim. Roella had found her way to Chestel's other side, and judging from her frown, she hadn't drunk the water either.

"Will you tell me what's so different about this water, even if I don't drink from your jar?" Chestel asked Penumbra.

"Gladly," Penumbra said, "but you'll only hear words." His eyes flitted to the nearby pilgrims passing his jar, before returning to Chestel. "The water from Vinelain River isn't like other water on Mirlane Isle. This water washes what is inside, not outside."

Chestel's eyes narrowed. "And I need washing, you think? Because I'm a slave?"

"I think all Mirlaners need the Vinelain River."

Pallo knew his family certainly did. Until now, he hadn't realized how much each of them had borne the weight of Lania's death. A shroud of guilt had covered Belany Castle for three years, but Penumbra's water would change all that.

Pallo turned to tell Norla of this new freedom, and to learn why she still frowned, but she had disappeared. Along with Chestel, Roella, and the Book, which she had tucked in her sash.

CHAPTER EIGHTEEN

Pallo's pulse thumped hard.

"The Book," Pallo whispered to Gen.

"She has it?" Gen whispered loudly.

Pallo gritted his teeth. They couldn't let Penumbra know of Norla's thievery. Pallo would have to find her before Penumbra noticed the Book's absence.

Over his shoulder, Pallo saw the trio riding east into the shadowy horizon. Roella was astride her stallion, and Chestel and Norla rode Senna.

"Draxton's queen," Pallo cursed. He'd throttle that horse thief as soon as he caught up to him. He turned to leave.

"She has my Book," Penumbra said.

Pallo's chest pounded. He slowly faced Penumbra.

The drayza was watching the trio's escape, not with anger, but with sorrow. His gaze drifted to Usak, standing to Pallo's right. Although no words were spoken, Usak nodded and moved to his large chestnut stallion at the edge of the crowd. In a moment the robed man had mounted his beast and, along with three dozen riders, begun galloping eastward.

Penumbra's men moved with unearthly speed. They would certainly catch Norla and the others. And then the six of them would all face the consequences of Norla's reckless plan.

"I'm sure it's a misunderstanding," Fira said quietly. "Norla wouldn't leave without us."

Gen shoved his hand eastward, where Norla and the others had taken flight. "There is no misunderstanding that."

Pallo rubbed the back of his neck. He could scarcely believe Norla had left. Without word, without explanation. She had just left. What did that say about her? About him?

He hadn't known the girl that long, really. She didn't owe him anything. Yet he had thought they shared... more. He hadn't anticipated this strike. Norla had bested him exquisitely.

And she had endangered herself by taking from a man like Penumbra.

Pallo swiped sweat from his forehead. Perhaps such madness had been Chestel's doing. But Norla's will was strong as marble; Chestel would have had a difficult time persuading her. Pallo would have heard such an argument.

No, Norla had left willingly. But surely she hadn't been deceiving him from the start. Surely she hadn't *planned* to abandon him...

Pallo felt as though he were slipping, deeper and deeper, into the gravely sand underfoot.

~~~

Norla tried to ignore the squeezing sensation in her chest. Instead, she focused on the steady rhythm of Senna's gallop and the feel of Chestel's taut muscles as she clung to his waist. She had wanted to take her own horse, but since she had never ridden before, she was forced to share with Chestel.

Chestel kept his body tucked low, angled forward, and Norla tried to mimic his posture. Her fingers went for an instant to the Book, making sure it was still tucked safely in her sash. She glanced over her shoulder. Penumbra's camp grew smaller in the purple light of evening as Senna carried them eastward.

Pallo. The band in Norla's chest squeezed tighter. She wouldn't think of him—or the betrayal he surely felt at her hand. She hadn't meant to hurt him. But she had seen the change in him, and she had seen it in Gen and Effira. Even their eyes had altered somehow. Norla was certain Penumbra had bewitched them for some purpose of his own. She dared not trust the trio after the water had changed them.

Thankfully, Chestel and Roella hadn't been fooled by Penumbra's demeanor. When Norla had begun to slip towards the back of the crowd, Chestel and Roella had followed without question. They too had recognized Penumbra's power—and the need to escape his presence.

Norla's only thought then had been fleeing. Now, in a panic she realized the insanity of such an escape. They had left only to have Penumbra's riders recapture them. Usak's familiar chestnut stallion was already departing from the pilgrims' camp, and he approached with at least three dozen riders.

Chestel prodded Senna's sides. The mare flew forward, passing Roella's white stallion. Roella yelled and dug her heels into the beast's sides, forcing it to match Senna's speed.

In half an hour they flew past Clovesdell Oasis and raced southeast under the rising moon. Usak and the rest of Penumbra's riders were keeping a tight pursuit, if not gaining on them.

Norla wished she were wearing trousers instead of a dress. Her skirt refused to stay tightly tucked around her legs, and her cloak offered little warmth as it flew out behind her. She closed her eyes, burying her head against Chestel's back. His woolen cloak scratched at her cheeks, and Norla had the overwhelming urge to sob.

She had ruined everything with her impulsive stupidity. Chestel and Roella would face Penumbra's punishment because of her, and maybe even Pallo and the others. How had she been so reckless? Even for Mia's freedom, Norla had risked far too much. And she had done so without thought of how her actions would affect her friends. Norla pictured Gen with his ridiculous hat and Effira's frazzled curls. And, of course, Pallo.

Norla thought of Pallo's small smile, as if he was shy to show his teeth, and the way he took off his hat whenever he needed to think. And, despite herself, she thought of Pallo's firm lips, and of how close she had come to touching them.

"Vaskel's crown," Chestel shouted, breaking into Norla's thoughts. "We're outracing them."

After several more grueling miles, Chestel and Roella reluctantly slowed the horses to a trot. The beasts were too tired to continue in a gallop. Oddly, their pursuers slowed too.

An hour passed by in a haze of silvery sand, but the desert riders didn't gain.

Norla felt a glimmer of hope. Maybe her reckless plan would succeed. But even if Senna did outrun the other horses, Norla was leaving behind Pallo and the others to face Penumbra's certain anger. And she would still have to persuade Chestel against using the Book to attempt to free the entire Weltang class.

The familiar sound of horse hooves sounded from the east.

Norla's pulse quickened. More riders approached. Asaltanis? They attacked at night, and the ever-darkening sky signaled that their hunting hours had begun.

The riders appeared at the top of an eastern hill, a thick line of silver cloaks. Swords raised, they sped down the hill's slope and erupted in battle cries.

Their screeching chorus sent shivers through Norla's limbs. They chanted in a tongue she had never heard.

They were trapped with asaltanis before them and Penumbra's men behind them.

Chestel's body tensed. "Sartania's king," he whispered.

He eased up on Senna's reins, and to Norla's right, Roella slowed her stallion and let out a colorful stream of curses.

Behind them, Usak and his riders advanced. Norla welcomed the sight, realizing she would rather face the penalties of Penumbra than death at the asaltanis' hands.

Usak and his riders gained ground at an unfathomable speed.

Norla inhaled sharply. She dared not breathe. The snatchers were practically upon them.

In a whirl of flapping mitzahs, Usak and his riders thundered past Senna and the white stallion. And Norla saw their unsheathed blades for the first time. The swords were made of pure gold, an imposing sight in the hands of their masters.

None of the riders even glanced at Norla, Chestel, or Roella as they passed around them. Their faces were intent on the riders ahead. The asaltanis had broken formation, veering northward and southward. The snatchers did the same and pursued the groups of asaltanis into the inky horizon.

Norla's pulse hammered. She snapped her head from left and right, trying to watch the scene unfurling before her. The asaltanis had disappeared behind hills, and with them, Penumbra's riders on pursuit.

Chestel and Roella brought the horses to a stop. No one spoke. In the distance, they heard swords clashing, riders shouting, and horses baying.

When Chestel wrapped his freezing hands over Norla's, she realized she was trembling. She had never heard a battle before. It sounded oddly similar to the slopes of King's Moun-tain.

Questions whirled around Norla, like the cold wind. She didn't understand why Penumbra's riders had trailed them, mile after mile, when they clearly had the power to outride them. And why had they ignored Norla and the Book to attack the asaltanis? Wouldn't they rather reclaim the Book and then worry about Vaskel's men?

"We should keep on," Chestel said.

"The snatchers will catch us," Roella said, urging her stallion toward Senna. "You saw what they're capable of. They were toying with us before."

"Want to surrender?" Chestel asked. "Just like that? We have the Book!"

"Not for long," Roella said, nodding northward.

Beside the nearest hill, riders in copper had come into view, their golden swords raised in victory. Usak's powerful silhouette was impossible to miss. From the south, another band of snatchers was racing back toward Norla.

Chestel's back stiffened, but he didn't kick Senna's sides.

Norla tried to still her shaking body. But as the eerie riders neared, her trembling grew. They flew as if the wind carried their horses. Their swords moved as if by magic. And the moon's light reflected so strangely on their skin, in small clusters instead of even plains.

Usak, riding at the front of the returning party, was the first to reach Norla and the others. He brought his stallion to an abrupt stop and sheathed his sword.

"You are safe," Usak said. "We have seen to that." His eyes glowed with victory.

Norla waited for him to demand the Book, but instead, he was assessing her and her companions with furrowed eyebrows.

"You are unharmed?" he continued.

Norla swallowed. No one spoke.

"Well, you appear unharmed," Usak said, reclining upon the saddle in his relaxed way. He waited for one of them to respond, but Chestel and Roella seemed as shocked as Norla. The man was more concerned with their well-being than with retrieving the Book.

"Penumbra sent you after us," Norla ventured.

Usak nodded. "To see to your safety."

"But I took the Book," Norla said. She snapped her mouth shut, amazed at her own stupidity.

"Draxton's queen," Chestel muttered. He tightened his grip on Senna's reins, and the mare tossed her head.

Roella remained silent, but Norla could picture the look on her face.

"You speak the truth." Usak smiled softly. "But that is not why Penumbra sent us."

"Then why did he?" Chestel asked.

"Your protection has been our charge since the beginning."

Roella and Chestel raised their eyebrows at each other.

Norla shared their confusion. Penumbra's riders had seemed like captors, not protectors.

"Penumbra wanted you to protect us from asaltanis?" Chestel asked.

Usak shook his head. "Though we are familiar with your king's assassins, those are not the men you just saw. The riders we faced tonight answer to another master."

~~~

163

Pallo kept his eyes on the dim horizon as Gen and Fira set up tents, alongside the rest of Penumbra's pilgrims. Pallo's arms and legs stung with cold, but he dared not fetch his riding cloak for fear of missing Norla's arrival. He would have to defend her from Penumbra the moment she returned.

In truth, Pallo was shocked it had taken Usak so long to catch Norla. Pallo took pride in Senna's abilities, but Usak had shown the power to move with unearthly speed, both on and off his horse.

The minutes stretched on, and still no horses appeared over the dark dunes of sand. Around Pallo, pilgrims had created a bustling campground, guarded by Penumbra's armed riders along its rim. The smell of fire and the sound of drums flooded the air with pulsing warmth. People milled from tent to tent, which flickered from lanterns lit within.

Their joyous spirit rankled Pallo. He would be celebrating as well, if it weren't for fear of what awaited Norla. Penumbra was a kind man, perhaps kinder than anyone Pallo had ever met. But Norla had stolen from him.

Penumbra joined his side, and Pallo's muscles tensed.

"You're afraid for her," Penumbra said.

The man's directness made Pallo blink.

"Yes," Pallo admitted. Concealing the truth from Penumbra was fruitless; the drayza had a way of knowing. "What will you do when she returns?"

Penumbra raised one of his thick eyebrows. "Why do you think she'll be returning?"

"Won't Usak capture her?" Pallo asked.

"He has no orders to."

Pallo frowned. Surely the drayza desired his Book to be returned.

"I don't need a book to remember the path of Vinelain River," Penumbra said. "I care much more about the young woman carrying it." He kept his gaze forward, surveying the desert with a grim nod. "Foreign riders hunt her."

A chill ran down Pallo's back. "What? Why?" he asked.

"My enemy wants what she carries."

"Which enemy? Vaskel?"

Penumbra shook his head. "This creature goes by many names, but I call him Foe."

CHAPTER NINETEEN

A hot sensation spread through Norla's middle as Usak spoke of the terrifying riders. She still shared Chestel's saddle as the harsh wind beat against her and the others astride their horses.

With a shiver, Norla recalled the silver riders' ghastly chants as they rushed down the hill's slope. They had sounded like ghouls, inhuman and chilling. No one on Mirlane Isle spoke in such a tongue.

"Where do the riders hail from?" Norla asked. "Where do *you* hail from?"

Usak slid his sword into its sheath in one fluid motion. His green eyes lit in amusement.

"Have we failed to blend into your world?" Usak asked.

"A little," Norla admitted.

Usak laughed. "We hail from Elyarn Isle, my lady. As do the riders we faced this night."

Norla blinked. The faraway isle.

Chestel glanced over his shoulder to meet Norla's eyes. In his face she saw their shared memories of Mia's reading lessons and stories of Elyarn.

"Do you believe him?" Roella asked Chestel, gesturing to Usak.

"Yeah, I do," Chestel answered. "Haven't you seen what I've seen?"

Chestel assessed Usak with a flick of his eyes. "Are you a sprite?"

"I am a warrior," Usak replied. He paused, a smile playing on his lips. "And a sprite."

Norla shook her head in confusion. She hadn't expected sprites to ride horses or have beards. But everything about Usak, his unearthly grace and agility, the way that light danced on his skin, marked him as Elyarnian.

"Do I disappoint you?" Usak asked, eyes on Norla. Apparently he had noted her appraisal.

Norla's cheeks flamed. She hadn't meant to offend the man... or sprite.

"I'm sorry—" Norla began.

Usak waved away her apology. "You may save your words." His eyes gleamed with laughter. "I know how I look on Mirlane Isle. But if you came to my land, you would see me as I truly am."

"You are immortal?" Roella asked Usak.

Usak nodded. "I still wear my Elyarnian cloak. It holds immortality and my gifts as a warrior. However, you would not see the cloak's thread with Mirlanian eyes."

"Those riders are immortal as well, then?" Roella asked.

"Yes, but their cloaks hold deception. They are forever disguising themselves—as asaltanis, even as us. They wear copper robes and snatch Mirlaners for lives of slavery." Usak paused. "Their master is called Foe, and he is the greatest deceiver of them all."

Norla shuddered at the name. What kind of master could command such riders? And how could he come from Elyarn Isle?

Norla glanced at Usak to ask, but the fierce sorrow in his eyes silenced her. She had never seen someone look so wholly grieved. Even Chestel must have sensed Usak's powerful emotions, for her friend remained quiet as well.

Norla considered what Usak had told her about Foe's riders. Though she was still hesitant to trust Usak, she had seen the shrieking riders with her own eyes. They, not Penumbra's band, were the snatchers.

Norla shuddered. If what Usak said was true, then both asaltanis and Foe's riders hunted them.

Oddly, Norla no longer considered Penumbra's riders a third opponent. Usak had the ability to easily kill or capture them—yet he hadn't. And if Penumbra's riders weren't a threat, Norla wondered about their master.

But Penumbra's water *had* changed Pallo and the others. They hadn't been themselves afterward. And the drayza had tried to manipulate her as well.

"Better ride through the night," Chestel said. "The sooner we're out of this desert, the better."

"Foe and his riders are not contained by desert sands," Usak said solemnly. "They roam every corner and crevice of this isle." His stallion whinnied, and Usak's eyes darted past Norla.

Norla gripped Chestel's cloak. Her mind rang with memories of the foreign riders' chilling cries.

"But fear not. We will travel with you," Usak said.

"You know where we're traveling?" Norla asked. Whether she or Chestel ultimately won the argument, both of their plans involved the same destination—Vaskel Palace.

Usak nodded.

Roella's eyes narrowed, and Norla sensed the girl's unspoken questions. Norla didn't understand the rider's intentions either.

"Why are you helping us?" Chestel asked.

Norla sighed, and Roella shook her head. Chestel didn't know how to keep his thoughts to himself. He never had.

"We follow the orders of our master," Usak said, with a faint smile on his lips. He seemed to have developed a fondness for Chestel.

"We don't trust your master," Chestel said.

"That does not change who he is," Usak replied.

Chestel studied Usak for a long moment.

"If we head southeast, we will reach the savannah in a short while," Usak said.

Chestel nodded briefly, and after turning Senna east, guided her into a walk. Roella did the same, her stallion beside Senna. A group of riders rode behind them, and a group ahead. Usak led the party, his mitzah guiding them eastward like a red flame atop a lighthouse.

Norla tried to calm her heartbeat to match Senna's gait. But she kept replaying the sight of those silver cloaks streaming down the hill like a terrifying mist. She was shocked the fiendish creatures hailed from Mia's beloved Elyarn Isle. Of course, Usak and his riders called the same land home, and they were far from fiendish.

Norla leaned her head against Chestel's back in exhaustion. She savored the familiar, ordinary smell of hay on his cloak.

"Thank you for coming with me, Chestel," Norla said. She spoke quietly so Roella wouldn't overhear.

"Of course," Chestel said, with a grin in his voice. "Think I'd let you leave me behind?"

Norla laughed. "I mean it, Chestel. I know we don't agree on everything, but I still… "

"I know." Chestel dropped the reins with his right hand, and slowly, brought his hand to Norla's exposed shin. Norla sucked in her breath. Even though Chestel wore gloves, the gesture felt far too intimate.

Norla held her breath until Chestel returned his hand to the reins again. Her face felt flushed. Why had he touched her so? Maybe he only meant to comfort her. But he had never comforted her in such a personal way before. Did he believe something had changed between them?

Norla remained silent and focused her thoughts on the silvery landscape. Soon, grassy plains replaced the sandy hills, and the wind grew less fierce.

Ahead of them, Usak brought his riders to a halt, and Chestel and Roella followed his lead. Norla noticed how Senna wheezed. They would have let the horses break miles ago if Effira had been with them. But Norla couldn't let herself think of Effira either.

Chestel descended from Senna and held Norla's hand as she dismounted. She kept her gaze averted and turned to leave, but Chestel wouldn't release her.

"Norla, wait." Chestel's voice was soft.

Roella dismounted her stallion and gave them a quizzical glance. Her gaze flickered to their joined hands before she led her horse on to graze.

Norla's cheeks burned. She tried to break Chestel's hold, but he held her all the tighter.

"Chestel—" Norla began.

"Norla, I know it's been hard between us, and I know you don't care about freeing all the Weltangs like I do. But the real reason I want all this... is for us."

Norla froze. The thick emotion in his voice frightened her.

"I want you as my wife, Norla," Chestel said, his eyes narrowed in determination. "I want us to be free... together."

Norla's lips parted. Her tongue was suddenly heavy and clumsy. The shock was too much. Chestel had never shown that kind of interest in her. He had never spoken romantic words or wooed her. And now he proposed marriage?

"I know this isn't the right way to do this," Chestel said, peering over his shoulder at the nearby riders and Roella. She was busy unsaddling her horse, but Norla caught Roella's gaze before the woman quickly looked away.

"But see, I've had it in mind to marry you for a long time, Norla," Chestel continued. "And I wanted to tell you before we arrived at the palace. I thought, if you knew, maybe you'd understand why I want to free whole class."

His brown eyes had no trace of their usual defiance. "I don't want to flee to some foreign island with our families like we're exiles. I want to stay in Reislan, our land, and live near friends. As *free* man and wife."

Norla said nothing.

Chestel wanted Norla to view him as a man, not just a friend. And so she did. She took in the firm set of his shoulders, his muscular frame, and his strong profile. Norla knew her best friend drew the gaze of women. But Chestel's beauty to Norla had always transcended the physical.

Chestel had remained fiercely loyal to Mia and Norla despite the village gossip. He had doted on his younger brother and sister, teaching them how to keep their spirits alive despite the strangling atmosphere of the mountain. There was no kinder or more faithful man in the village. Yet, Norla had never counted herself among the girls who desired Chestel... and in her heart, she knew that hadn't changed.

"Chestel," Norla began.

Chestel stiffened, clearly able to read her tone as well as her eyes.

She gulped. "I'm sorry."

"Because of that count?" Chestel asked, his voice rising.

"This has nothing to do with Pallo."

Chestel shook his head. "Oh, it's 'Pallo' now, I see. You'd rather be Pallo's harlot than my wife?"

Norla slapped him. "I'm not his harlot!" she snapped, her heart pounding.

Chestel's eyes widened. His hand went to his cheek.

"I belong to no man," Norla said.

"For now."

"What does that mean?"

"It means your count will come looking for you."

"I won't return to him."

Chestel scoffed. "Won't you?"

~~~

Pallo's neck tingled as he stood with Penumbra at the camp's edge. Norla was in danger.

How long would it take to saddle Hickory and go after her? Why weren't his limbs already moving to do so?

"Usak will protect Norla," Penumbra said.

"I'd rather protect her myself," Pallo said, turning to the drayza.

"I know." Penumbra's eyes warmed. "You've tried to protect all who are dear to you, ever since Lania departed."

Pallo looked away, marveling at the man beside him, and at his impossible knowledge. As a child Pallo had been taught that the Vaskel kings were of divine ancestry, but he had recognized Waylan Vaskel for the charlatan he was years before.

Pallo studied the dried mud on Penumbra's cheeks, his windswept hair, and the slight sunburn on his skin. No, for all his transcendent knowledge, the drayza seemed wholly human.

Penumbra smiled, as though he had heard Pallo's assessment and found it amusing. The drayza raised a thick eyebrow, urging Pallo to ask the question on his lips.

"Who are you?" Pallo asked.

Penumbra's grin widened. "Who do you think?"

"I think you're a drayza like no other," Pallo said, echoing the desert woman's words from the oasis. "And I think you know more than you've said about the Vinelain River."

Penumbra nodded. His eyes brightened, and he looked far younger than he had only moments earlier.

"My father and I forged the river," Penumbra said.

"Forged it? I thought men *discovered* rivers."

Penumbra laughed. "My father is King Lumin of Elyarn Isle."

"Elyarn Isle," Pallo repeated, blinking. He had read storybooks of the fabled land and its sprites as a child, but he had never given the tales credence... until meeting Penumbra.

"Your father is king of the entire isle?" Pallo asked. That would make Penumbra not only a sprite, but also a prince.

"Yes, and he's the rightful ruler of this isle, too," Penumbra replied.

Pallo whistled. No wonder Vaskel wished to silence this man. Treason came to Penumbra as naturally as walking.

Pallo's storybooks had described King Lumin as a powerful god-king, a sprite who had spoken Elyarn Isle into existence. But those books had never mentioned Lumin's authority extending to Mirlane.

"There are many who would disagree with your claim," Pallo said carefully.

"That's the work of Foe and his riders." The drayza turned his back to the desert and surveyed the camp of pilgrims. Nearby, a group of lads had started a bonfire outside their tent. The warm glow illuminated their grinning faces as they leapt over the flames, hoping to impress a group of girls.

Pallo saw a mixture of joy and sorrow in the drayza's watchful gaze.

"Foe's lifework is to keep Mirlaners from Vinelain River," Penumbra said. "When this isle was still young, the river ran above ground. All of Mirlane recognized my father as God-King."

Pallo had never heard this version of history.

"How long ago was your father King of Mirlane?" Pallo asked.

"My father still *is* King here," Penumbra said, returning his gaze to Pallo.

Pallo noted the drayza's determination and changed his question. "How long ago did the river run above ground?"

"Many ages ago," Penumbra replied. "My father and I carved a river's path that stretched the entire span of Mirlane Isle. Lumin instructed the Mirlaners to drink from the river. As long as they did, the headwaters would gush and never still, and Mirlaners would enjoy the very waters of Elyarn."

"But what headwaters would behave so?" Pallo asked.

Penumbra tilted his head to the side, as though his response involved great thought.

"The love of the Elyarnian throne is very difficult for Mirlaners to understand," Penumbra said. "Our love creates things... its expression has tangible results." He measured Pallo's expression, and Pallo nodded for him to continue.

"My father's love created the headwaters," Penumbra said.

Pallo rubbed his forehead, trying to imagine how someone's love could power an underground river. And as he wrestled with the impossible idea, he realized the vast disparity between the Elyarnian prince and himself.

If what Penumbra said was true, then Lumin had *created* Mirlane Isle.

Chills rushed across Pallo's skin. With a shaky breath, he stepped away from Penumbra.

"You don't need to be afraid," Penumbra said gently. "I left my Elyarnian cloak behind, Pallo. I'm here as a Mirlaner."

173

Pallo risked a glance and found a crooked smile on Penumbra's face. The drayza did look remarkably ordinary.

"You are human?" Pallo asked.

"In your land, I am."

Pallo nodded. No one speaking with Penumbra would doubt his authority. Even with dirt in his hair and sand on his robes, the drayza radiated power—not the seized, corrupt power of Vaskel, but power nonetheless.

"So why did the headwaters dry up?" Pallo asked.

"The headwaters haven't dried," Penumbra said, his voice firm. "But in order for the river to flow aboveground, Mirlaners had to drink the water. Foe knew that, and thus he began his deception.

"Foe asked the ancient Mirlaners if they enjoyed bowing down to a king from another land. He said if they wished to be their own kings and queens, they need only cease drinking from the river. The Mirlaners listened to Foe, and the river dried in its bed.

"Foe thought he'd bested my father, but he didn't realize the river would still run underground," Penumbra said, eyes glittering. "For ages, any Mirlaner who's thirsted for Elyarnian water has found it through digging wells."

It suddenly made wonderful sense. "So you have come to dig them," Pallo said.

"Exactly." Penumbra reflected Pallo's smile.

"But why is Foe so concerned with an underground river?" Pallo asked.

"Spite. He hates those my father honors." Penumbra rubbed his hands against his arms. "Foe was once a high commander in my father's army. But when Foe schemed to steal the throne, my father banished him and his conspirators from our lands."

The drayza's gaze turned pensive, and Pallo guessed the drayza missed his father's court. Pallo had seen his home and the southern shores only months ago, and yet he ached for them. He imagined Penumbra had been away from Elyarn Isle much longer.

Penumbra took a few steps toward the camp, his eyes studying one pilgrim after another, as if he savored the tiniest detail. He squeezed his fists together. "Do you see how just a taste from Elyarn affects them?"

Pallo nodded, thinking instantly of Norla. His stomach squeezed. Surely she, of all people, deserved to drink from Vinelain River.

He had only added to her pain; he knew that now. He had snatched her from home, from her mother, all because he was an Uyandi and she a Weltang. He might have asked for her consent to assuage his conscience, but deep down, Pallo had known he held the power to demand her servitude. And the thought, though sickening to admit, had pleased him.

Pallo dropped his head. All the days of their quest, he had still considered Norla his property. Even when she had asserted her freedom, Pallo hadn't accepted it. No wonder she had left him behind.

Pallo felt Penumbra's penetrating gaze, and wished to hide from the drayza. He had no right to stand beside the Prince of Elyarn Isle.

"You're seeing a little," Penumbra said.

Pallo gave a hollow laugh. "I'm seeing what a fool I've been." He closed his eyes and focused on the sounds of the camp, the beating drums, and the children's laughter. Cold wind slapped his back, but it felt strangely exhilarating. He knew what he had to do, and there was no point in even trying to hide his thoughts from Penumbra.

"She might leave when I release her," Pallo said quietly. She would be free to choose Chestel—and to walk out of Pallo's life without ever glancing back.

"That choice is hers," Penumbra said.

Pallo nodded. He had a choice as well, and he knew his decision.

Penumbra clapped Pallo's shoulder and laughed, reminding him of Gen.

"Ride with me at dawn and you'll see her before nightfall," the drayza said.

CHAPTER TWENTY

Norla and Chestel didn't speak as the riders built a dozen red tents in mere minutes. Norla watched, feeling useless. Their inhuman speed still awed her.

Despite herself, Norla kept remembering her friend's proposal in her mind—and their argument afterward.

A sudden picture of Pallo drifted to Norla's mind. He was twirling that piece of imaginary hair at the nape of his neck, lost in thought. But thinking of him only filled her with remorse and other emotions that were better left alone.

Norla shook her head and focused on the newly built camp.

"We will rest here the remainder of the night," Usak announced. A ring of riders remained seated on their horses, facing outward and keeping watch over the green plains beyond.

"What if I don't want to rest?" Chestel asked as he unsaddled Senna.

His angry tone grated Norla's nerves. She marveled at Usak's ability to remain impassive.

"You plan is to ride through the night?" Usak asked. He gestured to Senna's bare back. "Your actions suggest otherwise."

Chestel scowled and dropped the saddle by their bags. "Guess we can rest a few hours." He turned abruptly to lead Senna out to graze, muttering under his breath.

Norla sighed and walked to the nearest tent. She'd let Chestel tend his wounds alone. He clearly did not seek further conversation with her.

Once inside, Norla removed her cape and slippers and grabbed an orange blanket. A single lantern bathed the cozy room in flickering light. She tucked the blanket around her numb legs and savored the soft feel against her bare feet.

Roella slipped inside the tent then, and Norla stiffened. It made sense for them to share a tent, but Norla craved solitude. Her mind and body felt as tattered as her slippers.

Norla grabbed the nearest pillow and lay on her side. Shutting her eyes, she prayed Roella would do the same.

"You don't deserve him," Roella said.

Norla kept her eyes closed.

"He's loved you as long as I've known him," Roella said, her tone as flippant as ever. "We were lovers, you know, and still he spoke of you. It was pathetic to see this boy, so full of fire, drone on and on about some callow girl."

Norla's cheeks and ears began to sting. She opened her eyes to find Roella lounging on her side, with a golden pillow propped beneath her head.

"I didn't know how childish you were until I met you, of course," Roella said. "I couldn't believe this man considered you his equal."

"You've no right or power to judge me," Norla said coolly.

Roella laughed. "Have I hurt your feelings, fair Norla? Perhaps your count will defend your honor."

"He's not my count—he never was," Norla said.

"Oh, I think he is. You're mad for him."

Norla sat straight up. "You're wrong," she snapped.

Roella smirked. "I can see by the color on your face how wrong I am."

Norla cursed her skin for coloring so easily.

"My mother was like you." Roella turned towards Norla and cocked her head to the side. "She lived to please my father, but it was never enough. He punished her just the same, according to his law." She glanced away and smoothed her dress over her hips. "And my mother let him," she added. "After all, she was his suryan."

"I'm nothing like your mother," Norla said.

"You think not?" Roella tapped her chin in mock thought. "From what I've seen, you follow your count's lead like any obedient slave."

Norla's blood stirred. The air felt tight and hot.

"I left him behind." Norla hissed and grabbed the Book from her sash. "I stole the Book for myself, not him."

"How noble."

"I'm freeing my mother," Norla said. Sensing the defense in her voice, she refused to say more. She didn't need to justify herself to Roella.

"One person. When the Book could free so many more. I said callow, and I mean callow." Roella's loathsome smirk vanished as she rolled away from Norla.

Norla's mouth hung open. She wanted to eviscerate Roella, to make the hateful girl feel as small as she had made Norla feel. But she was scarcely able to think, let alone speak. All she saw was red.

Norla's body shook with trapped anger as she lay back down and replaced the Book in her sash. She wasn't a mindless slave who did Pallo's bidding. She had clearly chosen the Book over him, and Roella's accusations didn't change that.

It didn't matter if Roella thought Norla so far beneath her. Norla had spent her whole life surrounded by girls who viewed her that way. Norla had never cared before, and she wouldn't begin now. Soon enough, she would be free of anyone who viewed her so. She and Mia would flee to Luwista and build a new life together as free women.

Norla closed her tired eyes and let thoughts of clean air and turquoise waters lull her to a deep sleep.

When she awoke hours later to a burst of shouts outside, Roella had disappeared—and the Book was gone. Norla sprang up, heart pounding.

"Give it to me!" Chestel's voice yelled. "I know you have it, Roella. I can see its corner in your sash."

"Chestel, do you mean to attack me?" Roella's voice said.

Chestel snorted. "I thought you were on my side. But you just wanted to bargain the Book for your father's castle."

"And the comrades," Roella added calmly.

"You lied to me," Chestel bellowed.

"Don't act so innocent, Chestel. Neither of us can pretend that anymore."

Roella gasped. "How dare you! Release me immediately!"

Norla jumped to her feet, threw on her slippers, and raced through the tent flap. A heavy mist of dawn clouded the scene before her.

Chestel was lunging for Roella's sash. With a cry, Roella dug her nails into his cheek. Chestel yelped and released her. As Roella stumbled back, he grabbed her by the shoulder and made another swipe for the Book.

Norla watched, motionless. Chestel had earned a reputation on the mountain as a ruthless fighter, but she had never seen him attack a woman. Roella fought with equal fury. She scratched and bit like the fiercest of Weltang slaves.

Where was Usak, and why wasn't he stopping them?

Norla ran through the camp and found the lead rider on the eastern edge of camp, gazing into the green horizon. She saw then what had drawn his eye.

Norla's breath lodged in her throat. An army of silver-cloaked riders approached beneath the rising sun, at least one hundred men wide and several rows deep. This army didn't screech.

~~~

Pallo dreamed of Norla and the river again that night. The strange man emerged from the river, wearing the same sleeveless white tunic. His bronze arms bore faded fang marks, as Pallo remembered. Only this time, Pallo recognized the man's beautiful eyes. Penumbra.

The drayza came closer, and Pallo didn't attempt to draw out the venom himself this time. He knew Norla would be safe in Penumbra's hands.

179

With a gulp, Pallo pulled away from Norla as the drayza leaned in, his eyes glistening. He gathered Norla in his arms and spilled tears over her swollen skin. Norla groaned in pain.

Pallo's stomach clenched. He jumped to his feet, prepared to stop anything that caused Norla pain, but Penumbra held up his hand. Pallo stilled. Every fiber within told him to trust the drayza, yet Norla looked more in pain than ever.

Sinking to his knees, Pallo held Norla's clammy hand in his. She looked so small, so fragile. Her dark eyes were fixed on Penumbra, wide and searching. The drayza's deft fingers rubbed his salty tears into the snakebites until Norla's expression turned serene.

A burst of joy welled up from somewhere deep inside Pallo. Norla would live! Though he suspected she would bear scars like Penumbra's.

Norla dropped Pallo's hand. She pushed herself off the grass, her legs wobbling as she stood. Pallo reached out to steady her, but it was the drayza she grasped for balance.

~~~

Pallo sat astride Hickory as another wave of riders in copper appeared on the brightening dawn horizon. It seemed the Prince of Elyarn Isle commanded far more soldiers than Pallo had expected. And all of them were warrior sprites.

They had come in droves over the last hour, before Pallo had mounted Senna. Though Pallo welcomed the additional allies, he kept envisioning Norla surrounded by Foe's riders. He longed to depart.

Pallo took a drink from the jug he'd filled with Elyarnian water. His attention returned to the vast army of sprites gathering around the camp. These fearsome riders rode with Penumbra, and Penumbra wished to protect Norla. Pallo exhaled slowly, as he felt the powerful assurance that Norla's safety didn't depend on him.

Gen and Fira waited beside Pallo, each astride black mares Penumbra's followers had given them. Since Pallo's carriage would have slowed the party, he had decided to leave it behind.

Fira chuckled, drawing Pallo's gaze. She was bent over her mare's neck, stroking its shining coat. A group of pilgrims had provided her with a blue riding robe whose generous swaths of wool concealed her legs from the sandy wind. A matching mitzah protected much of her head and the back of her neck.

Pallo scarcely recognized the robed woman before him. Since their departure from the palace six days ago, Fira's skin had tanned, and she had shed her hat, cape, and purple sash. The daring look suited her far better than palace finery.

"We should have let Fira ride years ago," Pallo murmured to Gen. This new Fira reminded him strongly of Lania, but the memory didn't carry its usual sting.

"Penumbra beat us to it," Gen said. He patted his sash where he'd tucked his journal. "It's impossible to capture all of this. Especially him." He nodded toward the well, where Penumbra was lowering another jar.

The drayza was talking with a small boy and girl, probably brother and sister, who were watching the rope with eager eyes. Penumbra nodded them forward, showed them where to hold, and let the children finish lowering the jar.

"He's nothing like I expected," Pallo agreed. "I wish he moved a bit quicker."

Penumbra remained at his well. An elderly woman from a nearby tent brought the drayza a plate of fruit and cheese, and Penumbra took it with eager thanks, his face brightening. Pallo found it strange that the Prince of Elyarn Isle—privy to banquets with foods so rich they filled the stomach with a mere whiff—would find delight in simple desert fare.

Hickory edged toward Fira's mare, and Pallo shook his head. The gelding certainly had a propensity for mares.

"Oh, Hickory," Fira said, nudging him away from the mare. She removed her glass vial from the saddlebag and rubbed ointment on her own horse's forehead under its bridle.

Pallo held his breath. The potent ointment smelled strongly of cinnamon.

"That mare couldn't possibly have any sores yet, Fira," Pallo said.

"It won't hurt her," Fira said. "Besides, I think she likes it."

The mare nickered and lowered her head.

Pallo shook his head and smiled. That little mare had no idea how lucky she was to call Fira her rider.

Scanning the camp, Pallo saw that the drayza still stood beside his well, lowering a jar for another family of nomads. It seemed the man had no immediate plans to leave his beloved well.

"I'll go and see whether we're leaving before noon," Gen said, with a quick glance at Pallo and Fira. He nudged his horse, and they trotted away towards the well.

"You're anxious to find Norla," Fira said quietly. She focused on spreading more ointment onto the mare.

"Yes," Pallo said.

"Do you love her?"

Pallo stiffened. Fira had never broached the subject of Norla before, and suddenly she asked of love.

"I, er... " His tongue felt swollen and slow.

"It's all right, Pallo," Fira said, drawing his gaze. Her eyes were moist, but her gaze was steady. "I wish to know the truth."

Pallo swallowed. He knew his answer to the question. And he knew it would hurt Fira. He saw acceptance in her eyes, but also a faint flicker of hope. What a cad he had been. "I should have spoken with you sooner." Pallo exhaled slowly. "I do. I do love Norla."

Fira gave a brief nod, biting her lip. She returned the ointment to her saddlebag as a few tears slipped down her cheeks.

Pallo nudged Hickory closer. "Fira—"

"I've known for some time, of course." Fira brushed her cheeks with the back of her hand. "But I appreciate hearing it from you." Ducking her head, she guided her horse forward and left Pallo, just as Gen returned.

Pallo eased his heels into Hickory to follow, but Gen spoke.

"Leave her be," Gen said. "Would you wish for another's company if you were her?"

Pallo studied his friend's stiff shoulders and the way he clutched the pencil in his hand.

"Have I offended you?" Pallo asked.

Gen snorted.

"I apologized and told her the truth," Pallo said. "What more would you have me do?"

"Nothing," Gen muttered. "Penumbra says we'll depart any moment."

Pallo watched as Gen pulled out his journal and reviewed a few pages, wondering at his friend's fierce defense of Fira.

At last, Penumbra moved from the well toward a giant black stallion. Riders in copper surrounded him, and Penumbra talked with them as he walked. Before he mounted his horse, his gaze drifted over the camp, still alive with firelight and chatter despite the early hour. Pallo noticed the same mixture of joy and sorrow in the drayza's eyes that he had seen earlier.

As Penumbra mounted his stallion, Pallo straightened in his saddle. The time had come.

Penumbra approached Pallo and the others. "Stay close," the drayza said. He scratched behind his horse's ears. "I'm taking a different path."

With a slight tap of his heels, Penumbra urged his horse eastward, toward the savannah. Pallo and Gen did the same, as Fira caught up to them. Her green eyes were narrowed and her lips pursed as she eased her mare into a walk.

Behind them, dozens of pilgrims and hundreds of riders followed in a stream of copper robes and golden mitzahs.

Pallo itched to bring Hickory to a trot. Each time he thought Penumbra was about to prod his stallion's sides, the drayza maintained a steady walk. Pallo gritted his teeth. How in Vaskel's name did Penumbra plan to catch Norla if he insisted on such a leisurely pace? They hadn't even neared Clovesdell Oasis yet.

As the minutes stretched into hours, Pallo realized they should have already passed the oasis. Yet, judging from the low sun on the horizon, they were definitely still heading east, or perhaps more southeast. The ground had begun to change as well. Within what seemed like moments, the horses were plodding over grass instead of sand, and the air had grown damp.

Strangest of all, the sun still sat low on the horizon.

The skin on Pallo's neck raised. The drayza had spoken of a different path, but Pallo had not expected such a path to bypass the rules of time.

The sun slipped behind the clouds. A heavy mist hung in the air and violet streaks bled across the sky, casting a purple glow on the grass and oaks ahead—and what appeared to be a silver cloud moving on the ground in the far distance. A silver army.

A bolt of fear shot through Pallo. *Norla.*

"Asaltanis," Pallo whispered.

"Draxton's queen," Gen cursed.

"Are you certain?" Fira asked. She rode on Gen's other side. Her hand went to the sword she had fastened to her saddle.

"Yes," Gen said, eyes grim.

Pallo kicked Hickory's sides, startling the gelding into a gallop.

"You said we'd reach her in time," Pallo shouted, coming astride Penumbra.

"We will," the drayza said.

"What if Vaskel rides with his company?" Pallo asked.

Penumbra's eyes flickered, and Pallo knew.

"He does," Pallo said. A hot sensation clawed up his throat. "You promised Vaskel wouldn't capture Norla."

Penumbra shook his head. "I promised you would see her before nightfall. You shall."

CHAPTER TWENTY-ONE

Norla sat behind Chestel astride Senna, as the morning mist turned to rain. The others had mounted their horses as well. They waited at the eastern edge of the camp as the horde of asaltanis approached.

Norla, Chestel, and Roella, astride her stallion, were flanked by Penumbra's riders. Usak waited directly to Norla's left.

Roella still held the Book in her sash. There hadn't been time to retrieve it before mounting Senna. Still, Norla had no intention of remaining quiet while Roella bargained away the Book for the rights to Yintpa Castle. No one would stand between Mia and freedom.

At the front of the approaching army, a rider clothed in purple velvet rode a giant bay stallion. Norla had only seen King Vaskel once, but she knew it was he. The billows of fabric in the king's garments made Gen's wardrobe look modest by comparison.

Norla felt oddly numb at the prospect of encountering the king. She scarcely noticed the savannah's wet breeze on her cheeks or the ringing in her ears.

"Don't worry, Norla," Chestel said stiffly. "I won't let them hurt you."

Norla blinked. Her throat tightened at his loyal defense, even after the night before.

"But I'm using the Book for the Weltangs," Chestel continued.

"I have other plans," Norla said.

Chestel nodded toward Roella, only feet from them. "So does she."

Roella patted the Book in her sash. "How right you are."

"Hide the Book, Roella," Chestel hissed. "We won't have anything to bargain if the king can just take it for himself."

Roella pretended to ignore him, but she did tuck the Book deeper into her sash.

Norla craned her neck around Chestel's back. The asaltanis were almost on top of them.

Her whole body trembled as King Vaskel brought his bay stallion to a stop in front of them. He wore a silver crown, inlaid with sapphires and crystals, and silver thread lined his cloak. His horse stood several hands taller than Senna, yet the mare held her ground. With a snort, she shook her head and laid her ears back in warning. Next to Senna, Usak's horse mimicked her, while the lead rider himself maintained his impassive expression. A look to Usak stilled Norla's trembling.

King Vaskel's dark eyes already glittered with victory. Norla gritted her teeth, annoyed rather than cowed by his arrogance. After all, she had Elyarnians among her companions. They yielded golden swords and magic from another land. Surely that counted for something.

"Fair Norla," the king said in his booming voice. He cupped a glove over his auburn beard, feigning surprise. "Whatever are you doing so far from home?"

"I came to deliver your Book," Norla answered.

King Vaskel's eyes widened. He exchanged a glance with the man beside him, clothed in silver, and then laughed heartily.

"How extraordinary!" he said. "I come with companies of soldiers to attack Penumbra and reclaim the Book—and a slave girl has beaten me to the task."

"Yes, and I expect my mother's freedom in return," Norla said. "As you promised—"

"The Weltang lies," Roella said. "The Book is mine. I alone know its location, and I shall retrieve it for you, in exchange for Yintpa Castle."

"That's not—" Norla said.

"Enough," the king snapped, his eyes on Roella. His lips tipped into an amused smile as he admired her from head to toe.

"And what is your name, my lady?" the king asked.

"Roella of Yintpa," Roella said, head high. "I'm the daughter of the late Duke Yintpa."

The king's eyebrows shot up. "The duke has died? We received no notice of his death."

"Consider this your notice," Roella said.

King Vaskel's lips twitched. "Duke Yintpa has no daughter," he said in a clipped tone. "None he deemed appropriate to present at court, anyway."

"I *am* his daughter, my King." Roella squared her shoulders and gave the king a coy smile. "If you want the Book, grant me my father's province."

King Vaskel didn't return her smile.

"The Book isn't hers to give," Chestel said, urging Senna forward. "It belongs to the Weltangs. But if you free them, I'll give it to you."

"No, the Book is for my mother's freedom," Norla argued.

"Yes, for Mia and every other Weltang's freedom," Chestel argued.

The king's sharp laughter sliced through the air.

"Do you lot truly mean to command me?" King Vaskel snorted. "A couple of slaves and the illegitimate daughter of a duke?" He swept his hands out to illuminate his massive army. "I am King of Reislan. I'll give nothing in return for what's rightfully mine."

Norla shook her head, her cheeks growing warm.

"You gave your word," she said.

The king chuckled. "Fair Norla, you are beautiful but not so wise, are you? I promised to free your mother if *Pallo* brought me the Book. Since you did not follow my instructions, I'm afraid your mother remains enslaved."

His gaze roamed over Norla as the mist gathered into soft rain. "As do you," King Vaskel added with a crooked smile.

A hot flush spread from Norla's face down to her chest. "Why does it matter if I bring the Book, or if Pallo brings it?"

The king guided his stallion forward.

"Tell me, fair Norla, where is your count?" he asked softly. "Dead?"

Norla's body pulsed.

"He's very much alive," she said coolly.

"I see," the king said. "Why don't I act as your guardian until his return?"

"I'd rather—"

"That wasn't a request," he said.

Norla gulped. The king's guardianship could mean only one thing. Why did Usak and the riders stay silent?

"You aren't her guardian," Chestel said.

The king laughed and turned his gaze to Chestel. "You mean to defy me, slave? I hold your life in this hand." He held up a gloved hand. "You speak another word and see what I do."

Chestel's back stiffened. He stared ahead, silent.

Norla glanced at Usak, but he was watching King Vaskel with a deep frown. The king followed Norla's gaze but didn't acknowledge the sprite with so much as a nod.

"Give me the Book," King Vaskel ordered Roella. "I know you keep it close. You weren't expecting us."

"In exchange for—" Roella began.

In a swift movement, the king unsheathed his sword. "Produce the Book in exchange for your life," he said, aiming his blade at Roella's chest.

Roella hesitated.

"Draxton's queen," Chestel whispered. "Give it to him, Roella."

"Fine." Roella grabbed the Book and tossed it to the king without warning.

King Vaskel's eyes flashed, but as his fingers clutched the Book, all seemed forgotten. "I hold the key to the isle's throne," he murmured.

The king gazed at the bark cover like it was a meal to devour. "I'll unite the kingdoms… Our children will never know war."

He opened the Book and pored over its content, as though he were in a library instead of the wild savannah. Judging from his surprised murmurs, Penumbra had told the truth. Vaskel had never seen the Book before.

As Vaskel's excitement mounted, so did Norla's anger. How could the king dismiss his promise so cavalierly? All her planning and all the risks had come to nothing. Vaskel, as dishonest as he was ruthless, had tricked them.

Cold rain beat against her cheeks, mounting in strength.

Why had Usak's riders done nothing to help her? Hadn't Penumbra ordered them to protect Norla and her friends? Norla had expected more from warrior sprites.

She turned to meet Usak's gaze and found him watching her with a slight frown.

"You might have defended me," Norla said in a choked voice.

Usak's eyes softened. "Your defender comes." He gestured over his shoulder, and Norla turned to look behind them.

A throng of copper robes spilled across the savannah's western horizon, like a stampede of flames.

Chills raced down Norla's back. She had never seen an army so grand, so terrifying. So wholly spellbinding.

King Vaskel laughed, and the sneer in his voice made Norla cringe.

"Just as I was told," he said. "Penumbra approaches with his meager band of followers." He tucked the Book into his cloak pocket.

Norla glanced between the king and Usak. Didn't the king see the thousands of riders with Penumbra?

King Vaskel waved his hand impatiently in Norla's direction. "Take these three as my prisoners," he told the nearest asaltani. "And keep the slave girl near me."

~~~

Pallo squeezed Hickory's reins in rage. Pallo scoured the approaching mass of silver for Norla. His body pulsed with energy. He gripped his sword, ready to fight every one of those blasted asaltanis until he found her.

Hickory's powerful gait infused Pallo with a sense of strength as he rode beside Gen and Fira. He followed close behind Penumbra's black horse. Riders flanked both of Penumbra's sides, and with a glance over Pallo's shoulder, he saw that another couple hundred sprites had joined them.

Pallo had never guessed the breadth of Penumbra's army. Of course, he hadn't imagined that Vaskel had trained so many asaltanis either. With two such forces colliding, the coming battle would be as bloody as the great wars sixty years prior. The sprites might have cloaks of immortality, but Pallo and the rest of the Mirlaners certainly did not.

Pallo frowned at the drayza directly before him. Penumbra's bare hair, loose in the rain, flew behind him like a mitzah. His copper robes were still soiled with dirt from the wells, and he wore no sword in his grimy sash. He was hardly the type of commander Pallo would have preferred.

Penumbra squared his shoulders. "Victory is near." He spoke the words quietly but with fierce determination.

The massive armies halted mere yards from each other, and through the rain, Pallo saw Vaskel himself at the head of the asaltanis.

Pallo searched frantically for Norla, but only caught glimpses of Chestel, Roella, and Usak. Why was Norla not with the others?

"So this is Penumbra?" Vaskel asked. His smug voice pierced through the patter of rain.

Pallo marveled at the king's arrogance. Vaskel may have assembled a grand company by Reislan's standards, but Penumbra still outnumbered him ten to one. The very air felt charged with the presence of the Elyarnian warriors.

"I imagined you'd look a tad grander," Vaskel continued, surveying Penumbra's robes with a raised brow. "But perhaps you've fallen on hard times now that I've retrieved the Book. Have most of your infamous riders abandoned you?"

Gen and Pallo exchanged glances. Somehow, Vaskel didn't see the thousands of sprites; he saw only the pilgrims.

"I see Lord Trilstoy and Count Belany ride with you," Vaskel said, tipping his head to Gen and Pallo. His gaze glossed over Fira in her mitzah. "Perhaps they are prisoners? It hardly matters now, I suppose. I have the Book. The throne of Mirlane Isle is rightfully mine."

"My Book doesn't make anyone king," Penumbra said. "It maps the river of the true king."

Vaskel laughed, but there was an edge to his voice. "What a fantastic tale," he said. "And who is this king?"

"King Lumin of Elyarn Isle," Penumbra replied. "My father."

Vaskel's eyes widened, and for a moment they flickered with uncertainty. "How extraordinary," he said, grinning. "And I suppose that makes you a sprite as well?"

Vaskel waited for Penumbra to reply, but to Pallo's surprise, the drayza said nothing. Vaskel studied Penumbra for a long moment, measuring his opponent.

"I was told that you would say strange things," Vaskel said. He reclined in his saddle and folded his arms across his chest. "I'd charge you with treason, but I'd rather kill you in battle."

"I didn't come for a battle today," Penumbra replied.

"Why do you confront me if not for battle?" Vaskel asked.

"To free the three prisoners you keep," Penumbra said.

"Why would I do such a thing?" Vaskel asked.

"Because I'll surrender myself to you if you do," Penumbra said.

CHAPTER TWENTY-TWO

Norla peered over the shoulder of the burly asaltani who sat in front of her upon his horse. She needed to see the man who so calmly discussed her freedom.

Penumbra looked just as he had before her flight, only soaked with rain. Same thick eyebrows and broad shoulders. Same unkempt hair and beard. He looked so common, hardly Elyarnian, but he spoke to the king without a trace of fear.

"You're a traitor, Penumbra," King Vaskel said to the drayza. "You are already my prisoner."

"You won't take me as a prisoner unless I go willingly," Penumbra said.

Norla expected the king to laugh or make a smart retort, but he remained silent. His shoulders had stiffened, and he no longer reclined in his saddle.

"Free your prisoners and let them remain free forever-more," Penumbra said, his gaze unflinching. "Take me instead."

"Without a battle?" King Vaskel asked. His voice held no trace of its usual mockery.

"Yes," Penumbra replied.

Norla didn't understand. If the drayza was intent on rescuing her, why not vanquish the asaltanis with his army of sprites? Why surrender?

Her eyes drifted past Penumbra to Gen, Effira, and Pallo. All three were drenched and covered in sand. They looked a far cry from the nobles who had departed from the palace only six days ago.

"Very well," King Vaskel said at last. He turned towards the burly asaltani. "Bring forward the prisoners."

With a jolt, the horse started beneath Norla, bringing her to King Vaskel's side. Norla kept her head down. She couldn't meet the eye of the man she'd stolen from, or the friends she'd abandoned.

"Here is your prize, Penumbra," King Vaskel said, grabbing Norla's arm. "What pleasant times we would have had," he murmured. Then he yanked her from the saddle and flung her onto the wet grass with a thud.

Asaltanis dumped Chestel and Roella just feet from her.

Norla didn't look at them. She stared at her feet and clutched her stinging arm. Rain soaked through her slippers, but she didn't move.

Penumbra had no reason to surrender for her freedom. What hidden motives did he have?

Penumbra's soft footsteps approached. She heard him murmuring to Roella and Chestel, but she couldn't make out the words. Then she felt his gaze on her.

"Norla," Penumbra said. His voice was soft and near.

Norla's stomach turned. She had to speak to him. She had so many questions. She slowly glanced up and found only warmth in the drayza's eyes. "I don't understand," she whispered. They were the only words she could find.

"You will." The drayza placed a warm hand on her shoulder, then walked the short distance to King Vaskel. He looked so small before the king's giant beast.

King Vaskel tilted his chin and grinned at the nearby asaltanis. They promptly murmured their praises and congratulations.

Norla shook her head in disgust. Penumbra had given himself freely, and yet the king acted as though he'd subdued the drayza after some great struggle.

Then, in a whirl of robes, Usak and his riders galloped into the open space between the armies.

Norla felt a rush of excitement. Now King Vaskel would see the limits of his power.

But the sprites made no moves to strike. What restrained them? A soldier was hoisting Penumbra onto his horse, and still the warriors refused to act.

Norla let out a frustrated groan and ran to Usak. "Why don't you help him?" she demanded. Cold rain pelted her face.

Usak glanced down at her, and Norla saw her anger mirrored in his eyes.

"Our master has commanded otherwise." Usak's voice was thick, strained. He nodded toward the king. "Vaskel takes him now for a public execution."

The king had turned his horse, and his asaltanis were parting down the middle of their formation, making a path. King Vaskel's stallion accelerated into a gallop and the rest of the soldiers followed suit. Penumbra's copper robe quickly disappeared in the silvery mass.

Except for Usak and his three dozen riders, the pilgrims and legion of sprites departed in fast pursuit. Chestel and Roella ran after them, and Norla urged her feet to follow. But the wet grass felt like the mud on the mountain, impossibly thick and binding. She didn't have the strength to move.

~~~

Pallo didn't know how long he remained frozen astride Hickory. He could only think of the resolve he'd seen on Penumbra's face as the asaltanis carried him away.

Pallo's hand went to the leather jug on his saddlebag. He drank the Elyarnian water, slowly at first, and then in vicious gulps, letting the cool liquid coat his throat. When Pallo finally yanked the jug from his mouth, gasping for breath, Penumbra's words drifted to mind.

The drayza had said victory was near.

Pallo repeated this promise, over and over, until the snake of fear uncoiled in his gut. Penumbra would escape Vaskel's plans somehow. The drayza might have left his Elyarnian cloak behind, but he still commanded a throng of sprites. Vaskel would surely never best the Prince of Elyarn Isle.

Rubbing his forehead, Pallo turned to Gen and Fira. Both peered straight ahead and neither spoke. Beyond them, Usak and his riders remained planted in what had been the gap between the armies. Norla stood several feet apart from everyone, hunched over her stomach, as though each falling raindrop added to her burden. Her gaze was fixed on the disappearing cloud of copper robes.

Pallo's chest tightened. Norla had never looked more lost.

He grabbed the jug of water and dismounted Hickory. Thankfully, neither Fira nor Gen joined him as he approached Norla.

As he neared, Norla's back stiffened. Pallo kept walking. Even if she hated him, perhaps she would accept Penumbra's water after all she'd just seen.

"Here," Pallo said, offering her the jug. "It's water from Penumbra's well." He stood beside her, gazing into the dreary horizon as well.

"No," Norla whispered. Her voice was hoarse, and Pallo knew she'd been crying. He set the leather jug in the grass and moved behind her, wrapping his arms around her shoulders. He didn't care if she misunderstood the gesture; he wouldn't let her stand there alone.

"I've made such a mess of things," she whispered. He could barely hear her over the patter of rain.

"Penumbra will still have victory," Pallo assured her. "He promised as much. He said victory was near."

"When?"

"I don't know," Pallo admitted.

Norla's shoulders sagged, and Pallo rubbed her arms. To his surprise, she didn't shy away. He held onto her shoulders, angling his body over hers to block the rain. With a sigh, Norla leaned her head back against his chest.

Pallo inhaled sharply. His entire body warmed with her softness. He tucked her deeper into his arms, savoring the smell of rain on her hair.

"I broke your trust," Norla whispered. "I'm sorry." Her voice cracked, and Pallo knew she was crying.

He gave her a gentle squeeze. "I forgive you," Pallo said, and he knew he spoke the truth. "And I seek your forgiveness as well. I've been such a cad, Norla."

"You're a count," Norla said. "The traditions of your class are not your fault."

Pallo shook his head. Norla still saw him as an Uyandi. He knew what he had to do—what Penumbra would have him do—but then she could leave him. And if she did, he would never know the feel of her again.

Pallo slid his fingers down Norla's arms and gently turned her towards him. He had come to know her face so well. The flush of her cheeks, the faded scar on her left temple, the way her eyebrows were perpetually drawn together in thought. And her eyes… were presently wide and fixed on his lips, seemingly expecting a kiss.

Pallo's mouth tingled. He would love to fulfill that very expectation, but he would do so as her suitor, not her captor.

"Norla," Pallo said softly. He traced a raindrop's path across her velvet skin. She shivered and closed her eyes, her breath coming in soft puffs.

Pallo paused to savor his effect on her. It was the effect she had had on him since the moment he first saw her.

"Norla, you're freed from my household," Pallo said. "I no longer consider you my suryan."

~~~

Norla's eyes flew open. A pounding sensation filled her ears.

Pallo had dismissed her.

She drew back, untangling herself from his arms, and averted her gaze. Her hands trembled and she quickly folded them across her chest. Pallo's words seemed to freeze the rain on her skin. She had abandoned him at the oasis, and now, despite his words of forgiveness, he was abandoning her in turn.

Cold rain beat against her skin, but Norla hardly felt it. Her gaze darted to his eyes, so warm and bright. He looked different than he had before they met the drayza. He was still Pallo—only his brisk formality had all but disappeared.

Norla's eyes went to the jug. She didn't deserve to drink water from the faraway isle. Not after she had stolen from Penumbra. As the prince, he had undoubtedly attended the very Elyarnian balls Norla had once pretended to attend. He had walked through forests with stars for leaves. He'd felt wind that carried song in its many folds. What magic did water from such a land contain? She deserved neither the prince's magic nor the count's affection.

Norla turned her head before Pallo could see her tears.

"Norla, that's not all I would say to you," Pallo said. His voice sounded hurried.

Chestel and Roella approached on their horses. They had apparently realized that Vaskel's army would be better chased on horseback than on foot.

Norla watched Senna's familiar gait. She didn't want to hear Pallo's voice anymore.

"Chestel!" Norla called out. Her oldest friend waved in return.

"Norla—" Pallo continued.

"I can't, Pallo," Norla snapped. He didn't want her. She understood him perfectly. Why did he insist on discussing it?

"You can't?" Pallo asked.

"No."

CHAPTER TWENTY-THREE

Norla hurried forward as Chestel and Roella reached them. Chestel leapt from Senna and wrapped his wet arms around Norla.

"Penumbra... " Chestel said.

Norla trembled. Even the drayza's name shook her. "We can't let Vaskel kill him," she said, pulling back from Chestel.

"Vaskel won't," Pallo said. His voice was quiet. His eyes were flat, fixed on the horizon. He didn't look at Norla or Chestel.

"How can you be sure?" Norla asked.

"Because Penumbra said he'd have victory," Pallo said.

"But what if he needs our help?" Norla said.

Pallo gave a humorless laugh. "Penumbra can defeat Vaskel whenever he chooses. Didn't you see his army?"

Norla nodded. "But the king didn't."

"Vaskel has chosen not to see us," Usak said, urging his stallion forward to join them. "Our Elyarnian cloaks veil us from his eyes."

"I have to speak with Penumbra," Norla told Usak. She had many questions for the drayza.

"So be it," Usak said.

"Any enemy of King Vaskel is my ally," Roella said. Her eyes blazed like twin torches as she sat astride her giant horse. "I go as well."

"And I," Chestel said. "He freed me from returning to the mountain."

"And I," Pallo echoed. He finally looked at Norla, his eyes full of sad resignation.

Norla didn't understand his sorrow. He had chosen to release her; she hadn't forced his hand.

Pallo glanced westward, where Gen and Effira were advancing with Hickory in tow.

Effira looked stunning in her flowing robe and mitzah. She looked bolder, somehow stronger, than before. Surely she would be thrilled to discover Norla's dismissal. Or maybe Effira already knew. Maybe Pallo had released Norla so suddenly because he aimed to marry the lady sooner rather than later.

"We'll bed at Yintpa Castle tonight," Chestel announced. "Ride with me, Norla?"

Norla nodded, refusing to look at Pallo as Chestel assisted her onto Senna's saddle.

"You plan to ride my horse?" Pallo challenged.

"Want to switch?" Chestel asked. "Or you want to be on our way?"

"I prefer to ride my own horse," Pallo said coolly.

"But Senna prefers me." Chestel rubbed Senna's neck in long strokes, and she lowered her head in pleasure.

Pallo scowled at the mare. He swept his hat from his head and rubbed the back of his neck.

"Fine," he said. "She's mine once we stop for the night."

~~~

Norla and Chestel talked little as their band crossed the savannah's wet grass. Her mind swam with thoughts of Penumbra and his certain execution, and speaking those thoughts seemed impossible.

Gen regularly offered everyone a sip of Penumbra's water from his leather canteen, but Norla refused. Chestel and Roella did as well.

The party stopped at Yintpa Castle for supper. Unlike before, Pallo and the other Uyandis joined the comrades at the long banquet table for a simple meal of rabbit and carrots.

Throughout the night, Wendel fussed over Chestel like a nursery maid. Chestel grumbled, but he still basked in the old man's attention. He kept asking Wendel for more wine and biscuits while he pleaded their case to the comrades.

"We can stop Vaskel if we free the drayza and his Book," Chestel was saying. "The king thinks he can rule the whole of Mirlane Isle with the Book. That means inescapable servitude for all."

Norla poked at her carrots with her fork, but she had little appetite. She kept sneaking glances at Pallo across the table. He sat between Gen and Effira and his gaze was filled with sorrow like before, but also something like anger. She didn't understand. He had dismissed her—without care of what became of her, she might add.

Norla knew that, whatever did become her fate, she first needed to free Mia from the mountain. She had to. First, she'd elude King Vaskel and convince Penumbra to escape. Then, she would free Mia somehow, and the two of them would begin anew in Luwista.

Maybe Usak would help her. Surely he would understand Norla's desire to free Mia. He and the other warrior sprites had opted to remain outside the castle for the night. No doubt, they had formed a ring around the castle, protecting it against other riders in the night.

With a shudder, Norla thought of Foe's riders.

She tried to put them from her mind as she mounted Hickory the next morning. Effira had rubbed some of her ointment on the gelding's coat, and the beast smelled strongly of cinnamon. Norla breathed through her mouth as Chestel joined her on the front of the saddle.

Despite his efforts, not a single comrade had joined them. Norla didn't blame them. She understood their desire to keep far away from the king.

The horses moved at a trot's pace that day and the next. Norla spoke little. Even though people surrounded her, she had never felt lonelier. She kept recalling Penumbra's surrender to King Vaskel. The drayza had looked so certain, so confident.

Norla had to speak with him.

Chestel guided Hickory beside Usak's stallion, and Norla blurted the question that had reverberated through her all day.

"Why did your master free us?" Norla asked the rider. "I don't understand."

"My master loves teaching as much as he loves digging in the desert," Usak said, with a smile. "Ask him anything."

Norla nodded. "I will."

By afternoon of the second day, the entire party pulsed with energy. Horses kept their heads high, sensing the tension of their riders. King's Mountain was within sight, and beyond it, the green slopes of Vaskel Mountain.

Chestel gazed northward at the quarry, where he had spent so many years freeing rocks from their beds. Norla's eyes went to the summit of King Mountain. She didn't see Mia from this distance, but she knew her mother was straddling her scaffold, chisel in hand, as she had done nearly every day since Norla could remember.

They passed King's Mountain, and the sounds of hammers and breaking stones grew fainter. The sky dimmed to dusk, and the horses mounted the leafy path through King's Forest. Keenwood trees climbed into the sky, dwarfing the oaks and cottonwoods with their mossy trunks. Through the leaves, a great clamor came from the palace above.

Norla gripped Chestel's middle. She could guess at the cause of the assembly.

The horses accelerated into a gallop. Hickory's sides heaved with sweat as he worked to keep pace with Senna.

When they reached the palace clearing, Norla marveled at the thousands of people scattered among the oaks and marble pathways. It looked like all of central Reislan had gathered for the spectacle. They all faced the pale purple façade of the palace, which gleamed with an ethereal glow in the twilight. It was the balcony above the palace's grand entrance that held their attention.

Uyandis stood closest to the palace in their feathered hats. Behind them, Norla spotted Linyads in their elaborate hats without feathers. And nearest to Norla, a few Tintals lingered on the outskirts of the crowd, wearing flat caps like Chestel's and Roella's. Not a single Weltang besides Norla and Chestel made up the crowd, and none acknowledged them or Usak and the warrior sprites.

The vast assembly reminded Norla of the king's power. He had seemed impotent compared to Penumbra and the sprites, but King Vaskel did rule an entire kingdom. And he still held the power to enslave her. Norla gulped.

"This way," Usak said. "The time draws near."

As Chestel followed Usak, Norla had never felt more thankful for the sprite. She hadn't thought of how difficult it would be to reach Penumbra when he was King Vaskel's prisoner.

Usak led them along the edge of the grounds, and not a single person glanced their way, despite the sprites' foreign dress and swords. They hurried to the back of the palace, and Usak took them down a marble path leading to a gated service entrance. Norla wondered briefly if Usak had ever been to the palace before—he seemed to know its every corner.

Everyone dismounted, and Usak walked straight for Norla. He smiled, his eyes crinkling.

"Penumbra waits on the third story," he said. "Follow me."

Norla nodded, feeling her heartbeat quicken. She had told Usak that she wanted this, she reminded herself. She needed answers.

Usak swung the gate open as if the iron weighed no more than straw. Norla followed him into the black marble entryway. Chandeliers lit the corridor, which was much smaller than the grand entrance.

Norla pressed her palms together and realized they were clammy.

Usak led her forward, into a small room with cream walls and a winding staircase in its center. Judging from the number of stairs, the staircase led to all twenty stories.

Norla's hands shook as she grabbed the wooden banister and mounted the steps behind Usak, who was climbing with the unnatural speed she had come to expect. With a glance over her shoulder, she realized no one had followed her. Not even Chestel.

How strange. Chestel had seemed so intent on taking Penumbra and his Book back from King Vaskel. What restrained him?

Norla focused on her feet and tried to still her racing mind. Each step brought her closer to Penumbra. She had to keep climbing.

Above them, a pair of cloaked men entered the stairwell from a much higher floor. Norla expected Usak to stop, but he didn't even slow his pace.

The men's voices drifted down to her.

"I've been heeding your advice since boyhood," King Vaskel's voice snapped. "And you have been deceiving me these twenty odd years."

"Why do you believe that?" a man's voice asked. His voice was impossibly sharp. He spoke each word with such distinction that it hurt Norla's ears to listen to him.

"You promised peace for my kingdom if I stole the Book and killed Penumbra," King Vaskel said. "You said the Book held ancient magic. But I have scoured it, and all I see are blasted maps!"

"There is more to those maps than you know," the crisp voice replied. "Do the maps not show all of Mirlane Isle? Is it not your dearest wish to rule all four kingdoms? The holder of the maps also holds every kingdom depicted in them."

A moment of silence passed before King Vaskel exhaled. "I hadn't realized that."

"That is why you have a servant such as me." The man chuckled quietly, and in the folds of his laughter, Norla heard a faint screeching.

Her breath caught. She recognized that sound.

"Come," King Vaskel said. And with a whirl of their robes, the men departed.

Norla didn't move. She felt feverish.

"Foe," she whispered.

Usak glanced over his shoulder at her. His eyes blazed. "Yes. My master's enemy."

Without another word, Usak resumed his ascent with an almost furious intensity. Norla willed her legs to move. She had to keep up.

So Foe was the force behind King Vaskel. That fiendish creature had orchestrated everything, and now he would personally see Penumbra killed.

Norla had to persuade the drayza to fight back. He had the strength. He was Prince of the entire Elyarn Isle.

She and Usak reached the third floor in a moment. Usak led her to a closed wooden door, guarded by a pair of asaltanis. They stared straight ahead and seemed oblivious to both Norla and Usak.

Norla hesitated. She knew who waited on the other side of the door.

Usak pulled on the door handle, and despite the padlocks, the door clicked open. Norla wasn't surprised. She knew enough of Usak to expect that locks wouldn't restrain him.

Stepping inside, Norla noticed the emptiness of the room first. Unlike Pallo's ornate suite, this room boasted no furniture or paintings. Penumbra stood in the middle of the bare floor, facing the sole square window. When he turned, his wet eyes brightened. He rushed forward to embrace Usak.

Norla shrank back, feeling like an intruder.

"I'm glad you're here," Penumbra said, pulling back. He braced the sprite's massive shoulder, and Norla noticed the shovel had been removed from his sash.

"Do you still mean to surrender to the sword, master?" Usak asked.

"Yes," Penumbra said. And then his eyes went to Norla.

CHAPTER TWENTY-FOUR

Norla froze. Penumbra was smiling.

He didn't move toward her but instead held out his hand, inviting her to speak. Dirt lined his fingernails, reminding Norla of her own hands. Until recently, she'd spent nearly every day of her life with grime on her Weltang skin.

But this man was no slave. He was the Elyarnian prince.

"Why... " Norla began. Her voice came out in a whisper. She had spoken with Penumbra before, but not since learning of his true self. How did she speak to someone like him?

"Norla, ask your questions," Penumbra offered.

Norla gulped. She kept her gaze averted. "Why are you determined to die? You can't dig more wells if you're dead."

"There's a plan," Penumbra said. "Trust me, Norla."

Norla tensed. "Is that why you pleaded for the king to release me? To steal my trust?"

"Trust cannot be stolen. It's given freely or it's denied."

"But I can't trust what I don't understand. Why remain a prisoner when you could escape?"

"I have nothing to escape."

Norla rubbed her temples. Penumbra's answers only stirred more questions, but she knew they hadn't much time.

"Foe is here," Norla said.

Penumbra nodded.

"He plans to kill you," Norla said.

"Yes." Penumbra glanced down and tightened the sash around his waist.

Norla shook her head in frustration. The drayza was resigned to die. "Don't you want to fight?" Norla demanded. "Your army must be near."

Penumbra laughed, a sound that made him seem far younger than his years.

"Yes, they're very near. I doubt I could keep them away if I wanted to."

"Then why don't you do something?" Norla asked. "Why let Foe just take your life?"

"Foe can't take anything from me." Penumbra stepped toward her. "He cannot take something that I choose to give."

"*Why?*" Her throat throbbed.

"Because my father and I care far more for Mirlane than you could possibly imagine."

"Why should you care about us?" Norla asked. Surely the Elyarnian king and prince had pleasures enough in their own land to stay content.

"My father created this isle, Norla," Penumbra said. "The love Mirlanian parents feel for their children is only a shadow compared to our love."

Norla frowned. If King Lumin and Penumbra cared so much for Mirlane, then why had they allowed the hardships on the mountain?

The drayza's eyes filled with sadness, which only stoked the anger inside her.

"Where were you, then?" she asked. "You didn't help when the foremen whipped me for sport. Or when my hands bled from blisters. Or when my father was sold away." Tears wet her cheeks, but she didn't care. She wanted the drayza to see the pain he cared so much about.

"Did you help Mia grieve?" Norla asked. "I'm the one who made sure she ate and washed and woke. Always me. Just *me*."

Norla glared at Penumbra, flicking tears off her cheeks. She had much more to say, but her throat ached. All of her ached.

"You have never been alone, Norla," Penumbra said softly. Like hers, his eyes brimmed with tears. "Our love feeds the river, and you can't separate us from our love. We never left this isle."

Norla shook her head. Water, even Elyarnian water, wouldn't change anything. Besides, Mirlaners would never see a glimpse of that water. Foe probably had the Book by now, and he would keep the river's path concealed. All was lost unless Penumbra called on his army.

Penumbra slowly stepped towards her. He held her gaze and cupped his dirtied hand on her shoulder. His beautiful eyes were full of longing. He wanted her trust, but Norla had nothing to give. She felt as empty and useless as a broken jar.

Outside the door, the sound of marching boots grew louder.

Norla started. She glanced from Usak to Penumbra, wondering if she should attempt an escape, but she couldn't bring herself to leave the drayza.

In seconds, two dozen asaltanis piled into the room. They paid no attention to Norla or Usak. They marched straight for Penumbra, and with harsh hands they shoved him to the door.

Norla started. They had no right to handle Penumbra so! She looked to Usak for help, and though the sprite gripped his sword, he didn't raise it.

Moving into formation, the asaltanis marched Penumbra out the door and down the hall. Their boots slapped the marble, leaving an eerie silence in their wake.

Only then did Usak let out a single sob.

Norla shuddered. The sprite's anguish felt like a living presence in the room, writhing and coiling around her.

"Come," Usak said thickly. "It is time."

Norla nodded numbly and followed him out of the room. They moved down stairs, through marble hallways, into evening air, and yet Norla didn't feel the tick of a single second. Time had departed from her.

She sensed more people around her, and realized she had reached the back of the front grounds, off to one side among the Tintals. Chestel's arm draped over her shoulder, and she was vaguely aware of Pallo's voice, asking if she was well. She felt far from well, but she remained silent.

The sky had grown dusky, but was still bright with bursts of orange shading the clouds. On the balcony, King Vaskel was waving at the crowd. He wore a purple cloak, his elaborately jeweled sash and hat, and a broad smile. Beside him, a tall man stood in a bright silver cloak edged thickly in black. Unlike Reislaner cloaks, this garment came only to the man's elbows, revealing forearms that looked unnaturally smooth, as if his body was covered by silk instead of skin.

Norla recognized him at once.

"Foe," she whispered.

She heard Usak confirm the man's identity for the others.

"Draxton's queen," Pallo said. "When will Penumbra defend himself?"

Usak gave no answer, and Pallo continued to badger him.

Norla ignored Pallo's rising voice. She focused on the balcony as the asaltanis brought Penumbra into view. The throng of people erupted in victorious shouts.

"I give you the traitor, thief, and murderer Penumbra!" King Vaskel exclaimed. His booming voice showered over the crowd. "Today, we execute an enemy of the crown. And with my recovery of the Book he stole, Reislan shall become the throne of all Mirlane Isle." He paused as the grounds vibrated with a fresh wave of applause.

"Penumbra is innocent!" Norla shouted, stepping forward. But no one heard. The yells of others drowned out her voice.

"Penumbra is no traitor!" Pallo yelled in vain.

On the balcony, Foe whispered something in King Vaskel's ears. The king nodded and cleared his throat.

"It is time to put this traitor to death!" King Vaskel unsheathed his sword, and the crowd roared with bloodlust.

"Penumbra should stop this," Pallo said. His voice was hoarse. "When will he stop it?"

The king faced Penumbra and pointed his sword directly at the drayza's heart.

~~~

Pallo kept waiting for Penumbra to break free and claim his victory. When would he fight back? One word, and his army would readily defend him. They had to be near.

Each second stretched in the air, impossibly long. Senna whinnied behind Pallo. Beside the king, Foe was grinning at Penumbra, baring his impossibly white teeth. Vaskel adjusted his sword, and Pallo tensed.

Penumbra gazed below at the throng of Mirlaners, his arms loose at his sides, as the blade pierced.

Pallo squeezed his eyes shut.

The crowd erupted in shouts and applause.

Pallo's skin stung. Anger welled deep within him. How had Penumbra let this happen? The drayza had done nothing to defend himself!

Pallo grabbed the hilt of his sword. He would kill Foe— even if Penumbra had refused to.

On the balcony, Foe and Vaskel stood on either side of Penumbra's limp body. They held the drayza upright for all to see. Penumbra's hair fell over his face, and blood trickled down his robe, dripping onto the marble ledge.

Pallo urged his legs to move. He had to challenge Foe to a duel. But Pallo stood transfixed, watching Penumbra's blood form a trail from the balcony to the dirt below. Pallo could look at nothing else.

When the first drop of blood met the grass, a soft rumble sounded in the distance.

The ground began to shift.

The back of Pallo's neck tingled. He'd heard of earthquakes on Sartania's coast, but he'd never experienced the sensation of tremors underfoot.

The crowd quieted. Everyone stared at the ground. On the balcony, Vaskel grasped the ledge while Foe frowned at Penumbra's body.

Fira grabbed Pallo's arm. He held her and instinctively moved toward Norla. Gen inched closer, until their band had formed a tight clump, even Roella and Chestel. No one spoke.

The earth's trembling grew, and horses whinnied. Screams burst from the crowd. People fled the palace grounds. A frenetic energy flooded the air.

Pallo wondered whether their group ought to move, but Usak seemed content to stay. Hundreds of others stayed behind as well, all watching the ground in eager expectation. Pallo studied them closer. Despite their Linyad hats and cloaks, Pallo suddenly recognized the golden swords on their waists.

Rock began to split.

Pallo's ears rang with the tremendous sound. Twenty paces to his right, a fissure snaked down the middle of the lawn, from the road through King's Forest toward the palace.

High above, Vaskel and Foe had laid Penumbra's body across the balcony's edge. The asaltanis had already deserted the balcony, but when Vaskel turned to leave, Foe grabbed his arm.

"What did you do?" Foe roared.

"You saw exactly what I did!" Vaskel shouted.

Below, the snaking fissure collided with Vaskel Palace. Columns shook. Vaskel flung himself away from Foe, toward the balcony's rail. And the momentum of his body carried him over.

Norla gasped. Pallo pulled her near to him as Vaskel plummeted to the ground.

Pallo swayed on his feet. He had considered Vaskel his enemy, but seeing the man's fall brought little pleasure.

Vaskel's crumpled body lay sprawled across the palace steps. A small cluster of asaltanis sprinted to the body and bore it away, to the safety of the forest.

On the balcony, Foe had vanished. Only Penumbra's body remained, draped over its edge like a bloody banner. The sight sickened Pallo.

The earth's rumbling intensified. Trees crashed to the ground. Vaskel Palace trembled and shook as though it had sprung to life.

The fissure now stretched beyond the palace, into the forest's eastern edge.

Pallo's skin was slick with sweat. He clutched Norla and Fira with each arm. He wished to lead them into the forest, but Usak gestured for him to stay.

A ripping sound tore through the air.

Vaskel Mountain was tearing down its middle. Huge chunks of stone broke free from the palace and fell into the growing gap, now ten feet wide. Penumbra's body began to slide.

"No!" Pallo screamed. He watched helplessly as the drayza's body plunged from the balcony into the depths of the crevice.

Hundreds of Elyarnian riders erupted in cheers. Their faces gleamed with an ethereal light. Usak and his riders mounted their horses and raced past Pallo in a whirl of horsehair and golden swords. With cries of joy, they rode their horses over the gap's edge and followed Penumbra's body into the depths below.

Pallo and the others gasped. It looked as though the sprites were following their master's path into death. But surely immortals could not die, no matter how great the plunge.

The rest of the palace crashed into the crevice in a series of avalanches. And then, after a final long sigh, the mountain stilled at last, leaving a newly formed gap, twenty feet wide with jagged edges of rock on either side.

The sudden silence left Pallo's ears ringing. Slowly, his ears discerned a new sound deep below. Rushing water.

~~~

Furious screeches pierced the evening air with growing fever.

Chills shot down Norla's back, and she knew it was Foe's voice that filled the twilight sky. The intensity of his anger felt like palpable waves slamming into the broken mountain.

Norla and the others remained huddled until, after a long moment, the screeching finally ceased.

Gen broke their formation first. He mounted the black mare given to him by the nomads.

"I must report to my commander," he said solemnly.

Pallo raised an eyebrow.

"All captains have such orders after a major calamity," Gen explained. "I imagine that includes an earthquake and the king's death." He exhaled heavily. "Then I must search for my brothers."

Effira moved from Pallo's side. "I'll come with you," she offered.

Gen nodded, his eyes brightening, and Effira mounted her mare. Together, the pair disappeared into the remains of King's Forest.

Norla unbound herself from Pallo and Chestel and walked to the gap. Peering over its ragged edge, she saw a river rushing deep below. Her heart pounded. She knew the name of that river.

Pallo rested a hand on her shoulder. She sensed others around her too, all peering at the water below, with its freshly formed cliffs on both sides.

"Do you have your jug, Pallo?" Norla whispered.

Pallo nodded and handed the leather jug to Norla. A soft wind caressed her cheeks. With a shaky breath, she brought the water to her lips and let it coat her dry throat.

She took another gulp, closing her eyes, and images from the mountain washed across her mind. At first, Norla saw the elderly women who had tormented her and Mia so many times. But then the women's wrinkled skin smoothed, and their crooked backs straightened. They looked years younger. And oddly, they were back on the mountain, working while foremen struck them with whips. Welts lined their arms, their backs, their necks and shoulders.

Norla flinched. She knew that stinging sensation too well.

Slowly, the women aged in Norla's mind. They were transported back to the village, and as they hurled insults at Mia, whips came from their mouths instead of words.

An invisible band loosened slightly across Norla's chest. She saw the chain of hatred. So much beating, so much pain.

And then Norla felt a hand on her arm, bringing her back to Vaskel Mountain.

"Are you all right, Norla?" Chestel asked, frowning.

Norla considered. She didn't understand why Penumbra had to die. Or why King Lumin had allowed the Weltangs to suffer so. But she saw more than she had before, and she guessed that was something.

"I'm fine," Norla said.

"You look... different," Chestel said.

Norla felt her face break into a grin. She *was* different. She still felt the sorrows she'd endured, but the sound of gushing water gave her hope.

She thought of Penumbra then, and tears welled in her eyes. He had wanted this for her.

With a deep sigh, Norla turned and found Pallo watching her with his hat in his hands. His eyebrows were furrowed and his lips pressed tight—the face he always made when he was deep in thought. She had become so fond of that face.

Norla swallowed the knot in her throat and turned westward, toward King's Mountain. She wouldn't think of Pallo or how he had dismissed her from his life. She'd focus on finding Mia. Since the earthquake had uprooted so many trees, Norla could see the river's path across the moonlit savannah below. It flowed directly past Weltang Village.

"Mia," Norla said. "Can we find her?"

Pallo nodded and tossed his hat to the ground instead of replacing it. In a moment's time, he had mounted Senna and was extending his hand to Norla.

"Would you care to share my saddle?" he asked.

Norla's cheeks warmed.

"Norla rides with me," Chestel said. He'd mounted Hickory and was holding out his hand expectantly.

Chestel's assured tone chafed. As much as she loved her friend, she would never have another chance to be near Pallo. After they went to the village, she'd likely never see him again.

"Much thanks, Chestel," Norla said, "but I'll ride with Pallo."

CHAPTER TWENTY-FIVE

Chestel's eyes darted towards Pallo.

Roella chuckled. "Looks like the grand count bests you again." She lounged on her horse, appearing far too calm after what they'd just seen.

Norla avoided Chestel's scowl and took Pallo's hand. His skin was bare.

A tingling sensation began at the base of Norla's neck, shimmering down her back. His hands were warm despite the cool air, and the feel of them flooded her with heat.

She didn't meet Pallo's eyes as he cupped her waist and easily lifted her onto the saddle. To her surprise, he placed her toward the front and then mounted the horse behind her. His torso pressed against her back, and Norla inhaled sharply.

Pallo slid his arms around her to hold the reins, and Norla tensed.

"Shall we?" Roella asked, with a smug smile. "I think a trip to Norla and Chestel's little village could be quite entertaining."

"We shall," Pallo said. His voice sounded hoarse. He prodded Senna's sides, and the mare ventured into King's Forest, down the western slope of the mountain.

Stars gleamed overhead as they followed the cobbled path, now littered with branches and trees. It looked as if a giant had stomped across the mountain's face.

They heard only the occasional wisp of chatter through the thick keenwood trunks and the cottonwoods' yellowing leaves. But the sounds of conversations grew louder as they neared the mountain's base and discovered three makeshift camps. The classes had divided amongst themselves. They stood in clumps, talking and gesturing wildly to the devastated mountain and the freshly formed river to their left.

Soldiers were already mounted on horses, keeping watch over the various camps. Norla marveled at the army's swift response. Still, despite the attempts at order, Norla sensed the people's fear. The spirit of unrest wafted about the camps.

From the Uyandis' camp, Norla heard a familiar voice.

"Don't you trust me?" Gen was asking. Effira stood beside him, nodding vigorously with her hands on her hips. "The water hails from Elyarn Isle."

Gen held out his journal to three lords, and Norla recognized the men as Gen's brothers.

Pallo and Gen exchanged a wave, but Gen quickly resumed telling his brothers about the Elyarnian water. Effira watched Pallo for a moment, and then averted her gaze without a word.

Norla frowned at the pain she'd seen flash in Effira's eyes. Was she mourning Penumbra's death, or had she and Pallo quarreled?

Pallo wove Senna among the frenzied camps and guided their group straight for the rushing water, now twenty feet wide. The river ran flush with the grass and was sufficiently deep so that Norla couldn't see its bottom.

Pallo led them along the riverbank toward King's Mountain. He prodded Senna into a trot, and Norla eased back slightly. She breathed in the smell of sand and sun on him and felt his taut muscles beneath his cloak. His whole body radiated an earthy strength.

Norla's blood stirred. His touch drenched her senses, like a relentless wave. She could scarcely feel the night wind against her skin. Or Senna's powerful rib muscles beneath her. She felt only him, so near.

He was no longer the count to her. He was the man who had confided in her. Who had forgiven her when she'd abandoned him to an unknown fate.

But then Norla's mind rebelled. She recalled his dismissal, and the urge to cry out rose in her throat. He had discarded her so easily, as if she were a cloak he no longer desired. And his single betrayal had hurt more than the thousands of barbs she'd endured from the villagers.

She swallowed. She shouldn't have taken this ride with Pallo. She had finally found someone she longed to love, but he didn't want her.

Norla inched forward, attempting to break Pallo's hold on her. Her chest throbbed in protest, but she took a deep breath and forced her thoughts on the scene ahead.

The river had carved King's Mountain in two, turning the temple into a heap of ruins on the summit.

Norla smiled, savoring the view of Vaskel's demolished temple. But then her thoughts turned to her mother. All of Mia's beautifully intricate artwork, the fruit of her love and toil, all destroyed.

As they neared, Norla saw the Weltangs had responded to the earthquake like the other classes. They'd clumped together. Some talked, but most stared at the river in silence.

Their threadbare tunics and dresses fluttered in the night breeze. Dirt lined their faces, their necks, their hands. Many of their backs were stooped from years of labor.

Norla felt like she was seeing them for the first time. They looked scared, as vulnerable as children as they gawked at the river. Penumbra would have loved to glimpse Elyarnian water rushing at their feet. But then, Penumbra had said he and his father had never left this isle. Maybe some part of him remained still.

Foremen stood guard with their whips, but their faces held no trace of their usual arrogance. They gaped at the river alongside the villagers.

"Chestel!" a woman shouted. She burst from the crowd, and Norla saw it was Metrie, Chestel's aunt. "Chestel has returned to us!"

Villagers shouted and raced to greet Chestel.

With a grin, Chestel dismounted Hickory and disappeared in a huddle of embraces. A few people glanced back at Norla, but if they recognized her, they didn't show it.

The foremen watched, making no move to stop the reunion.

"Home," Norla murmured.

Pallo's arms tightened around her. "We'll find Mia," he assured her.

Norla nodded, but his voice only reminded her of his coming departure. The band in her chest squeezed. Her gaze drifted to the river.

Norla pulled herself free from Pallo's arms and jumped to the ground. Her feet landed harder than she expected. Shoots of pain raced up her legs, but she ignored them. She raced to the river, knelt in the mud, and with feverish hands, lapped Elyarnian water into her mouth.

Icy water coated her throat, and Norla remembered Penumbra's touch during their final goodbye. She felt as though he was cupping her shoulder again, and slowly, the fear of loneliness ebbed from her.

"Norla!" Mia cried. She burst from the crowd and ran to Norla. She yanked Norla away from the river and enveloped her in strong arms. "Don't drink that, child!"

"Mama," Norla whispered. Her throat stung.

Mia smelled of sweat and smoke, just like Norla remembered.

"I missed you, child," Mia said through tears. "King Vaskel has brought you to me."

Norla pulled back. "King Vaskel?"

Mia wiped her face. "I prayed to him every night," she said. "I asked to see you again one day." She held Norla's face with her blistered hand. "And here you are."

Norla moved her hand to cover Mia's. "Mia, King Vaskel is dead," Norla said.

Mia's eyes widened. Her gaze drifted beyond Norla's shoulder to Chestel, who had freed himself from the throng.

Chestel cleared his throat. "It's true, Mia. We saw him die with our own eyes."

Villagers near Chestel began to murmur at the news.

"No," Mia whispered. She dropped her hand as fresh tears spilled down her cheeks.

"He was no god-king, Mama." Norla gestured toward the summit. "Just look at his temple. Penumbra's river toppled it."

"Penumbra?" Mia asked. "The criminal?"

"He isn't a criminal," Norla said. "He's Prince of Elyarn Isle, and this river is Elyarnian."

Surely Mia, of all people, would find excitement in that.

Mia's eyes narrowed. "According to whom?"

"Well, Penumbra himself," Norla said.

Mia shook her head, freeing hair from her bonnet. "Penumbra is a common criminal."

"But just look at his river." Norla nodded toward the glistening water. "It split an entire mountain, Mia."

"I know." Mia's voice grew thick. "I saw the temple fall."

She brushed fresh tears from her cheeks, and Norla realized her mother was grieving. Mia had devoted her life to serving King Vaskel through her sculptures. She'd found purpose and beauty in a land of whips and sweat. To defame King Vaskel was to defame Mia's lifework.

"That river is evil," Mia said. "It destroyed a holy place."

"A holy place?" Chestel asked. "It's this mountain that's evil, Mia. How many women and children have been beaten here? How many men have died on its slopes?" His voice trembled with rage. "Only a fool would call this place holy."

"Chestel!" Norla said. How dare he criticize her mother?

"Those were sacrifices," Mia argued. "The life of a Weltang is hard, but we serve a purpose beyond ourselves."

"What purpose?" Chestel challenged.

"We bring honor to the king. I taught you this, Chestel. Don't you remember our lessons?"

Chestel's face softened. He exhaled slowly and rubbed the back of his neck.

"Mia, I loved our lessons," he said, "but I've seen enough to know you're wrong about King Vaskel."

Mia shook her head in protest.

Norla reached for Mia's hand. "If you would only drink—" Norla began.

"I'll never drink from a river that destroyed the king's temple," Mia snapped. She turned on her heel and weaved through the crowd, down the lane toward their hut.

Norla felt the urge to follow, but she didn't. Mia had set her heart against Penumbra, and Norla didn't know how to convince her otherwise.

Pallo approached Norla tentatively. He offered her a small smile, but Norla looked away. His kindness only stirred the ache in her chest.

Her eyes drifted to the nearby clumps of Weltangs. She sensed the difference of the village compared to Clovesdell Oasis. There was no music here. No warmth or peace or sense of hope.

Norla sank to her knees and felt damp mud seep through her dress. She lapped the river's water to her lips, and as she swallowed, ribbons of color burst across her mind's eye. Oranges, reds, yellows, every dazzling color of the sunset. The ribbons scattered and flew past every hut in the village— including Mia's.

Norla leaned back on her heels and smiled to herself at the picture. Then she noticed Pallo. He had knelt beside her, dirtying his cloak and trousers, as he too drank from the river.

Murmurs rose from the crowd.

Norla glanced over her shoulder. Villagers had moved closer to the river. Children squirmed in their parents' arms, eager for a drink. But it was Janya, an elderly woman, who stepped from the crowd toward the riverbank.

The woman didn't meet Norla's eyes, and Norla knew why. Janya had spat at Mia and Norla too many times to count. Still, as the old woman stumbled to her knees, Norla felt compelled to offer her hand. Janya didn't take it.

As the crowd quieted, she dipped her gnarled hands into the water and brought water to her lips. Then, slowly, she let out a weary sigh and sat back on her haunches. For a long moment, she didn't move or speak. She just stared at the rippling water.

Then she glanced at Norla, uncertainty in her old eyes.

Norla nodded. She certainly didn't feel like embracing the woman, but she couldn't deny the gladness she felt. Penumbra would have wanted Janya to taste Elyarnian water.

Janya returned Norla's nod and then waved her family over. They hesitantly followed. More and more Weltangs came to the water then, and before long the hum of chatter had washed over the village. Norla didn't spot Tylon's wife or other children among those on the bank, but she hoped they would come.

Many others remained back, watching those by the river with anxiety. Among them were Roella and Chestel.

Norla rose to join them. Pallo followed her, and she felt a mixture of excitement and dread. She wanted him near, yet his closeness stirred the ache in her. He would be leaving soon.

As Norla neared Chestel, she noticed that his eyes were tired and bloodshot.

"You look happy," Chestel said to her. "What does it feel like?"

Norla considered his question. "Lighter," she said.

Chestel and Roella exchanged a glance, and Norla sensed his unspoken disapproval. She raised an eyebrow. "What?" she asked him.

"You've been bewitched, Norla," Chestel said. "Can't you see that?"

Norla shook her head in disbelief. "How can you say that about Penumbra's river?" The drayza had offered himself to free Chestel from the king.

"Penumbra's death just caused an earthquake, Chestel," Pallo said.

"I'm sure he's powerful," Chestel said. "He's Prince of Elyarn Isle. But that doesn't mean his water isn't enchanted, and I won't surrender my sanity to him."

Chestel turned his back and joined a group of his cousins.

"Chestel," Norla said. But he wouldn't turn around.

"We're not like you, Norla," Roella said. She had pulled her gray cape tightly around her.

"What do you mean?" Norla asked.

Roella gave a shrill laugh. "The water isn't for people like us."

Norla shook her head in protest. How could she make Roella understand? "Penumbra wanted every Mirlaner to have Elyarnian water," Norla said. "He said as much before he died."

Roella frowned. Her eyes darted to the river. "I'd probably contaminate it." She laughed, but the sound was hollow.

"If I didn't, then you won't."

Roella gazed past Norla to the river. With a shrug, she tossed her hair and started toward the bank. She didn't glance back at Norla or Pallo. Her steps were slow, and when she reached the riverbank, she watched the others for a long while before bending to her knees.

Norla glanced away, knowing it was what Roella would prefer, and found herself peering directly into Pallo's warm eyes.

"Norla," he said softly.

Norla's heart thudded. She blinked to keep her tears from showing, but the gesture felt false. How often had she hidden her feelings from Pallo? So many times she had diverted her thoughts and swallowed her ache. Anything to keep her emotions at bay.

She had always prided herself on what had seemed like strength, but now she saw how cowardly her pride had been. She had only been trying to hide the truth.

Opening her eyes, Norla saw Pallo had moved closer. He looked so humble with his dirtied cloak and bare head... so different from the man who'd chosen her on the summit.

Tears welled deep within her, but she didn't fight them.

"I don't... I don't want you to leave, Pallo," Norla whispered.

CHAPTER TWENTY-SIX

Pallo stood in silence, spellbound by Norla's words. Tears slipped from her dark eyes, so full of hope. So honest. She had never looked more beautiful to him.

He remembered how it had felt to hold her in his arms astride Senna. He had wanted to keep riding, as far as Senna's legs would carry them, if it meant he could hold her longer. He'd assumed their time together was coming to a swift close—that Norla and Chestel would make a life together while Pallo returned home.

He had all but abandoned the thought of a future with her. She had been acting so cold the last two days, as icy as when they'd first met. But then she'd uttered those impossible, beautiful words.

"Norla," Pallo said, taking her hands.

Norla sucked in her breath, but he didn't release her. He stroked her callused palms, so small in his, and then brushed his thumbs over her wrists.

Her eyes were wide and fixed on him.

Pallo's heart thumped. He leaned closer until the edges of her cape whispered against his cloak.

"Norla... " Pallo felt his voice tremble. "I wish—I ask—to have you as my wife. Will you consent?"

Norla's lips parted in surprise. "Is that allowed?"

Pallo laughed before he could stop himself. "Is that your response?"

"No!" she exclaimed. Her cheeks flushed. "My answer would be yes."

"Yes?" he asked.

Norla nodded vigorously. She beamed, and fresh tears spilled down her flushed cheeks. Her hair danced in the breeze, brushing against his arms, inviting him near.

Pallo laughed and squeezed her hands. He felt such joy, and to share it with Norla was a wonder he'd never known.

At last, he lowered his head and pressed his lips against hers. Norla started, and Pallo told himself to move slowly. Yet her soft kiss only made him all the more ravenous for her. He had dreamt of this very moment so many times.

For a long moment, he drank deeply of her, savoring her sweet taste. But then, reluctantly, he pulled away to look into her face.

Norla's breath came out in soft gasps. Her lips were pink from his kiss, which made him want to kiss her all over again. Instead, he brought his hand to her hair and brushed a tendril from her forehead. The black lock slid through his fingers like strings of silk.

"I had hoped," Norla said, leaning her head against his chest.

"No more than I," he said.

~~~

Norla awoke early the next morning. Even before she opened her eyes, the familiar smell of smoke reminded her that she'd returned home last night. After the foremen had recovered from the shock, they'd ordered everyone back to their homes. A few Weltangs had tried to escape in the interim, but none had succeeded. Soldiers from the palace had offered the foremen additional reinforcements.

Part of Norla wondered if she had failed Mia. For the last week, she had been plotting Mia's escape from the mountain. Once she'd tasted Elyarnian water, though, she had thought only of showing Mia the river.

But Pallo had said he believed freedom was coming for the Weltang people. Penumbra's water had already begun to ignite change the night before. Villagers had sung and danced, many for the first time, like those awakened from an age-old sleep. And the more they awakened, the stronger they had become. Norla wanted to aid them in whatever way she could.

She thought of the drayza's face, streaked by dirt, and her chest tightened. He would have loved watching the villagers dance.

Norla had the sudden urge to visit his river.

Rising from her mat, she pulled on her cape and crept to the door, casting a final glance at her mother. Despite her grief over the temple, Mia had been delighted the previous night when Norla and Pallo had told her of their engagement. But then she had asked how such a marriage could be. Would a priest even perform such a ceremony?

Pallo had assured Mia that any number of priests would be eager to help a count. That had comforted Mia enough for her to offer her congratulations.

No one had mentioned Penumbra or Vinelain River.

Norla hoped Mia would see in time. And Chestel. Pallo thought they would in time. He had whispered as much before he'd left for the night.

Norla smiled to herself, remembering the feel of Pallo's lips near her ear. She still could hardly believe that Pallo would be her husband. He was challenging every convention imaginable by marrying a Weltang, and she along with him. For now, he camped with Gen and the others in the savannah, just outside the village.

Norla slipped outside and headed down the muddy lane. She kept to the shadows, hoping to avoid any foremen who might be on patrol. Thankfully, she didn't encounter a single person as she weaved through the village, toward the trading post.

When she turned the final corner, she saw that a small group had already gathered on the riverbank for an early morning drink.

Pallo! Norla recognized his tall frame instantly. She sprinted the rest of the way, right into his arms.

He laughed and hugged her.

"What are you doing here?" Norla asked.

"We all found each other here," Pallo said. He gestured to the others, and Norla saw that Roella, Gen, and Effira were all watching them.

Norla blushed. She had embraced Pallo just feet from Effira.

Gen strode to her. "I'm terribly offended you didn't greet me with such enthusiasm," he said, feigning offense.

Norla's cheeks flamed. "Well, er… "

"He's only joking," Effira said. "And being a scoundrel, of course." She shot Gen a pretty scowl and then faced Norla.

Norla steeled herself. She deserved whatever barrage was coming. Almost from the start, she realized, Effira had tried to befriend Norla. Her seeming nosiness had been one attempt after another to know Norla better, to understand her. The girl had offered food, wine, even kind words, but Norla had remained cold and unyielding.

"I'm so sorry," Norla blurted. She peered into Effira's green eyes, bracing herself, but saw only warmth.

"You haven't wronged me, Norla," Effira said. She still wore her desert robe and a mitzah over her curls.

Norla inched forward. She wanted to explain how much Effira's forgiveness meant, but even the idea of such a conversation brought a flush to Norla's face.

"And congratulations on your betrothal," Effira added. She smiled broadly, but her gaze flickered.

Norla cringed inside. She had hoped to spare Effira that heartache for a few days yet. Why had Pallo told the one person who would hurt the most from their engagement?

Norla turned to Pallo in question, but Gen cleared his throat.

"I may have shared your news," Gen said sheepishly. "I couldn't help myself once Pallo told me."

"In confidence," Pallo added. "I told you in confidence, Gen."

"And I can confidently offer you my best wishes, Norla." Gen took Norla's hand and gave it a hearty shake.

Norla nodded but kept her gaze on Effira. The girl offered another smile, and though Norla saw the trace of pain, she also saw joy. Effira was genuinely happy for her.

Norla swallowed and returned Effira's smile. It was a small gesture, but it was something. More than Norla had given before.

Effira beamed and held Norla's gaze until Gen interrupted. He took Effira's hand and led her right up to the river. Without a word, Pallo went to Norla and did the same.

As Norla bent to drink, her eyes caught a sloop approaching from the west. A man sat near the stern, steering the boat with a wooden tiller.

"Penumbra," Effira whispered.

Norla's heart thumped. She shook her head. "That's impossible."

She had seen him die. She had seen his body fall into the pit.

Yet the man looked eerily familiar. Especially his beautiful aqua eyes.

"My friends," the man said, stepping from his boat onto the shore. His voice was Penumbra's voice.

Norla's hands began to tremble. The man she'd mourned was all breath and warmth before her. He looked just as she remembered. Except his robe was a pristine white and no grime dirtied his skin.

Norla reached out to brush his tunic. Its woolen hairs tickled her skin, and she quickly drew her hand back.

"How are you alive?" Norla whispered.

"Foe's blade couldn't keep me dead," Penumbra said. "As long as my father lives, so do I." The drayza paused, his eyes gleaming. "My father and I are joined in a way that Foe can never understand."

"But I saw your body," Pallo said. His voice wavered, and Norla knew she wasn't the only one in shock. "There was no life in it."

"That's true," Penumbra replied. "I had to die as a Mir-laner. It was the only way."

"The river?" Effira asked.

Penumbra nodded, smiling.

"But why die?" Norla asked. "Why not unbury the river some other way?" He was the son of the river's creator. He could have called the water to the surface with a single word.

"The love of the Elyarnian throne has powerfully tangible effects," Penumbra said. "Remember? When Foe killed me, he released the highest form of my love." His eyes shone. "And nothing short of that love could have caused the headwaters to erupt as they did."

The drayza's joy was a tangible glow that warmed Norla's skin like summer's light.

With glittering eyes, he let his gaze drift to all who had gathered on the bank. When he turned to Norla, time slowed to a crawl. He looked thrilled, bursting with joy to be there with her, beside his river in the violet morning light. His expression didn't hold any expectation, only pride.

Tears pricked Norla's eyes. She wanted to thank him, but as she searched for words, she sensed Penumbra already knew her desire. The smile in his eyes said as much.

Penumbra turned his gaze to Roella next, and though their moment seemed quick, Norla guessed it had felt longer for Roella. As it had for Norla.

"So now you return home?" Pallo asked as the drayza moved toward his sloop.

"Yes," Penumbra replied.

"Take me with you," Effira said, stepping forward.

Penumbra's gaze softened. He reached out and squeezed her hand. "Not yet," he said. "You are my wells to Vinelain River now."

Norla exchanged a glance with Pallo. How could a person be a well? And the river ran above ground now.

"And Foe?" Gen asked.

"He still haunts Mirlane Isle. He will set himself against you," Penumbra said. "But you won't fight him alone. I'll send help from Elyarn Isle."

"Why won't *you* help us?" Norla asked.

"I will," Penumbra replied. "Wait with patience and see."

Norla shook her head. She didn't understand.

"I'll return for you in time," Penumbra added softly, "and bring you to my home."

Norla felt a rush of excitement. "To Elyarn Isle?"

Penumbra laughed. "Yes, and I'll teach you the dances of the sprites. You won't be contained by a hut then."

Norla's cheeks flamed. She'd never guessed her clumsy dancing with Chestel had been seen by the Prince of Elyarn Isle. And she'd certainly never guessed that he would teach her his dances one day.

"Your sister waits for you there, Pallo," the drayza said.

Pallo's eyebrows shot up. "Lania?"

"Oh yes. I led her home years ago," the drayza replied.

Pallo blinked in surprise. Slowly, his lips parted to reveal that small smile Norla had come to adore.

Penumbra peered over his shoulder then, as if he'd heard a call the others couldn't. When he turned back, his eyes shone impossibly bright.

"Goodbye, friends," Penumbra said. "I'll see you soon."

With that, he climbed into his small boat and set the sail eastward. The river's gentle current carried him away from them and into the savannah beyond.

Pallo stood behind Norla and wrapped his arms around her shoulders. Together, they watched Penumbra's boat grow smaller in the distance.

"He didn't look back," Effira said.

"But he's alive," Norla said.

"He really left," Pallo said.

"But he'll return," Norla said. He had promised as much.

"Who also brings me out from my enemies; You even lift me above those who rise up against me; You rescue me from the violent man."—2 Samuel 22:49 (NASB)

A percentage of all net profits generated from *Penumbra* are donated to Mission: RECUELIFE, a ministry of LIFE Outreach International. To learn more about this program, visit:
http://lifetoday.org/outreaches/mission-rescuelife.

Made in the USA
Lexington, KY
03 January 2013